Other books by Susanne Aspley
Illustrated by Lucas Richards

Bilingual children's books:

I Know How to Hola

I Know How to Ni Hao

I Know How to Bon Jour

www.iknowhowtobooks.com

In fond memory of Scabby

To help end the suffering of street dogs and
the brutal dog meat trade, please consider supporting
Soi Dog Foundation, Phuket, Thailand.

www.soidog.org

Ladyboy and the Volunteer

A Peace Corps Writers Book
An imprint of Peace Corps Worldwide

Copyright © 2014 by Susanne Aspley
Cover art by Tatiana Davidova
All rights reserved.
Printed in the United States of America
by Peace Corps Writers of Oakland, California.

Names, characters, places, events and incidents are used in a fictitious
manner. Any resemblance to actual persons, living or dead, or actual
events is purely coincidental.

Peace Corps Writers and the Peace Corps Writers colophon are trade-
marks of PeaceCorpsWorldwide.org.

ISBN-13: 978-1-935925-54-5
Library of Congress Control Number: 2014954014
First Peace Corps Writers Edition, November 2014

A PEACE CORPS WRITERS BOOK

Ladyboy and the Volunteer

Susanne Aspley

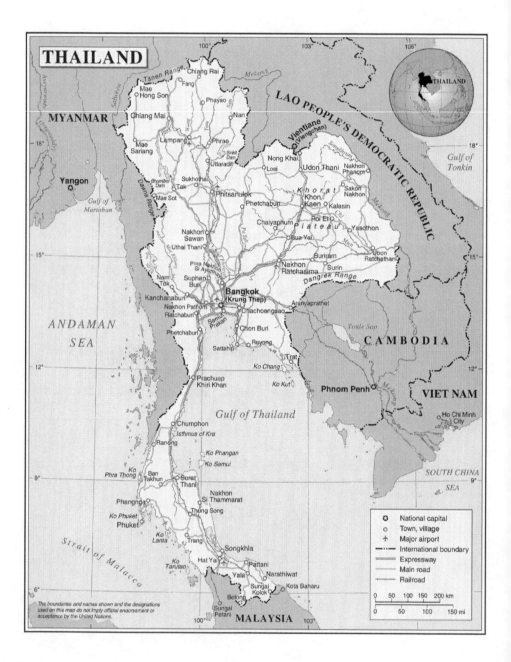

Dedicated to

The men and women of
Group 94, Thailand, U. S. Peace Corps
1989-1991

Chapter One

The Prince Hotel in Hot Yai resembles a Hitchcock-perfect movie set, uncanny and slightly unsettled.

The vases on the tables are not centered in the middle, but pushed to the far edges, ready to topple off. The magazines are all stacked covers down. The chairs face a bleak wall, instead of out toward the reception desk and windows.

There are three framed pictures next to the elevator; a photo of the King of Thailand, a photo of a golden, reclining Buddha and one of Mel Gibson. I think Mel's on the wall because when they made the movie, *Air America,* it was filmed here in Thailand. Then again, maybe the owner just thinks he's cute.

Christine recommended this hotel to me when I first met her. It's also where she brings her customers for the day, night or hour.

In my room, a carnation pink fan rumbles overhead. The desk mirror looks like it would be ideal to tape on a suicide note, molting gray around the edges, cracked and askew. The walls are painted puke green with bile yellow trim.

Perhaps the only regal touch that gives reference to the hotel's ill-fitted name are the musty gold curtains covering the barred windows. Outside the window of my room is the blinking neon hotel sign missing a few letters. It reads: **The PRI CE HO E.**

I'm getting ready to take a quick shower after the dusty bus ride from my village, digging through my backpack.

In the bathroom, the shower head is a foot in diameter, however, for being so wide, the water trickles out in one pathetic drip. The drain in the sink isn't connected to anything. It's just a small hole that spills out onto the floor and runs toward a hole in the corner about two feet away.

"Susan!" I hear from the hallway, then several excited knocks on my door.

That was quick. I checked in about ten minutes ago and already someone has told Christine I'm here.

"I know you're in there, Susan! Open up, it's me!" she yells in her silky, husky voice.

(She pronounces my name, Sue-sahn, like most Thais do.)

Christine is from my small southern fishing village of Sichon where I'm assigned for work. Confident and statuesque, long hair so black it shimmers blue, she smells of Love's Baby Soft perfume and cigarette smoke.

She is a ladyboy, which is the third sex in Thailand. Born with a penis but as the Thais like to say, "Has a female heart."

The term ladyboy refers to any transgendered person originally born a male, whether they like to occasionally cross-dress or completely undergo gender-reassignment surgery.

Thais take the Buddha's view on sexuality, be it hetero, bi, homo or trans. Sexual orientation is considered karma, neither good nor bad, but simply cards of fortune the person is dealt.

In the States, if a young boy picks up a Barbie doll, many parents grab the Barbie away and make the child go play with a truck instead. If the boy cries, he is told to stop being a sissy and get over it.

In Thailand, if a boy would rather play with dolls instead of rattan ball with the neighbors, it's not a big deal. The child is not hauled off to therapy or shamed. He just might be a ladyboy.

When I open the door, Christine wraps her arms around me in a tight hug, grabbing a fistful of my blonde hair. She smells it, almost inhaling it, then pushes me aside, talking non-stop.

She sashays into my room wearing a stunning white Marilyn Monroe type halter dress and shiny lavender pumps. Prowling to the desk like a kitten to catnip, she starts pawing through my makeup bag and cosmetics.

I always bring extra girly items because I know she will take half of them. Rather, she will take all of them.

Taking a seat on the bed, I watch her purr over my lipstick and eyeshadows, deodorant and lotions.

"Susan, why you never wear lipstick? I can borrow lipstick? Okay? You never wear mascara either," she says as she tucks the tubes into her purse before I can answer.

Christine continues smelling, spraying and applying everything that I brought with me. All that I have, she stuffs in her purse, which is what I expected her to do.

We speak in English because she is fluent, I imagine from all the practice with foreigners here at the hotel, but is unable to write. She often uses inappropriate words, sometimes lost in translation, sometimes on purpose. Occasionally, she innocently uses insensitive or racist labels, and I have to correct her.

Floating over to my backpack, she begins to pull out all of my clothes.

"Susan. You dress like a village rice farmer. You wear tee shirts and shorts. Your shoes are for handicapped people. They are retard shoes."

"They are hiking sandals. And don't use the word, *retard*. In America, we say *special needs*," I explain.

"There is nothing special about those shoes," she states.

"They are comfortable."

"Comfortable for handicap people," she adds.

"Enough about my shoes and that word, Christine. Let's just stop talking about this," I answer curtly.

"Why don't you wear high heels?" she asks.

"I have other shoes, not just these."

"No, you don't. Flip flops don't count. They aren't heels."

"I have size ten feet, Christine. There are no high heels in Thailand that fit me."

"I find heels in Bangkok that fit me. Or Koh Samui. I buy you some next time I go," she says, and kicks my foot.

"It's one hundred degrees here, all the time. I live in a mud village with dirt roads. I can't do heels in this."

"Flip flops are for poor people. They are bad for your feet, no support," she tsks.

Flitting to my bed, Christine plops down next to me and gracefully crosses her legs. She has elegant legs, but her kneecaps are huge. They are man-sized kneecaps, but that doesn't matter. She knows well enough to always cross her large, manicured hands on them to keep them less noticeable. A previous boyfriend paid for her breast implants a few years ago, so she's fully stacked.

Pulling out a crumpled love letter from her purse, she asks me to help write a reply to a man in Australia.

The letter is from a former tourist, and from what I can tell, had more than just a paid one-nighter with her. He obviously wants to continue the relationship with her somehow.

"I want him to be my boyfriend," she coos. "I meet him here at this hotel."

She then catches a glimpse of herself in the mirror and winks at the reflection.

"A customer or a boyfriend?" I ask.

"He customer first, but maybe soon be my boyfriend," she answers. "He very rich and cute."

Christine does quite well in the world's oldest profession, but doesn't keep much of the money she makes. She sends most of it back to her impoverished family in Sichon. Not only does she support her own immediate family, she supports half a dozen extended family members as well. Being the oldest child, she feels it's her duty to do so. This is often the heartbreaking reason why many sex workers here do what they do.

Christine hands me a sparkling pink greeting card and a red marker she pulls from her purse.

"Tell him I love him and I miss him and I want him to send money to me so I can go to Australia to see him," she gushes.

"Christine, really?" I ask, suspiciously.

"Yes, Susan, really!"

"You don't love him," I say.

"Yes, I do!" she protests.

"Are you sure he's not just another sexpat tourist like most of your customers?" I ask.

Sexpat is a play on words to describe an expat, (expatriate) who are foreigners living, temporarily or permanently, in another county. In Thailand, there are many who come for the abundance of available sex for sale. I simply hate them.

She laughs, shakes her head, and says, "No, Susan, this one might be different. Just write the letter for me."

"Fine," I say reluctantly.

I've seen how Christine uses prostitution and the men as a sad means to her still hopeful, happy ending. Desperately searching in each customer for one that may result in a loving relationship, and lift her out to a better life. She also mentioned once she'd like to open her own clothing boutique, but is unable to save the large chunk of cash needed for the initial investment. I had tried to get funding through the Peace Corps for a small business grant, but was unsuccessful. So, Christine keeps working, keeping her hope alive that maybe, someday, her dream will come true.

Warily, I write the letter, expanding it a little with flowery adjectives. I then suggest to Christine to put more lipstick on and kiss the bottom of the page. She giggles with approval.

She smiles giddily, then remembers to thank me for writing the letter. Grabbing a hand full of my hair, she buries her face in it again. She then stands up and swishes out the door to begin her work night.

I hate that she is a prostitute, however, I stand in awe and admiration of her *coming out*, being who she is, being the third sex. She is the most joyous person I have ever met. I can tell she loves being who she really is, a ladyboy.

I leave soon after and walk to the movie parlor around the corner. From the outside, it looks like a video rental shop. Inside, there are three walls lined with bootleg copies of the latest Hollywood releases. In the back down a hall, there are ten small rooms, each with a VCR, big chunky TV, comfy armchairs and side tables.

For twenty baht each, I pick out a stack of three tapes, then lock myself in a room and watch them back to back until midnight. Afterwards, I return to the hotel and fall asleep. I plan to return in the morning to watch a few more videos before going home to Sichon.

~~~

Tap Tap Tap

Tap

Tap Tap

I look at my pink plastic alarm clock on the bamboo table next to my bed. The glow in the dark face reads 2:15. In the morning. Or night. Nonetheless, it's late.

Tap Tap Tap

Although soft, the sound is persistent and steady. I can tell that whoever is knocking on my door is using the padded tips of their fingers.

I hear a hushed, harried voice.

"Susan."

A few seconds pass. I roll over, hoping it's a dream.

"Susan. Please, Susan," I hear again, quietly.

Dear God, I think it's Christine. I watch the skitzy second hand twitch on my clock a few times more.

"It's Christine, please open."

What is she doing here at this hour? Something is certainly wrong. I stare at the blinking neon hotel sign outside my window for a moment, then get up and go to the door.

"Christine?" I ask softly.

"Susan. Susan. It's me, open please, just open the door and let me in," she whispers back.

I unlock the door and peek through the crack. Christine is waiting to get in, nearly tottering over in gold vinyl stilettos and a neon green mini dress. Her glossy hair is tossed and tangled. The lipstick she took from me earlier is smeared all over one of her cheeks. One false eyelash is gone, the other hanging off the end of the other lid. She is haloed in cigarette smoke and Love's Baby Soft perfume.

In a panic, she pushes her way into the room, shutting the door quietly. She leans against the door, and I rub my eyes with one hand and grab her arm with the other.

"What happened? You look like hell! What's wrong? Are you okay?" I gush.

"Susan, come help me now. I think I killed him," she answers, grabbing my hands desperately.

"What are you talking about?"

"My customer, please come, I think he..."

She then makes the universal sign of sliding her finger across her throat, tilts her head to the side and feigns death.

"What? Where? What are you talking about?" I whisper back.

She pulls me out the door, leads me through the hallway, and down four flights of stairs to another room. She quickly glances back and forth before pushing the door open while jerking me inside with her.

On the bed is a fat naked man, motionless on his back, covered faintly from the waist down with a sheet. I walk over to get a closer look. Oh gawd. He looks like an overstuffed bean burrito, the kind if you microwave too long, the mysterious filling oozes out the ends. I don't want to touch him, fearing he will pop at his bloated seams.

"What happened, Christine?" I say as calmly as I can, but it comes out in a whine.

"He like it when I choke him just before he cums. Many German men do, they like it when I choke them when they cum," she says, as if it's the most obvious thing in the world.

"I think you choked too hard," I whisper back.

With hesitation, I push two fingers into the fat rolls of his neck to check for a pulse. I don't feel anything but my own nausea. His lips are starting to lose color, slowly turning a pale, blueish purple.

"Mouth to mouth," Christine says. "You do mouth to mouth."

"*You* do mouth to mouth," I retort.

"I don't know how to mouth to mouth. You do mouth to mouth," she answers.

"I think you know plenty about mouth to mouth."

"Shut up, Susan. So do you. You do mouth to mouth."

"No, you, he's your customer," I argue back.

"No, you do it."

I stare at the rubbery lips. Two long chubby slabs pulled back exposing tiny, brown stained teeth. The sweat. He is covered in sweat. Dear Jesus, there is even sweat on the black hairs sticking out of his doughy nose.

I remember mouth to mouth resuscitation is to be the last resort, and simple chest compressions should be performed first. Leaning over the naked German, I put one hand on top of the other and plunge down with my palm right below his rib cage area. Then again and one more time. Nothing. No movement.

Christine then lunges toward the man, sticks her hand under the sheet, obviously grabbing his junk, and starts yanking it around violently.

The German man suddenly twitches, heaving and is gasping for breath in wheezy desperation. He is breathing. The fat burrito is alive.

Christine looks at me in amazement, her eyes round as full moons. I stare back, equally amazed. He's coming back to life quickly, too quickly.

"Let's go!" Christine says, and flicks me on the side of the head to hurry me up.

Before we sneak out, she takes his gold watch that is on the bedside table, a pack of Marlboros and pulls all the money out of his wallet. She then grabs a silver metal briefcase that is next to his bed, and heads for the door.

"Put that back!" I hiss.

She just smiles and shoos me out, leaving the fat man to clean up his own sorry predicament.

Chapter Two

Early the next morning, I check out of the Prince Hotel with no problems or signs of the fat German. I'm sure he didn't see me last night, but I don't want to take any chances.

I start walking the fourteen blocks to the bus station to catch one back to Sichon.

The Chinese influence in Hot Yai opulently takes over the busy downtown area. Newspapers, signs and conversations are often in both Thai and Chinese. The aromatic restaurants often serve Chinese style food more than they do Thai.

On the way to the bus station, I stop at the Kim Yong Market, the sprawling indoor and outdoor food wonderland. Kim Yong Market is named after the Chinese business man who developed the town in the early 1900s.

The smell of sweet fruit, fried fish and fresh vegetables hang in the humid air. Lined up and down the sidewalks, shoulder to shoulder and basket to basket are Muslim women, heads wrapped in batik scarves. They sell plums the size of oranges, oranges the size of grapefruit, grapefruit the size of cantaloupe, cantaloupe the size of watermelons, and watermelons the size of apples. Bags of oily cashews, thumb sized raisins, black mushrooms and white pomegranates are plentiful. On every corner are sputtering woks, glowing with hot rocks and roasting chestnuts.

The narrow, crowded food stands are stuffed with treats and sweets from Singapore. Crunchy gingerbread men frosted with chocolate, chocolate covered durian and chocolate coated crickets. British candy bars such as Flake, Twisted, and Double Deckers line the shelves. Rows and rows of oddly flavored Lay's potato chips such as Paprika Lobster, Salmon Teriyaki and Kyushi Seaweed are for sale.

Malaysian men come to Hot Yai for a weekend getaway from the wifey and kids, usually looking for prostitutes. The shopping opportunities also attract Chinese from Hong Kong who jet in for a day, along with wealthy Japanese tourists. These sleek, fashionable yuppies come for the abundance of inexpensive electronics and expertly made counterfeit Coach, Prada and Louis Vuittons.

I buy a skewer of charcoal grilled bananas and a hot waffle drenched in sweet coconut milk for breakfast. I always come hungry to this market and leave too full.

~~~

I get on the crowded bus back to my little village of Sichon, in Nakorn Sri Thammarat province. I have to work tomorrow and teach English at two rural schools. I'm not the most productive Peace Corps volunteer (PCV), but at least I can teach English.

A few hours later, I struggle to disembark, shimmying through the aisle to get out the door at my bus stop near Sichon.

My clothes are coated with rust colored dust. My nose is filled with rust colored snot. My freshly washed hair is muddy.

The bus rattles away. I stand in the rude, blue exhaust and angry, Siamese sun for a minute trying to get my land legs back after the cramped ride. I still have one mile to walk to the seaside village I call home.

At the intersection is the local convenience store made of corrugated tin and rotted wood. I call it the Jet Sipette, which is Thai for the numbers seven eleven. There are individually wrapped cough drops, bags of rice chips and warm bottles of Pepsi and Sprite displayed on overturned crates. Cigarettes, bottles of booze and newspapers line the wall.

The Jet Sipette is run by an old man with cataract-coated eyes and his beloved dog, Scabby.

"Sawatdee ca," I say to the elderly man, who answers with a "Sawatdee crop."

Scabby is laying near the old man's feet and lifts his head when he sees me. Scabby smells his butt, looks at me again, then goes back to sleep.

The old man makes sure Scabby always has fresh water and plenty of food. Scabby sleeps in a cool, shallow hole behind the building to shelter from the sun and rain. In return, the dog sits by the old man all day long, everyday, and gives him pleasant company.

Scabby has foam caked on the corners of his mouth but has the most lovely, luminous eyes. He often scoots along in the dirt and rocks on his callused butt, oared along by his two front legs while keeping his hind legs jutted out straight ahead. He has scabs that he constantly gnaws so they never heal. I would have been more than happy to help pay for a trip to a veterinarian for him, but after asking around, there are no vets in my province. Vets simply do not exist outside of Bangkok, and only there for the very rich and their imported purebreds.

Scabby is a *soi* dog, or street dog, which is a big problem in Thailand. Homeless, often maimed in traffic, mangey, surviving on garbage, these dogs are left to fend for themselves. Sometimes they are rounded up and sold over the borders of Laos or Vietnam in the illegal and barbaric dog meat trade.

When I first arrived in Thailand earlier this year, I asked the old man, "What is your dog's name?"

"Dog," he answered.

"I know it's a dog, but what's his name?"

"Dog. His name is Dog."

"More like Scabby," I said sarcastically.

I immediately felt bad that I had suggested such an insulting name for the poor creature, but the old man lit up and loved it.

"Scabby! His name is Scabby!" he answered. Scabby has been his name ever since then.

The old man then went on to say, "Ten years ago, Scabby just showed up, nothing but bones, skin and bones. So I feed him, and he never leave here. He is my guard dog now when I am not here. He's my best friend now. One time, someone stole him, but my neighbor told me who stole him. Someone was going to eat him. So I go find the thief, punch the thief in the eye and said, 'If you eat my dog, I will eat you!'"

Ever since, I have loved both of them.

The old man has ordered one Bangkok Post newspaper delivered to sell to me everyday. I buy the latest edition along with a bag of crab flavored crackers, and start walking toward home.

Dry, roasted rice paddies edge both sides of the skinny black-top that aims toward the coast. Deluding heat ghosts dance up from the pavement, wave in the sun and twist off. These spiraling spirits give me a headache. A thick blanket of pure heat wraps around my shoulders. I just keep trudging down the road.

Unable to meet me half way, the cool ocean breeze is trapped in the trees up ahead. The rattling wind is captured in the coconut groves covering the coast and clatters the tropical rooftop.

Finally, I arrive at my hidden fishing village scattered under the high palms.

The turquoise sea is soft, swirling and seems to go on forever toward an eternal horizon. Giant umbrella palms darkly shade the sand and the salty air is sharp and sticky. Humble houses lining the shore are clustered here and there, swaddled in the fumes of fresh fish. Racks and racks of stout bamboo are weighed down with squid, hung to dry. The squid are pale and pink, like deflated balloons, shriveling in the sun.

Nearing the end of the main road which leads further down the beach, I see Bong, the young man who lies in the middle of the intersection. (Bong means crazy in Thai.) He's here whenever I pass through, he's here whenever I pass back again. He's long limbed and a bit chubby. Laying on his stomach, he draws doodles in the dirt all day. The people and traffic simply drive or walk around him.

Bong is also like the town deejay. I think his parents at home must have a satellite radio to pick up some American stations or at least a cassette player, as he is always singing the latest top 40 hits of this year 1990.

"Sawatdee ca, Bong," I yell.

He stops drawing and looks at me.

"Bong, get out of the road," I yell again.

"You get out of the road, *farang* Susan!" he screams back.

"I'm not in the middle of the road, you are!"

"Nothing compares to U!" he screams.

"Nothing compares to U getting hit by a truck!" I yell back.

Bong goes back to his dirt doodling, now ignoring me.

Shaking my head, I keep walking to my house.

Along the village boardwalk is an open patio with a concrete deck filled with women and girls garbed in tank tops and sarongs. Squatting or perched on wooden stools, they peel poignant shrimp the day long. In two quick flicks of the fingers, the shrimp are perfectly plucked from their veiny shells and tossed into damp straw baskets.

Several women break from their work and wave to me. They motion to me to come over but I keep walking near the wharf. The last time I stopped to visit, their generosity left me with nearly five pounds of shrimp, three flat squid, a smoked fish and a small bag of deep fried crickets.

Gathered around the village dock and anchored to the mooring are the carnival colored fishing boats wafting in the waves. They are old longboats, thickly painted red, yellow, green and blue. Tangles of thick rope nets are webbed over the sides. Straw baskets are littered on top of the solid vessels.

Dark, spindly young boys are swinging from the masts or dangling from somewhere dangerously, constantly fixing something. The older men are weathered and deeply grooved, toasted beyond their years in the bitter sun. Most are shirtless with sinewy backs and heads wrapped in a rag or sarong.

A man with long, white hair and spider-like arms crouches on the stern of one of the smaller boats. His wide feet are splayed out beneath him like a duck. He rolls a cigarette, while he's gently rocked to the left and right. He waves to me.

All the villagers know me well by now, but still stop to watch where I go and what I am doing.

I was hoping to get back in time to stop by the small post office in my village to check for mail before it closes. However, I'm still about a quarter of a mile away.

A little motor scooter pulls up behind me, with the tin horn beeping madly.

"Susan! Susan!" two young teenaged girls scream.

They pull in front of me, almost tipping over as they come to a clumsy stop.

"Susan! Where you go?" they ask, giggling.

It's Nong and Lek, sweet girls from my village, on their way home from middle school.

"Come with us, get on, get on, let's go!" they beg.

I'm grateful for the ride and hop on.

With all three of us on the small scooter, we take off down the road. Three people on a motor scooter is common in Thailand, usually there are four or more. Whenever I see a single person on one, it almost looks empty.

Nong zips down the road. Lek is delighted to have me on board and helps hold my legs up, which are sticking straight out because there is nowhere else to put them.

Finally, we reach the post office. I get off and put my two hands together in front of my bowed head, and *wai* to thank them. I give them each a pack of Big Red gum in turn for the ride. (My dad always sends me Big Red gum, which I save to give out for moments such as this.)

Off the two girls zoom, the small engine of the bike pinging away into the distance.

I have a few letters to send back home to the States and a dozen more to send out to other volunteers in Thailand, to keep in touch and somehow feel connected. Letters, postcards and occasional telegrams are the only way we can communicate here.

Although there are several volunteers in my province, we are hours apart. I have gone weeks without seeing another American, much less speaking English. Luckily, many of us stationed in the South get together as often as we can, or I go meet others that live in the North or centralized Bangkok.

All volunteers are assigned to a Thai Government agency. I was assigned to the provincial Community Development office in Nakorn Sri Thammarat, the capital of the province. My coworkers love me and treat me as their American pet. I tagged along with them on their duties when I first arrived in the country, but now that I have been here a year, I only stop by to check in, do Peace Corps reports, get my Peace Corps mail, and be fed by my favorite secretary there, Nuang.

In Sichon, I receive my personal letters and packages because only official Peace Corps mail can go to my office in Nakorn. However, the weasly post office clerk in Sichon not only opens my letters and reads them, but opens my packages and takes what he wants, yet denies everything.

I began to have suspicions when I went to the post office one day and the Weasel was wearing a new Minnesota Twins jersey.

The next day, the Weasel was wearing a Minnesota Golden Gophers shirt. What a coincidence that my mom had just asked if I had received the Minnesota shirts she sent a month prior.

A week later, I walked into the post office and the Weasel smelled like Victoria's Secret Vanilla Sugar body spray, the same kind I use in the States, that I begged my girlfriend to send to me.

Finally, one day while I was sending a letter, I saw on the back counter behind the Weasel a can of Kraft Easy Cheese and a half eaten box of Ritz crackers. The same cheese and crackers my mom said she sent, but I never received. When I saw my beloved can of Easy Cheese, the can of cheese that was rightfully mine, I also saw red. I crawled under the counter, grabbed the glorious can of cheese, popped the plastic lid off, put the nozzle in my mouth and pushed it down. The wonderful squirting processed cheese filled my mouth completely. It was pure heaven. Then, I had turned my attention back to the Weasel.

"Mon't you mever meal my mail again, muver mucker!" I yelled, cheese flying out of my mouth and running down my chin.

Weasel took a few steps away and watched as I crawled back under the counter and stomp out the door.

Nonetheless, I am again in front of the post office at the bottom of the steps, digging through my big purse. I suddenly look up and see the most amazing thing walking out of the door toward me.

Oh, my goodness, what do we have here.

He stands on the top rickety steps for a moment, looks around, then notices me.

Wow.

The man is tall, broad shouldered, and is wearing a light brown Army tee shirt, black athletic shorts and tan military issued desert boots. Sweaty, tan and gorgeous. He would stop traffic just about anywhere. Special Forces. Definitely Special Forces. You don't get those biceps just any old way. I just stand at the bottom of the steps admiring him like a statue.

"Hi," he says, a bit surprised to see me.

I am speechless.

I continue to stand still, my mouth open, staring.

"You American?" he asks, smiling.

Holy apple pie. My mouth is watering hot. I melt inside as I turn my stare from his handsome face to his chest. I forget to swallow. I remember to breath. I have been in Thailand too long.

"...uhhh...uh," I answer.

I wipe some drool from the corner of my mouth.

"Yes," is all I manage to say.

He looks wonderful.

"Peace Corps, right?"

"Yes," I answer.

"I'm Mike," he says, and walks down the steps to stand in front of me. I can't believe this beautiful creature is so close to me. I can smell him. Sweat from working hard, not lazy sweat. He smells of Hawaiian Tropic sunscreen. I haven't smelled such a good-looking American man in, well, it seems like forever.

"Nice to meet you," he says, and holds out a hand.

Instead, I give him a *wai*. He then returns the *wai* and I stick out my hand. He finally grabs my hand to shake.

"You live here?" he asks.

"Yes," I say.

Then I remember to let go of his hand.

"Awesome. Say, my buddies and I are here training for a while, going a little further north today, but should be back in a few weeks. Maybe I'll run into you again," he says, grinning, showing his adorably imperfect teeth.

Run into me, please.

"Yes," is all I can say, completely tongue tied.

"I hope so. What's your name?"

"Smitten."

"Excuse me?"

"Ahhh..." I answer, unable to say Susan, unable to produce anything coherent.

"Okay, Smitten, hope to see ya soon," he says.

meow

With that, he turns around and walks to his pickup truck.

I stand motionless, staring, unblinking. The tingles inside me are ricocheting off every nerve. His back side is just as luscious as his front side.

If he looks back, I'll know he's interested. I plead quietly out loud to look back. Please. Pretty please. Oh no!

Dang it. I'm wearing my ugly hiking sandals. I'm thinking he won't look. He's outta here.

He turns around back before opening the truck door.

I can't believe he looked back, so raise my hand to give a little wave.

"It's Susan! My name is Susan!" I yell.

He smiles and nods, climbs into the Ford F-150 truck and takes off down the dirt driveway. I watch his arm hanging out of the truck window until it disappears around the corner.

Great job, genius, so glad you remembered your name, I grumble to myself.

Finally exhaling, I walk into the post office, not noticing that the Weasel is wearing a Minnesota Twins baseball hat and eating a package of Keebler fudge striped cookies, which is exactly what my mom said she sent to me last week.

Chapter Three

The next morning, I wake up in my hut and watch the geckos having sex on my ceiling. At least something is getting lucky in this village. I wish it was Mike and I instead. Those biceps. That smile.

Gawd, I get so lonely, sometimes it's unbearable. Seeing a handsome Western man here is a rare treat. I go for weeks at a time just doing my Peace Corps work, yelling at Bong, waiting for mail, staring at the ceiling or sitting by the ocean at the end of the day.

Enough moping. Mike is gone, so I might as well go save the world as a Peace Corps volunteer. Enjoy the toughest job I will ever love, or whatever the commercial said. So, I get up and go to my bathroom to get ready for the day.

My hut is on three foot stilts with a four foot porch on the front and one side. There is a small wide ladder I use for steps, or sometimes an overturned crate. The walls and roof are made of bamboo with plywood planks for the floor.

Inside, there is just one room, about twenty feet by twenty, with a twin sized platform used for a bed frame. Mattresses don't exist outside of hotels, and would certainly be too hot in this constant heat. Like most Thais, I sleep on a smooth, woven bamboo mat. It's pliable, cool and comfortable. However, I don't skimp on pillows. Besides about a dozen lining the walls around my bed to lean against, a friend from the States sent several memory foam pillows, so I always sleep well.

Opening the door to my bathroom, I'm greeted by my indignant cockroaches. Rather than skitter out of sight when the lights go on like their American cousins, they keep trudging about their business regardless. They don't mind if I'm around, as long as I'm respectful and don't intrude on their activities. Some of the more athletic ones fly across the room, crash into the wall and thud to the floor. They then barrel away unfazed.

I used to beat them with a broom when I first moved in, but that only pissed them off. They are my immortal housemates and I have accepted them as they have accepted me. Besides, I'd rather live with fat and happy cockroaches than angry, hungry ones.

My bathroom has two steps down to a concrete area with a drain in the middle of the floor. In one corner is a spigot with running water directly over a large clay urn holding the water for showering. Next to it is the squat toilet which is very efficient and sanitary compared to Western toilets. It is used exactly how it's named. Simply squat, pour down a few bowls of water to flush, and that's it. There is no toilet paper, just more water is used to splash and rinse.

The bathrooms throughout Thailand are incredibly easy to keep clean. For mine, I just splash water everywhere with a little soap, squeegee it into the drain, and it's done.

After a quick shower, which means pouring bowls of water on my head, I grab my backpack and walk over to Tong's house, my closest neighbor.

Tong is my age, about twenty-five years old, and mother to five cute kids. Her husband is away most of the time working on a salt farm a bit further up the coast. In the year I have been here, I have only met him a few times.

I pull out a bag of fat, black gooey dates and Japanese chocolate candy for the kids in the yard. I always bring something back from Hot Yai for them and they are always thrilled. I'm almost tackled by the kids as Tong tells me to sit down for breakfast. She insists on feeding me whenever she sees me, which is all the time.

Thais will make a feast with whatever they have available. Tong brings out a plate of fresh, steaming rice, three sunny side up eggs, and four bowls of leftovers: yellow chicken curry, red squid curry, green okra curry and sweet and sour vegetable soup. I eat until I am stuffed as the kids munch on their treats.

After breakfast, I start walking toward the Jet Sipette as a motorcycle taxi pulls in front of me. A motorcycle taxi is really just some guy with a motorcycle looking for easy cash, but I do need one now.

I climb on and sit sideways this time because I am wearing a long, flowing skirt. Off we go to a small village about twenty minutes inland. I often go to the schools there to teach English.

The motorcycle guy drops me off at the crossroads.

I take a well-trodden path toward the childcare center and can hear the preschoolers before I can see them. Two older girls from the middle school catch up from behind and escort me all the way to the gate. White scarves cover their hair. They have conservative shirts and ankle length skirts. Both are soft spoken, shy, yet strikingly beautiful. They are Muslim, as are a significant number of the Thais here in the southern peninsula.

"Can you eats spicy foods?" the taller one murmurs, unsure of her English, but eager to try it out on a real American. They love to practice on a native speaker. Her face flushes and she hides her chin in her scarf.

"Yes, I can. Can you eat spicy food?" I ask.

"Yes, Thai peoples eat spicy food," she giggles, and then both girls start giggling together with their arms around each other's waists when I correct her grammar.

The girls leave me at the planked fence of the preschool and continue on their way to their own school.

A loud crowd of blooming children hoot and holler when I enter the play yard. Their happiness beams through their dusty, sweet faces. They then shift back to their original entertainment already in progress.

A village mother has brought her pet monkey to show the children. I sit next to her and watch the terrified primate cowering in a papaya tree. Holding on by one tiny paw, it's trying to cover it's stricken ears with the other.

Screeching and throwing rocks, the kids are having a ball. The childcare attendant looks at me with a 'children will be children' muse and the village mother seems to agree.

"What is his name?" I ask, referring to the tormented monkey clutching tight to the tree. Suddenly, it spits on the mob below.

"Monkey," the mother says.

"I know it's a monkey, but what's his name?" I ask again.

"His name is monkey," she answers, seeming to wonder why I ask such silly questions. She pats my knee in consolation and adds, "Do you want him?"

The squealing kids scatter in all directions, laughing and screaming. Then, they reassemble. Monkey has just pooped on them and they want him to do it again.

"Let me think about it," I answer, with no intentions of taking the monkey.

The childcare attendant gives me a bottle of water, a dirty cup and five oranges for me to eat. Peeling the fresh citrus, she watches intently to make sure I devour each one. She doesn't want to discuss teaching goals or concerns right now. The most crucial item on her agenda is this: feeding the American and feeding her a lot because she is so big.

A couple of diminutive boys with identical crew cuts trample toward me. They have clear nutmeg skin, rosy lips, wide curious eyes and decayed teeth. One of them, Chok, proudly holds out a soiled hand within inches from my face. He has his own little pet to show off to me.

It's a beetle the size of a grade A egg with an aluminum tinted shell. Laying on it's back, the multiple thorny legs are slowly twirling in the air, trying to find traction. The glossy black head resembles a miniature rhinoceros, complete with a formidable horn protruding from it's forehead.

Chok drops the critter into my hand and I manage to swallow my shriek. The armored bug lands on it's back. I flip it over into my other hand. The legs start to rotate and claw at my palm.

"What's his name?" I ask.

"Insect," he answers.

"I know it's an insect, but what's his name?"

Chok shakes his head, hopelessly confused at my question.

"His name is Insect!" pipes the other boy.

Fine, Americans have this strange habit of naming their pets, Thais do not.

Insect is behaving himself properly in my care. I gingerly touch his horn and he nods for me. Chok pokes a twig into the space between it's head and body. Insect cocks his head forward, and with spring release action, snaps it back, violently crushing the twig between his neck. With insect still clenching the twig, Chok bashes him against the ground. Insect ultimately releases his crunching grip.

Curious and without thinking, I want to see how this intriguing defense mechanism works again, so reach down and touch it with my finger.

"Yaah!" I scream.

The lads scream louder in laughter. They dance a celebratory jig, thrilled that an adult would do something so foolish. I am foolish all right. Reverting to English and swearing very fluently, I instruct them to get the "GOD DAMNED BUG OFF MY GOD DAMNED FINGER!"

The boys tug and pull, but Insect is a stubborn creature and won't relent easily. Finally, the childcare attendant nudges them aside and lights a match near Insect, but directly on my finger.

Insect releases, taking along shards of my skin. My flesh dangles from the back of his neck. A steady stream of blood flows from my mangled finger. It's charred black around the wound from the match flame and visibly swelling. I pop the pulpy mess into my mouth. I have no intention of removing it for the rest of my life.

I want to slap the innocent kids, grind the bug into dust with my heel, bawl, scream and stomp home. Home to America with my stupidity.

Instead, the attendant snatches my other hand and pulls me through the yard and across the road. I follow obediently with my painful finger in my mouth.

Like all women around the world, in any culture Western or remote, she knows the best remedy for physical or emotional pain is fattening food.

The ice cream vendor, a scaly reptilian man from the village, has parked his rusty pushcart under the shade facing the childcare center. He knows where he's wanted.

The kids are still preoccupied with terrorizing the monkey, so we have the goodies to ourselves for the moment. The old man hands me a sundae. It's a thin paper cup filled with globs of sticky rice and on top a melting ball of homemade coconut ice milk, generously sprinkled with kernels of sweet corn and dosed with sweetened condensed milk. The attendant has chosen neon pink tapioca squirts to adorn her own.

My teeth shake from the sugar shock, but beyond all odds, it's delightful. It also obliterates the taste of blood and singed flesh from my mouth. The attendant buys the first round and I get the second and third.

A few of the preschoolers have spotted us and begin to straggle over. The attendant abruptly throws down her empty cups and rushes toward the desperate youngsters. Swooping down like a huge vulture, she swats anyone in reach as she corrals them back across the forbidden road.

They scream for ice cream but she screams louder.

Grabbing several of the kids in one arm, she directs me to rustle up the remaining. It's nap time instead.

The childcare center is divided into two rooms, with no furniture except a chair for the teacher and a table swaying from the weight of notebooks, oranges and coffee cups. The walls are sparsely covered with pictures of flowers, all drawn with the same few colors of crayons. There's a shiny poster of the King of Thailand gilded with paltry garlands above the door. A few broken toys are cluttered in the corner. An orchestra of crickets chirp from some secret hiding place.

In the other room, a short wooden bed frame takes up nearly the entire area. All the children climb onto the communal resting place and spread out their thin, wicker mats. Quickly falling asleep, they use buffed wooden boards as pillows. They snuggle together like a pile of jellybeans, content and rainbow-hued.

The attendant tiptoes out after much hushing and shushing. She beckons me to follow.

On the shaded patio, we at last discuss the childcare center and the problems. She is concerned mostly about the lack of an outhouse. They had one a few years ago when the center was first built, but couldn't afford the repairs when the plumbing went out. Besides that, the roof caved in.

She points to a dainty, barefoot girl. The child has gotten up from the nap and is squatting near the side of the building.

"Where is the bathroom now?" I ask.

"There, that's the bathroom."

"There?"

"There," she says again.

"The side of the school building?"

"Yes. There."

The girl stands up with her skirt hiked around her small oval stomach. She wipes herself with her hand. She then studies her palm for a few seconds and sniffs it. Deciding to rub it on the grass, she does while tugging down her skirt before scurrying back inside.

"The side of the building is the bathroom?" I ask again.

The attendant is almost annoyed with me now.

"Yes, yes it is. The villagers can build us a bathroom, but we have no money for the supplies," she explains.

"I will write a PC project proposal or maybe we can get a donation or something. I'll find out and let you know," I answer, hoping I can be true to my word.

This suggestion kindles a spark in her eye but leaves me strangely numb.

One bathroom at one school in one developing country is not what I had in mind when I decided to join the Peace Corps. I had high hopes to do much more, instead of saving the world one bathroom at a time.

"See if you can get us a refrigerator and a television too!" she adds and squeezes my hand. I wince in pain from the rhino bug attack over an hour ago.

A baby blue truck grumbles to a standstill in front of us. Deeper blue smoke wheezes from the exhaust pipe. It's Boonchu, my Thai Supervisor's driver from my office in Nakorn.

If I tell my Thai coworkers ahead of time where I will be working, and if my Supervisor doesn't need a ride anywhere, they send Boonchu out to drive me around.

Quite honestly, Boonchu just loves driving around smoking and drinking beer. Boonchu is a slender, middle-aged man with a menthol cigarette constantly slipped between his pursed lips. He's got skinny bird legs and a pot belly, which describes many older Thai men.

The ashes on his cigarette are nearly as long as the filter. There are several splotches where they have already fallen on his polyester pants. He's balding on top, but he lets his hair grow long on one side of his head and swirls it around to give the illusion that he indeed isn't balding. It makes his head look like a marble cake.

His hair falls askew in the breeze. So, he twirls the lost tendrils around his fingers and back to it's rightful position.

"Don't forget now, Susan," the attendant says as she kicks a chicken out of the way. She leans into my window once I climb into the truck. "A refrigerator and a television!"

"What? I thought you needed a bathroom?" I say, confused.

She squeezes my throbbing finger again and yells as we pull away, "And a bathroom! Good luck!"

Boonchu delivers me to the elementary school about three hundred yards up the ribbed road. I could have easily walked, but Thais love to show up to places with the *farang*, (foreigner). One time I was offered one hundred baht by a strange man to just walk with him down the street to a restaurant. I was going that way anyway, so did without taking his money. When we got to the restaurant, all his buddies stared at him and I, and thought he was the coolest dude in Thailand to arrive with a *farang*. I kept walking and never saw him again.

"Do you have dirt roads in America?" Boonchu asks, shifting his cigarette as well as the gear.

"No. They are all paved with gold," I answer.

He looks at me, grinning, knowing I am pulling his leg.

I continue, "There's no place in America that looks like Thailand, but yes, we have many dirt roads. I live in Minnesota, but grew up in Nebraska. One of my favorite things to do in Nebraska is drive really fast on the country dirt roads."

"I like driving fast on dirt roads too," he says speeding up. Nope, no, probably shouldn't have said that, now hanging on for dear life. Thank God we are not traveling far.

I *wai* him a thank you when we safely arrive.

The school is a long, wooden strip of a building secured on short stilts in a red muddy field. The classrooms are in a row with a rickety porch along the front as a hallway. Many of the floorboards of the porch are missing. No problem. The students have fun bunny-hopping over them as they scamper back and forth between classes.

An outdoor covered patio is the cafeteria, next to two outhouses. At the water pump, a purple plastic cup swings from a string and is shared by all who are thirsty.

A sludgy water buffalo pays no mind to me as I wade through the mud toward the steps. An arrogant bird is poised on the beast's back. It sees me and squawks at the sky, as if announcing my arrival.

I walk up the unsteady steps as a black rooster with flame-painted tail feathers and several red hens dash underneath the school. I'm welcomed by shy giggles, bewildered gazes and hidden grins behind grubby hands as I enter the first classroom. I remove my shoes as custom.

The English teacher, Peal, points to a tub of murky water.

"You, dirty foots," she proclaims in English.

"Yes, I have dirty feet," I answer, knowing I must wash them before continuing on into the classroom.

"Yes, you, dirty feets," she answers, proud of her English.

I rinse my feet and the crowd of kids hold me up. Some aid by splashing dark water on my legs and skirt. Some children are star-struck and intimidated by my presence and just stare at me. Some don't think I'm all that great, and only want to know what is in my bulky bag. A flimsy boy tries to pick up my supplies. Surrendering, he recruits two of his pals to assist. They drag my stuff to the front of the classroom.

Peal, like most English teachers in Thailand, cannot speak English well. The words she does know are often slaughtered beyond recognition. Her sentences are jumbled, disjointed and backwards. The textbooks are riddled with mistakes and old fashioned gender stereotypes. Young zooming minds are easily bored by the method of instruction which is dull memorization, dry repetition and copying words to paper without a clue of what they mean.

There is no wonder why sometimes nothing sinks in after six years of English classes except the abrasive words of "You! You! Where you go, *farang*?"

Peal scoots the rest of the kids out of her way and I pad behind with wet footprints. The students take their places by their wobbly desks, military style, and I take mine in front of the room.

"Goose money, teachah!" the kids yell in chaotic unison.

I cringe.

"Good morning, students!" I yell back, enunciating slowly.

"Goose money, teachah!" they repeat, only louder.

"Sit down, please!"

"Ten Que!" they reply.

"Thank you!" I answer.

Peal smiles primly at her properly behaved class. She presents a book for me to read out loud. This gives the students the rare opportunity to hear a native English speaker. The book is from the 1970s and is, well, just weird. The first paragraph I glance over describes *two bad men with guns* who get on a bus and steal purses and bags from *every people*. I decide to skip this literary gem and tell Peal I'll bring some better books to read next week.

I move onward to what I had originally planned. Making peanut butter.

"What is this? What is this? What is this?" I yell, holding up the oil, ground peanuts, salt and a spoon I remove from my bag one at a time.

Now that food has entered the lesson, I have the student's total attention. The kids flock forward and surround the table. Elbows are nudged and shins are kicked. They take anxious turns having the privilege of stirring the mess into edible paste while I insist they pronounce each ingredient in a complex sentence.

I then pass out sugar crackers. With great care, they spread the entire surface with our newly made peanut butter evenly and thick. A few children devour the treats instantly but most hold on to their crackers like precious pearls. They admire the foreign food from every angle. They discuss it in detail while occasionally touching the exotic morsel with the tips of their tongues.

There is half a bowl of peanut butter and two bags of sugar crackers remaining. Before I can offer the pupils more to eat, Peal snatches the leftovers.

She races to the teacher's office, screaming, "Come! Come! You!" over her shoulder to me. All I see are her pink heels and jet black bob disappearing around the corner. She apparently doesn't want to share anymore. Class is dismissed.

The one office for the headmaster and teachers is at the end of the long building. When I arrive, I am breathless from the pursuit. Peal is already talking excitedly to the other teachers and spreading the treats on the table. Break time here seems to be at random, or whenever someone has food.

I'm given bubbling dense coffee, a glass of green tea and a cup of red, warm soda. The teachers munch the peanut butter and crackers. A watermelon is sliced and papayas are peeled.

Being a 5'9", 145 pound American woman is amazon proportions in Thailand. Everyone assumes I require an enormous amount of food. Therefore, an assembly line is organized with myself on the receiving end. One teacher meticulously covers a rice cracker with bright yellow lard. It's gingerly passed to the next woman who layers on a coat of some orangish paste. The third woman tops it off with chunks of rock salt before she exaltedly hands it to me.

After seven crackers pile around my plate and in my lap, I convince them I have enough. Next comes rice, abundant bowls of curried fish and the inevitable common questions about America.

I'm met with disbelief when I explain that Americans love tanned skin and go to great lengths while spending much money to get it. My whiteness looks sickly compared to the cinnamon glow of Asians. I would trade tones in a heartbeat.

"Poor people in the U.S. have pale skin because they can't afford to vacation to sunny destinations like Thailand and work on their tans," I explain.

"Susan, you speak fun." Peal says and gently strokes my arm. The rest of the teachers chatter in agreement. White skin is beautiful, they say.

"Do you miss your family?" she asks.

"Yes, my family and my dog."

Silence instantly descends upon the room.

"A dog?"

"Yes, my pet dog. I have a pet dog in America."

"Why?" Peal asks, repulsion crossing her face. Most dogs in Thailand look like overgrown neurotic rats.

"Because it's a clean dog and it doesn't have any diseases. I miss sleeping with my dog."

"That can't be true," Peal answers.

Again, unanimous agreement. Thais simply can't imagine sleeping in a bed with a dog.

The air then turn noxious.

My nose recoils from the odorous assault. I start to gag and bury my nose in my elbow. The headmaster has dragged in a durian. Almighty God made His one and only mistake when He created durian for this otherwise magnificent planet.

It's a fruit the size and shape of a monstrous pineapple. The inner rancid flesh reeks of a clogged up garbage disposal. The color is vomit yellow. The taste is a raunchy sweet mixture of onions and strawberries. Mildewed melon. With garlic.

Lingering on the breath, the gusto lasts three days and a tube of toothpaste.

The shell is covered with deadly sharp spikes, perhaps at one time being a medieval weapon used to bash dragons. How the first person ever figured out how to open it and why they decided to eat it rather than flee in terror remains a puzzle to me.

They must have been hungry.

Considered a delicacy, I should be honored the teachers want to share this with me.

"You, eat durian you," a teacher says.

"Americans can eat rice and spicy food, but we cannot eat durian. I'm sorry." I explain holding my nose.

Peal pats my arm sympathetically while stuffing a piece of durian in her mouth. When I say, "Americans can't eat that," it usually gets me off the hook. I make it seem that it's an unfortunate American disability that just can't be helped. I'll eat stir fried ants, deep fried buffalo dung beetles, silk worm larvae but hell no to durian.

The stench is giving me a headach, so I announce I must leave. On my way out, a few students invite me to meet their school mascot out on the porch.

"What is his name?" I ask.

"Dog," Peal says.

Dog has lost most of his entire fur, is missing a front leg and does nothing but pant. It's rotted tail is curled up like a leather coil in the rear over it's body.

"I know it's a dog, but what is his name?"

She patiently looks at me and says again, "Dog."

"You should name him Tripod," I suggest of the three legged animal. When I explain what the word means in Thai, all the children yell, "Tipod! Tipod!"

Tipod gimps down the porch as the children part to make way for their untouchable friend. He stops, drops his weight, and rolls over in exhaustion.

The headmaster briskly walks over to Tipod and very businesslike, boots him off the porch. Tipod rolls down the stairs in a muffled ball, then crawls under the building.

The children escort me back through the red mud to Boonchu's waiting baby blue truck. There is hardly anything better in life than having a bunch of sweet Thai children gather around me and humbly render the traditional Thai *wai*.

"Goose pie, Teachah!" they pelt out, musically.

"Goodbye, students!" I answer, and *wai* back to them.

I get in the truck and see that Boonchu is already on his second quart of beer. He offers me one, but I decline. Someone in the truck should be sober, I just wish it was the driver.

Chapter Four

I spend the hour trip to Nakorn picking and itching my new mosquito welts. Making animated faces in disdain as I scratch, Boonchu hands me a small canister of potent tiger balm.

"Do you have mosquitos in America?" he asks.

"In Minnesota, yes, same-same, Boonchu," I answer.

"Do you drink Budweiser beer in America?"

"I wish I had one now!"

"Do you want some of my Singha beer?" he asks, passing me his half empty bottle.

"No, I'm good. Thanks though," I answer.

He finishes the beer and throws the bottle out the window as we speed down the road.

Once we get to our office, I sit down and plunk my head on my desk like a slumped over caterpillar. My coworkers usually arrive by six or seven in the morning, do the bulk of their work till about eleven, eat lunch and nap till about two o'clock. It's simply too hot to work in the afternoon. All the villagers in the places we work are taking naps at this time also, so it is pointless to even try. It's just too hot.

I try to doze as I wait for the mail.

About an hour later, the mail boy plops a thin magazine on my desk. I lift my head up and pull the magazine towards me. It's the latest edition of the *Diarrhea Dialogues*, courtesy of the Peace Corps. At least it's something to read in English.

On the cover are three close-up photos.

The first one is a photo captioned with, *Healthy stool*. The article inside further describes a healthy stool as *slightly moist with well-formed mounds and pliable to the touch.* Then it goes on to list a well-balanced diet a Peace Corps volunteer should eat to obtain a healthy and moist stool.

"Moist..." I mumble.

The next photo is captioned, *Sick stool*. This paragraph describes the turd as *often bubbly, gurgly and exits the body rapidly.* The article goes on to warn against eating raw and unwashed fruits and vegetables, which is what everyone here eats all day long, every day.

"Gurgly..." I whisper.

The next photo is of a *Dry stool*, with this description: *Flaky, pale and often disintegrates when plunged into water.* The paragraph encourages the volunteer to drink plenty of liquids to avoid dry stool.

"Plunge..." I say under my breath.

For the love of God, Peace Corps, why? Although I appreciate English words to read, *moist, gurgly* and *plunge* are not tops on my list. I know the U.S. Government is trying to be supportive, but sending full color magazines to us every month about bowel movements is not helpful. Who the hell touches their shit to see if it's *pliable to the touch*? Stop. Just stop.

I swipe the magazine off my desk straight into the trash can. Thunking my head back down, I snap my eyes shut. I bang my head on my desk one more time.

Boonchu walks over and pulls the magazine out of the trash. After a few seconds of perusal, with his first finger and thumb, he looks away and drops it back into the can with a grimace.

I don't think he can get away from the trash basket fast enough. Gawd. I bang my head on my desk again.

Mail preoccupies me. I want mail. I also want cheese. I would give anything for a piece of cheese. Colby longhorn. Swiss. A fresh bowl of iceberg lettuce with blue cheese dressing, sprinkled with cheddar cheese and bacon. Shredded mozzarella. Dill havarti. A pepper jack bacon cheeseburger. A Juicy Lucy from Matt's Bar...

I thunk my head up and down on my desk a few more times.

Thais are farmers and harvesters and hunters and gatherers and fishermen and gardeners. Much to my dismay, they are not cheese makers.

Every day I crave cheese. It's the one food I miss the most. I often pay outrageous sums to get a small brick of imported cheese in Bangkok at a fancy hotel's shop. I have friends and family send me Cheese Whiz and Kraft Easy Cheese that I eat with a spoon or put the nozzle in my mouth and suck the can dry.

With most Asian cultures throughout history, cheese and dairy were never a part of the diet. They have plenty of other food to eat, and when you think about it, cheese is really just a condiment to be on something else or with something else. This doesn't make me miss it any less.

The tropical climate is undoubtedly another reason. It would be too hard to keep dairy without a refrigerator, which only the very rich here have. There is shelf stable milk available, but it's nasty, even the chocolate flavored kind.

Once when I was out to eat with my coworkers, I was painstakingly removing my prawn from the shell to eat.

"Susan. That is not how you eat prawn. You eat it this way," Nuang said, and popped the entire prawn, shell, head and twirled little legs into her mouth and crunched away.

"Calcium, Susan. Shell has calcium," my Supervisor added. "You eat calcium."

I'd prefer cheese and real chocolate milk for calcium, but the Thais know how to get theirs, also.

I suppose my complaining about Thailand not having cheese would be similar to sitting in Paris and complaining the French don't eat rice and fish curry. 'What? Bread and cheese again? What's wrong with these people?'

The best advice I received during Peace Corps in-country training was this: Learn to eat Thai food. Simple and done, as most Thai food is delicious, fresh but spicy.

Eating in a group of more than one, everyone is brought a large mounded plate of white rice and a huge spoon to eat it with. No knife, no chopsticks, everything goes on the spoon.

To eat from the main dishes that are placed in the middle of the mat or table, you take one spoonful at a time, put it on a bit of rice and eat it. When you are ready for your next bite, you stick your saliva coated spoon with food particles attached back into one of the main dishes and retrieve another bite. Spoon to mouth, back into main dish, back into mouth.

Last month at lunch my coworkers ordered deep fried, whole baby birds, sizzled into all sorts of grotesque contortions, and a small bowl of raw garlic cloves. Nuang grabbed one by it's frazzled thin legs, bit off the seared head and crunched. Then, she followed it up with a clove of garlic as a chaser.

"Eat! Susan! Eat!" she urged, all the while the beak of lil Tweety bird was sticking out of her mouth. "Delicious!"

My other coworker said she didn't like fried baby birds, and told me not to eat them, making a face. Thank God that got me off the hook.

Nonetheless, I keep my head on my desk for another hour.

Then, I hear two of my male coworkers speaking rapidly in the southern Thai dialect. They use the southern dialect when they want to talk about me, knowing I don't understand it, as I only understand formal Bangkok Thai taught to us by the Peace Corps. At least I know when they switch dialects, they are going to talk about me.

I do pick up on the word, *farang*, which means me.

Here we go again.

I hear the word, nippen. Many, many, times, nippen.

One of the men walks over to my desk, but I don't raise my head.

"Susan. You. You. Nippen," he says in English.

I continue to keep my head on the desk and cover it with my hands.

"Nippen. Susan. You," he says again.

I know he won't leave me alone until I show some sign of life, so I answer, "What is it, nippen?" I answer in Thai.

"Nippen. You. Nippen," he answers in English.

"What is a nippen?" I ask louder in Thai.

The man snickers.

"Susan," he says in Thai. "What color are you nippen?"

I raise my head and ask, "I don't know. What is a nippen?"

He points to my boob, "Nippen."

"Nipple?" I ask in English.

"Yes. You. Nippen," he answers.

In English, most Thais cannot pronounce any word that ends in *le*. Apple is appen, simple is simpen, and now, nipple is nippen.

God forbid pronouncing three consonants together. A word like *straight* would be pronounced *ss taaa raight*. The *th* sound? My coworkers giggle when they say an English word that contains a *th* because it is so difficult for them to say correctly. Well, I know I butcher their language just as badly, if not worse.

"*Farang*s have three nippens," I say, and put my head back down on the desk.

One would think I would be offended by their question. More often than not, highly personal questions like this are merely innocent curiosity. I am, after all, the first American and/or white person they have talked to, much less seen, in their lifetime.

I remain face down at my desk till early afternoon.

At least there is hope that I have mail back in Sichon.

My mother writes to me every week. Frequent notes on Holly Hobby or some cute-puppy-in-a-basket-of-flowers stationary. She writes in exquisite cursive handwriting. She is the only person I know that can properly pen a capital cursive letter Q.

Her letters are wonderfully mundane chitchat of home; "Not enough salt in the tator tot hotdish." "The repairman is coming because the laundry sink backed up." "Snowed six inches today!"

My dad writes also, on a 3x5 notecard. Most people can't decipher his chicken scratch handwriting, but I can. He scrawls words of encouragement every week, such as "Life gets better if you let it!" or "Always carry a pocket knife!" or "Paddle your own canoe!" Every letter also contains a fresh twenty-dollar bill.

Two of my coworkers, beautiful women who work in the office as secretaries, approach my desk. My favorite, Nuang, is in a tight pink pencil skirt, pale blue ruffled silk shirt and high tan pumps with orange bows. She sits on the corner of my desk and gives me a bag of red papaya. The other coworker, Ping, is wearing a bright yellow and black skirt, white blouse and green slingbacks.

"Have you eaten rice yet or not, Susan?" Nuang asks.

Thais always ask one another if they have eaten rice, yet or not, as an informal greeting. It's similar to asking 'How ya doin...?"

"Already eaten rice," I reassure her.

"Eat rice!" Nuang screams and grabs one hand, and Ping grabs the other. They pull me to the back courtyard of the government building, filled with pushcart vendors, fruit stands and wobbly tables.

They buy me a plate of yellow curry with eggplant. I in turn buy all of us iced coffees.

"Susan, have you seen the Army boys in the province, American Army boys?" Nuang asks.

"Nope. No." I say, pretending I hadn't.

"Susan, they are your size. Big."

I about choke when she says that word.

"They are too big," Ping adds, making a scared face.

Nuang and Ping then abruptly excuse themselves, noticing it is time for them to go home for the day.

I'm finishing up my curry when I see her walk toward me.

Oh oh here she comes...

Chapter Five

Christine struts through the food court like a boss. A big, ravishing, flamboyant, swishy, peacocky boss.

She is radiant in a tight turquoise dress just past her hips, silver, strappy sky-high sandals and purple clutch purse. Oh, and a tiara. A silver tiara. Corral lipstick and green feather earrings.

"Susan! Susan! Susan!" she yells, flouncing towards the table.

"Susan!" she screams one more time.

"Sawatdee ca, Christine," I answer with a big smile and give her a traditional *wai*.

Everyone eating in the courtyard notices her, but pays little attention. There are no snickers or stares. Ladyboys in Thailand are tolerated, accepted, hardly unusual, and just part of life.

Christine pulls up a stool in the most elegant way, perches on top, crosses her long legs and folds her well-manicured hands on her lap like Queen Elizabeth.

Her Adam's apple is a bit large. Her nose is flat and she has a high forehead with clear, perfect skin. A brilliant smile. Thick, ebony hair spills down her sculpted back. She is a beautiful woman, just with a penis taped up between her legs.

Christine is from the small village of Sichon where I live but travels back and forth to Hot Yai for work. I met her at a disco in Hot Yai one night with my PCV friend Nori. The club was called The Emperor Disco.

The Emperor is about as majestic as the Prince Hotel, as in not at all, but gigantic in space and very fun. Nori and I were the only two white faces amongst the hundreds of partiers. At least we got plenty of free drinks and just stuck to dancing with ourselves.

During the evening, between the Madonna and Whitney Houston pop tunes, they cleared the dance floor for a drawing. The admission tickets had numbers and the stubs were put in a big bowl. A beautiful go-go girl drew the tickets and the lucky winners ran down to the floor like a contestant on *The Price is Right* game show. Then, they were ceremoniously presented with a large stuffed animal.

The whoop-dee-doo over the drawing and the passing out of the animals was the highlight of the evening. I can't imagine the crowd any more excited than if they were passing out bags of diamonds.

A gorgeous Thai woman and her cloud of Love's Baby Soft perfume slid into the booth next to me. Her beauty was strong and dazzling. She put her arm around me and snatched my ticket from my hand.

"Why don't you win?" she asked in very good English.

I shook my head, and said, "Bad Luck. I have bad luck."

"Oh no!" she exclaimed. "You have good luck! I'll bring you very good luck!"

She jumped out of the booth and took off through the crowd.

Ten minutes later, she returned clutching a fuzzy, white, stuffed rabbit with red velvet ears.

"You now have good luck. For you. My name is Christine," she said and proudly handed the rabbit to me.

"Thank you! What should I name it?" I asked.

"Rabbit."

"I know it's a rabbit, but what should I name it?"

"You name it Christine, after me," she said, and sat back down with me and Nori.

She grabbed a fist full of my blond hair and buried her face in it, sniffing it deeply.

After talking for only a few minutes, we discovered I live only about two miles from her mother's house in Sichon.

"I come see you!" she said excitedly, and squeezed my thigh almost painfully.

"Let's dance!" I said, mostly to get her to stop crunching my leg. We slid through the packed bodies to the dance floor.

We danced to Soul II Soul's *Back to Life*, the B-52's *Love Shack*, and the Fine Young Cannibals, *She Drives me Crazy*.

She then hugged me so tightly I could hardly breathe, sniffed my hair one more time, then disappeared into the crowd.

I went back to the booth. Nori was laughing hard and could barely speak.

"What's so funny?" I asked taking a big gulp from my cocktail of Sang Som (Thai rum) and Red Bull.

"Couldn't you tell?" she blurted out.

"What?"

"Don't you know?"

"What?"

"Seriously? You don't know?" she said again, and slapped her hand on the table.

"Huh?"

"Lola! L-O-L-A Lola!" Nori yelled over the music.

"Who?"

"Christine looks like a woman but...!"

"The Kinks?" I shouted. I couldn't figure out what she was talking about.

"Seriously, you couldn't tell?"

"Just tell me!" I screamed, starting to get annoyed.

"Girls will be boys etc? You don't get it?"

"Tell me!"

"Sue! She is a he!" she finally yelled, and threw her head down on the table, laughing.

I stared at Nori. She lifted her head and kept laughing.

"That was a ladyboy?"

"Oh my God, Susan, aren't you quick," she said sarcastically.

"Whatever!" I screamed above the music.

She screamed "That's about it, whatever!" back to me.

Before we knew it, it was almost two a.m. As we were leaving, I looked around as we walked out the door. I saw Christine on the mezzanine, sitting on some man's lap. She gave me a little wave and blew me a kiss. I pretended to catch it, put it on my cheek and waved goodbye.

~~~

Back in the food court behind my office building, Christine orders an iced coffee. She then lowers her voice and says, "I stopped by your house, but you weren't home."

"No, I decided to do some work today," I answer.

"You need to clean you house. There are empty cheese cans all over. You are going to get ants. And too many books Stacks of books. How many books do you read at time? You have too many books."

"It's clean, just messy."

"Why do you have so many books?" she asks again.

"Wait a minute, how do you know what the inside of my house looked like today when I wasn't there?"

"Susan, your house is a mess," she says, rolling her eyes.

"Did you go into my house?"

"Of course, I was looking for you."

"Didn't you knock? Its only one room and a bathroom. I would've heard you if you had knocked."

"You didn't hear me because you weren't there," she answers, like it was the most obvious thing in the world.

"I know I wasn't there! Stop talking in circles, Christine!"

"Do you want me to help clean your house? You will get ants."

"How did you get in my house?" I ask incredulously.

"Through the window, dummy," she says.

"Christine!"

"You act like that's a problem. I always go into your house when you're not there."

"What? Since when do you go into my house when I'm not there?"

"I go there to look for you. Look at your things. Take a quick shower. Sometimes I sleep there when you are gone."

"You are only now telling me this? Gosh, Christine, I can give you a key to the house. You don't have to break in."

"Why you never give me the key to your house?"

"Because I am only now finding out you climb through my window when you are more than welcome to come in the front door anytime?"

"You pay too much money in rent for that little place," she answers instead.

"You didn't take any of my Easy Cheese, did you?"

"No! Thais don't eat that nasty crap. How do you Americans eat that nasty crap?

"You Thais eat plenty of nasty crap too," I retort.

"Thais don't eat fake cheese out of a can."

"Americans don't eat stir fried ants."

"If Thailand wants to eat ants, they go to your house. Ants all over your messy house."

"Then why don't you fry them up and eat them?"

"They taste better than crap cheese!"

I take a deep breath. Conversations like this with her could go on forever.

"Christine. Tell me why you went into my house, please," I state, instead of asking.

"I left the briefcase under your bed."

"What briefcase?"

"Claus."

"Claus?"

"Claus."

"You mean case?"

"No, Claus, the fat German. His case."

What?"

"Claus. His case. My German boyfriend in Hot Yai."

My eyes grow wide. I can hardly move. I whisper, "Christine, I don't want anything to do with that. Nothing. I could get in very serious trouble. You could get in very serious trouble."

"You won't get in trouble. I take it away soon. No problem."

"I trust you Christine. I trust you will take care of that as soon as you can. I don't want to know what you do, just get rid of it."

"You forget about it. It's okay," she whispers with a grin.

"Promise?"

"Promise."

"Good." I answer, and push it out of my mind. I know Christine will take care of it. She's the most trustworthy thief I know.

"Good. Now come, lets go shopping!" she says, obviously wanting to change the subject as much as I.

Chapter Six

There is one small department store in Nakorn tucked between two noodle restaurants. It's a narrow three story building with clothing, shoes and accessories for both men and women. As we walk in, I see a basket of belts on a low shelf, so I gesture with my foot towards them, telling Christine to take a look.

She backhands me in the stomach.

"Susan, never, never point with your foot," she scolds.

"What?"

"Your foot. Rude. Rude. Foot is dirty. Head is clean. Don't point with your foot. In Buddhism, souls are in head. Feet are dirty. Don't touch people with feet or use feet to point."

I never realized how often Americans use their feet to point, gesture, or touch people or things. I do it all the time

Christine pulls me by the hand to the lingerie section. Cooing and cawing, she holds up one silky lacy bra after another. Soon, the shop girls surround us, wanting to help.

"Susan, you try, you try," she insists, throwing a purple thong in my face.

"No, Christine, no. I'm a Hanes cotton brief sorta girl. It's too dang hot here to wear anything else."

Then, the shop girls join in and load me up with bright pant-
ies and frilly bras.

"You never know when you might need them," Christine says
with a wink.

Almost everything is too small. I'm a normal size eight, but in
Thailand that is full-figured size, so the shop girls really have to
dig around to find items that might fit me and Christine as well.

Christine buys everything she likes and a few things for me
despite my protests. She does just fine soaking her customers for
cash or stealing from the ones she doesn't like.

Awhile ago, she told me how she *came out* as a ladyboy and
eventually turned to prostitution.

Her father once had a fishing boat and was able to support his
family by selling the daily catch at the market. One day, he was so
drunk that he fell overboard. Some nearby fishermen tried desperately to save him, but he quickly drowned. The fishermen were
able to pull the boat to shore, and the family sold it, but the money
didn't go far. Soon, the family fell into deep poverty without a
steady income.

Being the only son at the time, Christine quit school at age
fourteen and went down to the docks to help on the fishing boats.
Her two younger sisters quit school also, and went to work along
with their mother on the dock patio.

Christine didn't like being out at sea with the rough fishermen who drank all day. She preferred to work with her sisters,
mother, and the rest of the women on the dock. They worked long
hours on the patio peeling shrimp, preparing squid, and sorting
fish. The work was tedious, but the women sang, gossiped and
giggled to make the days go by fast.

She did this until she turned fifteen, and as she said, "grew
hairy down there and started to feel hard" in her penis. One day
after working twelve hours, she and another boy the same age
stole a quart of Mekong and sat under a palm tree out of sight.
They shared the entire bottle.

Soon, they began fondling each other. Christine then put her mouth on his part, and couldn't believe how much she enjoyed it. She said it was like a wall coming down exposing a new world for her. From that day on, she said, she realized she was a ladyboy.

She also explained that she always admired women and the beauty rituals of being a woman; hair, makeup and clothing. This is one reason why I think she always wants to go shopping as her outward appearance is very important to her. She wants to look the feminine part outwardly to match how she feels on the inside.

After we shop and try on clothes for several hours, Christine announces it's time to eat rice again. It seems it's always time to eat rice in Thailand.

A delicious aroma pulls us around the corner to a place serving turmeric rice and roasted chicken. Three gigantic black witches caldrons of deep golden rice are steaming on the pavement in front of the cafe.

A Muslim woman with a colorful head-covering dishes out plates of turmeric rice and chicken in rapid succession. After every scoop, she ceremoniously smacks the huge spoon on the side of the pot, sailing rice through the air, and digs in again to fluff up the steaming feast.

Towering across from the cafe is an Islamic mosque. It's an ornate and sturdy fortress covering one square block. There is a white fence surrounding the cement structure. Topping all corners are round turrets with teardrop caps. They are primary green and match the trim around the arching windows and doorways. During certain times of the day, an enchanting voice echoes out of the highest belfry and carries thru the air far above.

Once I bravely walked through the arches into the inner courtyard. As a Christian, every temple in Thailand I had been to and everything I learn about Buddhism comforts me, but that mosque gave me the creeps, and unsure why. I walked out as fast as I could.

Sitting in the mosque's shadow, we order a plates of turmeric rice and chicken. The cook walks over and hands me a dish of sumptuous yellow rice with a black chicken heart on top.

"She likes you, Susan. The hearts are the best, she saves them for special. Eat, eat it. It's delicious," Christine says.

"Sorry. No, I can't. Americans can't eat chicken hearts."

Christine scoops it off with her spoon and puts the whole thing in her mouth. She then smiles and pushes some of the chewed up goo out between her teeth, giggling.

"Stop it! That's nasty!" I scold.

"Not as nasty as you wearing hiking sandals," she says, glancing down at my feet.

"There's nothing wrong with my hiking sandals," I say.

"There's nothing wrong with chicken hearts," she answers.

"Can I ask her to give me a breast instead?"

"Boobies? You want to eat boobies?" she says, teasing me.

A few heads turn, apparently some of the men know what the word *boobie* means in English.

"Not boobies, breast meat. Meat from chicken breasts."

"Chicken boobies?"

"Christine, seriously, you know what I am talking about."

"Go ask her Susan, go ahead. Ask her for boobie meat."

Christine is just playing with me, but I am getting annoyed.

"You're no help so shut up," I say, grab my plate, and walk up to the cook.

I slump my shoulders apologetically in front of the smiling woman. I see a plump white breast on top of the rice, so I simply point to it and smile back.

The cook looks confused, and gives me another heart instead, obviously thinking I enjoyed the last one so much because I ate it so quickly, I must want another.

"No, please, that one there," I say, and point again.

She compassionately scoops the juicy, perfectly roasted piece onto my plate.

I slam my bowl on the table in front of Christine and sit back down. I'm still mad at her for teasing me.

We eat in silence for a few seconds, then under her breath, she whispers, "Boobie."

I try to stay angry but can't.

"Mine are bigger than yours," I whisper back.

Now that gets *her* mad.

She reaches over and hovers a hand above one of mine, while holding one of hers.

"Same-same," she says, defensively.

I bat her hand away and grin.

"Same-same," I answer, and we both start giggling and enjoy the rest of or meal.

As we finish, a teenaged boy with a vinyl headband drives his motorcycle over the sidewalk, through the restaurant and parks it in the back behind the last table. He has a greasy pompadour hairdo and is wearing a tee shirt that reads in English, *The more I know men, the more I love my dog.* Ordering a plate of turmeric rice and chicken, he asks specifically for the heart.

After we share an iced coffee, Christine and I walk to the bus station. She hops on one back to Hot Yai for work, and I get on one to my village of Sichon. Half an hour later, the bus spews me out on the side of the road at the Jet Sipette.

I buy a couple packs of cigarettes from the old man along with a bag of squid flavored chips and my Bangkok Post. I give a few chips to Scabby, who is busy smelling his butt.

"It's okay, Scabby, we all have our issues," I say to the dog.

He eats the chips, then goes back to smelling his butt.

I walk the hot mile to my house. Sitting on my woven mat in the middle of the floor, I light a cigarette and spend the rest of the evening reading the newspaper and watching the geckos having sex on the ceiling. I have completely forgotten about the briefcase.

Chapter Seven

A few days later, I am helping some older village girls with their English homework on my front porch. They love hearing a native speaker, and cling to my every word.

A motor scooter pulls up followed by a dozen tiny beeps from a cheap horn.

It's Christine.

"Come Susan! Let's go!" she yells.

She is wearing an orange mini skirt, lime tank top and yellow, high heeled pumps. With pink plastic sunglasses on, she has her hair pulled back tight in a high pony tail.

"Hi Christine! When did you get back? Where do you want to go?" I ask.

"We go to Tangmo's restaurant and suck snails with my friends!" she answers.

I make a face. I'm not a big fan of sucking snails, but excited to go along to spend time with Christine.

"Snails are good, Susan, you go suck snails," one of the girls says in English, trying to encourage me.

"Suck snails, Susan! Go suck snails!" the other chimes in.

"Get ready, hurry up!" Christine shouts. "But don't wear your ugly hiking sandals, please!"

I spend a few quick minutes inside combing my hair and change into less sweaty clothes, then jump on the back of her scooter. We tootle down the beach road to the end of the cove to Tangmo's restaurant.

A popular munchie food to eat while getting drunk are *hoi*, or snails. They are cooked in a thick spicy broth, and then put on a plate in the middle of the table so everyone can share. I almost feel like I'm back in the States enjoying an appetizer at TGI Fridays. Okay, not really, but it's fun nonetheless.

To suck the snail, you have to remove the operculum, which is the little flap that covers the opening, like a trap door. Then, you hold the shell to your mouth and simply suck really hard. The meat will slide out in one solid chunk, and has the texture of a rubbery oyster. Some people chew them, some people just swallow them whole.

When we arrive at the restaurant, which is an open patio under a thatched roof on the beach, Christine's two friends are already waiting for us. They have a bottle of Mekong, several bottles of coke, a bucket of ice, and a plate of *som tom* on the table.

One of my favorite dishes which I eat almost every day is *som tom*, unripe shredded green papaya salad.

Som tom is a good example of Thai, as well as many Asian dishes, using all five of the sensations of tastes. Most dishes include something sweet, savory, sour, spicy and salty. Thais do not use soy sauce, which is often associated with Asian cooking. It is fish sauce, or *nam plah*, which translates as "fish water." Fish sauce is from fermented fish, not salty, but adds a savory, rich taste to the food.

Christine's beautiful ladyboy friends welcome me with open arms and genuine friendliness. I don't know if most Westerners would be able to tell they are transgendered. However, anyone could tell they are prostitutes.

One is wearing a red snakeskin print pleather sundress, large gold hoop earrings and four inch spiked fuchsia pumps. The other is wearing a stretchy pink halter top, neon blue tube skirt, and purple sky-high heels. Proper Thai women do not dress this way, and in America, women don't dress this way either unless they are dancing in a strip club.

"This is Velveetah, and this is Samantha," Christine says, proudly introducing them to me.

We all *wai* to each other before I sit down.

"Oh, Christine, you weren't lying! The *farang* is pretty. Are her boobs real?" Samantha asks in Thai.

"She can speak Thai," Christine answers, and flicks Samantha in the head.

Samantha blushes a little and says, "Oh! Susan! You are pretty!"

Velveetah then blows me a kiss and winks.

"You are prettier," I say, smiling back.

"Are you named after the cheese?" I then ask Velveetah.

"Of course. Because I'm smooth and creamy," she answers.

I don't want to burst her bubble, but something certainly got lost in the translation there...

We all giggle, start to drink and chit chat.

Christine orders a plate of *hoi* and a quart of Singha beer for me, and another coke for her to drink with the Mekong.

Velveetah reaches over and hovers her hand above my breast, and then her own, making a face.

"Mine much bigger, Susan," she says, pursing her lips.

"Mine are big enough!" I answer.

"Mine bigger than all of yours," Samantha adds.

"No, mine are," Christine says.

All three ladyboys have breast implants, but Velveetah has gone all the way with a full sex change operation down there.

"No one can tell that I had an operation," Velveetah brags.

"Really?" I say.

"Same-same as you," she answers, smiling. "Doctor in Singapore, he does it for many ladyboys. Very expensive though."

Christine and Samantha kept their private parts, and tape them up between their legs. They weren't very big to begin with, they tell me.

"What happens when your boyfriends or customers discover that you're a ladyboy?" I ask.

"When I do tell them, they get more excited, because they have never been with a ladyboy. Susan, all men are a little gay. Homo in some way. They just don't admit it. When they travel to Thailand, no one knows them here, so they do things they would not do back home. Experiment," Velveetah explains.

We all cheer a toast.

Christine orders a plate of *lahp*, which is raw, heavily spiced minced meat. Usually it's made with beef and ground toasted rice, fish sauce, lime, chili peppers and mint. Served at room temperature, sticky rice and raw veggies are used to scoop it up to eat.

She also orders *tom yam goong* (hot and sour soup with shrimp), which is one of my favorites, and smells so good I want to hunch over it just inhale the sinus clearing citrus.

It's made with lemongrass, kaffir lime leaves, galangal and green onions. Galangal is blue ginger. The cook slices thin pieces off the enormous root to soak in the broth. Then, the cook throws in salt, sugar, hot chilies, fish sauce, whole mushrooms, and fresh jumbo shrimp.

The plate of snails is delivered to our table, and as we start to eat, a Ford F-150 pulls up to the restaurant.

With two big handsome guys in it. One is Mike.

I nervously pick up a snail to suck.

I fall into a trance when I see him, and sit quietly, smiling like a fool.

Mike and his friend walk up to the table as the ladies squeal, "Sit! Drink! Eat! You welcome!"

So they do. Mike's buddy is Captain Johnson, and Velveetah immediately sets her sights on him.

Remarkable. Mike. He smells like Irish Spring soap. I want to bury my face in his neck and breathe him in.

Then, I realize the snail I am trying to suck has attached to the inside of my lip. I can't get it out of my mouth. Jesus Holy Hell...then the pain sets in. The shell is firmly attached to the inside of my gum.

I try to be inconspicuous, but the agony is becoming unbearable. It's sucking the bottom inside of my mouth between my teeth. The thing is alive and hornier than me.

I keep my hand over my mouth, and try to say, "Hi Mike."

"Sawatdee, Susan, good to see you again," he answers, and sits down next to me, smiling.

I lean over to Christine on my other side, lift my hand from my mouth and whisper, "Christine, get this off my lip."

She lifts my hand further up and peers into my mouth, making a horrified face.

"Susan, that's not how you eat this!" she says with concern.

"I know! It's stuck to the inside of my lip! Get it off now please!" I squeak loudly.

Mike and the Captain are staring at me now, wondering what is going on. I try to act like nothing is wrong.

Christine looks again, then says very seriously, "That's a cone snail, Susan. That is not good news."

What she is telling me is this thing is not a simple snail, but a deadly cone snail that somehow got on the plate of *hoi*. It has suctioned onto the inside of my gum and is not letting go.

Velveetah and Samantha are wondering and worrying about what is going on with my mouth. They rush over and yank my head back and forth to get a better look.

Christine grabs my bottom lip and places her fingers on each side of the shell, twists and pulls. An awful popping sound explodes from my mouth as she rips the snail off. It hurts. It hurts too bad. Too much. It's not right how much it hurts.

I realize I am bleeding and bleeding a lot. There is now a huge hole in my gum with blood and saliva running down my chin.

Christine flings the cone snail shell off into the night. Then, Samantha pounces into action.

"Susan! Disinfect it! DIS IN FECT IT!" she screams.

She grabs the bottle of Mekong and pours it into my mouth, on my wound, but mostly down my throat.

Velveetah screams, "Stop the bleeding! STOP! THE! BLEEDING!" and wads up a handful of napkins and sticks them into my mouth.

More Mekong is poured in and more napkins shoved.

Because the booze Velveetah pours on the wound is going straight down my throat, along with the lack of oxygen from the huge wad of alcohol-soaked napkins in my mouth, I become cross-eyed dizzy. I can't breath. I am getting no air. I can't move.

Mike stands up, tells all three of them firmly to sit down and be quiet. He grabs my face in his hands and pulls out the booze-soaked, blood-drenched, packed brick of napkins.

He then slaps me hard on the back. I lurch forward and take a deep breath inward. I stand up, and puke all over his boots. Spray them, like a projectile vomit, booze and blood missile.

Not that I remember too much from then on out, I do recall getting into the Ford F-150, Mike driving with Christine sitting in the middle of us, like a protective mother hen.

He drives us back to my hut.

"She tired, Mike. You go now. You come back tomorrow if you want, but not now. You go," I hear her say as I pass out.

Chapter Eight

I open my eyes to the waft of Tong's sizzling garlic in her wok outside. The chickens are scratching in the dirt under my hut. I lift my head and see Christine sleeping on the mat on the floor, next to my bed, using a pile of laundry as a pillow.

The box of seashells I keep by the door are all perfectly lined up on the window's ledge, from large to small. She must have arranged them last night.

Christine is wearing one of my tee shirts and a pair of my shorts for pajamas. Her long black hair loops around the side of her face. She rolls on her back and starts to snore like a freight train, nostrils vibrating with each breath in and whistling honks on the way out. I realize how easily I forget she was born a boy, and now a woman of twenty-five-years old.

I put my head back on the pillow, but continue staring at her. She looks so very peaceful. Lovely.

I then hear a truck pull up. A minute later, a few light knocks on my door.

"Susan, good morning, are you in there?"

It's Mike. Holy big Buddha. I am sure I look like hell but don't feel very bad. As good as I can feel after last night.

Dear God, I am so embarrassed.

"I gotta leave Sichon today, probably go up north soon. Are you in there? Hello? Susan?" he says again.

"Hi Mike! Just give me a minute!" I answer, panicking a little.

Christine flips over to her side and continues snoring. I quickly run to the bathroom, rinse my face, brush my teeth and comb my hair as well as I can in two minutes. My inner lip is sore from the snail, and starting to swell a little.

I slip out the door silently, as not to wake Christine.

There he is, standing in front of me in all his masculine glory. Mike. Dang, he looks even better than he did last night.

"How ya feeling?" he asks, glancing at me sideways. "How's that mouth?"

"Not so bad. Sorry about last night," I mumble.

"I never had a date who got a snail stuck on her lip," he says with a grin.

Oh my gawd, did he just call me his *date?*

"Only in Thailand," I answer.

"Let's go get some breakfast before I leave, sound good?"

"Awesome, let me get my stuff!"

Off we go, back to Tangmo's restaurant for bowls of chicken, lemon grass and rice soup, sweet sticky rice with orange mangos, and dark iced coffee.

We talk, laugh and eat for almost two hours.

I told him I was in the Army Reserve for six years, and they paid for my college. My enlistment was up right about the time I graduated and was accepted into the Peace Corps.

"So how do you serve in the Army, then serve in the Peace Corps?" he asks.

"The Army does more good in Thailand than the Peace Corps, I'll tell you that much. A few years ago in my province before I arrived, the Army Corps of Engineers came here and built an entire school in two short weeks. Me, I teach English and sing Madonna songs, for two long years."

"You are doing fine," he chuckles, and brushes the hair out of my eyes.

Oh my Lord, first he called me his date, and now he just touched me.

He says he joined the Army right out of high school to get away from an alcoholic dad and mom addicted to prescription pills. She took the pills to get away from the dad, or at least escape in her head, as she was too scared to leave him.

I remember one of the first days in my own Army basic training, my drill sergeant screamed, "Y'all joined my Army because you are running from something or looking for something! Right now in my Army, you will stop running and find it!"

Mike says he had been running. He quickly went on to do amazing things he knew he could do if given the chance. The Army gave him that chance, and he went on to make it into the elite Special Forces.

He does drink some, but other than that, he is what I refer to as straight and narrow. I really have to downplay all the drinking and goofing off I do here, and I certainly don't smoke in front of him, as he would think that is disgusting.

He isn't self-centered, if anything, self-deprecating. Doesn't brag about his achievements. An easy sense of humor. The confidence. The total focus on me. Oh, my goodness, those arms...and chest...and hands...and just about everything. Blue eyes, sandy brown hair, his front two teeth slightly overlap one another, big nose, all dipped in scrumptiousness.

He says he is going up north to Chiang Mai for a joint training exercise the U.S. Army does with the Thai military every year later today. So, we get up to leave as he really should be going. He will be in touch, he promises.

Then we would meet up back in the States, run into each other's arms and fall madly in love. We were soul mates, destined to be together. The wedding would be small, but we would honeymoon in Thailand, of course. We would buy our first house together, and have one child. I would want a boy, so it would be like him. He would want a girl, so it would look like me, because we both think each other is perfect. We would then grow old together yet still feel the exciting tingly attraction toward each other as we do right now at this little cafe.

Or, maybe not.

I might never see this dude again.

I have to say something.

"Before you leave, would you mind coming back to my hut and just totally fuck my brains out?"

"Excuse me?" he asks, quite politely but shocked.

"You heard me," I answer softly.

"Sure, Susan. With pleasure," he says and laughs. "Let's go."

So we leave.

When I open the door, I see that Christine is gone, so we go in.

I turn around. He shuts the door quietly.

I suddenly don't feel so brazen anymore. I feel like jelly.

I can't believe this man is here. Ready. For me. I look down at him there. Oh goodness, he is ready.

I am standing barefoot with straight, scraggly hair. Dang, I should have shaved my legs. The manicure Christine gave me awhile ago has begun to chip off. I have callouses on my feet and those annoying little red sweat bumps on the back of my upper arms. I am wearing a white, practical bra.

He needs a shave.

His nose is a little crooked.

A hockey injury, I find out later.

He has sweat stains under his armpits.

I am starting to sweat between my thighs.

Would you make the first move, please. Because I just can't. You are too wonderful of a thing to touch.

He gently touches my shoulder and says, "Ah, ya know Susan, I would really like to kiss you, but your lip. I think you need to get that checked out, it's starting to swell."

He takes my head in both hands and tips it back a little to get a better look, then furrows his brow.

"Well," I say quietly, "in Thailand, they sniff kiss."

"What's that?"

"Sniff kiss. *Hawm*. They smell each other closely, but don't kiss with their lips."

He looks at me intently, then says, "I think I can do that."

With one hand around my neck, his other hand slowly lifts up my hair to one side. Then, he puts his nose behind my ear, inhaling all the way down to my collar bone.

Oh sweet Jesus, yeah, that's pretty much how it's done.

In about zero-seconds, we are on the bed, ripping each other's clothes off. Then he slows down before we actually do, which drives me crazier.

I feel like an open book and he is reading me. Every sentence. Every word. Every letter. Devouring my best parts. Skipping over the bad parts. Yet he smiles. I simply can't close him and put him down. Keep going. It gets better. Wait for the good part. It's coming. I want to turn the page. I am just about ready to turn the page, yes, just flip the page and close it, close it good, just slam the book down hard motherfucker and finish it....ah, gawd ...yes...just like that.

"Are you okay in there, Susan?" Tong screams, knocking on the shutters.

I bury my face in Mike's chest, cringing in embarrassment.

We were too loud.

Tong then starts banging on the door. I can hear her kids yelling outside, getting all excited about the commotion.

"Susan! Is there a lizard in there? Just beat the lizard with a broom!"

"No, Tong, no lizard, I'm fine!" I yell.

"You want me to kill the lizard? Beat it with a broom?"

"No, Tong, I am okay, thank you!" I yell back.

"Beat the lizard, Susan! Use a broom!"

Mike whispers into my ear, "Please don't beat my lizard with a broom."

"Shhh, shush, stop it, just be quiet," I whisper back, trying not to giggle.

Then I hear another neighbor yell from across the yard, "She has Army boy in there!"

"You know those American Army boys? She has one in there!" someone else chimes in.

"You have Army boy in there, Susan?" Tong screams through the shutters.

There is some rapid southern Thai dialect arguing back and forth between the neighbors outside, but I can't understand it. Then, dead silence.

I'm now positive the entire neighborhood is gathered around my porch, listening, only quietly.

So Mike and I do it one more time, this time quietly.

Then he says he has to go, and promises to come back again before returning to the States. We kiss goodbye, and he leaves. I listen to the Ford F-150 pull away.

It is the best morning of my life.

Chapter Nine

I get out of bed and start to pull out my dirty clothes to do laundry. I can't wait for Mike to come back, then feel panicky that he wouldn't. I sit down and put my head in my hands and start to think too much.

I then remember the briefcase Christine has hidden under my bed. I fall to the floor to look underneath it. A gecko scurries out, flitting toward the nearest wall, running up and away.

Sure enough, there it is. I pull it out and stare at it for a moment. There seems to be no way to open it. There isn't a combination lock, no latches, no key holes, no hinges, no markings, no brand, nothing but a sturdy handle. I shake it and it makes no noise. I realize this is not an ordinary traveler's suitcase, or business briefcase. The German tourist has something inside that he doesn't want anyone to get to, that's for sure.

Shit. Shit. Shit. I hope it's not drugs.

Shit.

I would go to prison for a long time if I get caught with something like that. Thais don't mess around when it comes to punishing drug traffickers. The Peace Corps or U.S. Government would be unable to do anything to help. If caught with this in my hut, the truth would be absolutely unbelievable:

Really, Sir, my best friend, a ladyboy prostitute, stole it from one of her clients after he almost died because she choked him too hard during sex and then she climbed through my window and hid it under my bed when I was sleeping at my desk at work.

I slide it back under my bed. I don't know what to do. Christine did say she would take care of it, but things could go wrong. Even when she gets it out of my house, what if she gets caught with it.

Starting to worry and even shake a little, I grab my cigarettes and go outside to sit on the beach to stare at the ocean.

I see Tangmo sitting in her chair down the beach in front of her family's restaurant. I walk over to sit by her. She is always here, and I often sit by her for hours. On weekends, sometimes we sit together all day.

Tangmo (her nickname meaning watermelon) sits outside on the beach more than I do. She is about ten, maybe eleven years old and inflicted with cerebral palsy. UNICEF or some church back in the States had delivered to her a wheelchair, which is fine in theory but not in practicality. It's impossible to wheel it around in this environment with the rocks, sand and muddy roads.

Every day, her older brother brings her down to the beach in the morning, and here she sits. They bring her back at lunch time and for a potty break, then bring her again to sit until dinner time.

I had asked her mother why they didn't send Tangmo to one of the state boarding schools for the handicapped, but her mother said no way. She explained the facilities are more like pantries to warehouse the disabled. There is not inclusive education like in the States, where the disabled go to school along with mainstream kids. Rural schools here just don't have the trained teachers, money or resources to handle kids with special needs.

Also, Thai Buddhists believe in reincarnation. If a person is mentally or physically handicapped, although treated with compassion, it is karma. The handicapped, or poor, or diseased person suffers because of a past failure in a previous life. They need to be allowed to go through the suffering now, with nothing added or nothing taken away, to eventually reach nirvana, or so it was explained to me by her mother.

Tangmo is much loved and well cared for, but will never do much else than sit all day in the shade on the beach, watching the able bodied do miraculous things like walk, talk and breath without drooling. Perhaps when she dies, and returns for her next time around, she will be an Olympic runner, or find the cure for cancer.

I pull over a beach chair, and we watch the ocean switching, changing, rushing in and out for a few hours. Whatever wave slips away from the shore, another new round of dancers gently replace it. Sometimes the watery ballerinas gracefully slide seaweed or leaves or sticks near our feet, like offerings. Sometimes they sneak away with them instead.

Tangmo and I stop staring at the ocean when we see a groggy little turtle searching it's way in the grass next to us at the shoreline, struggling with the weight of the world on his back.

The turtle reaches the edge of the grass and peers over the top to the sandy shore. He must have miscalculated the distance. Scooting right over the edge, he falls, landing on his back. Only about six inches, but that is quite a tumble for a little turtle. He twirls his chubby legs and keeps jutting up his head. To no avail. He lies there and slugs away into the air, trying to find traction.

Tangmo makes a throaty groan and gurks her head around, as if trying to tell me to help him. She even lets her arm drop off her lap and down the side of the chair toward the struggling turtle. I just watch her, watching him.

Within reach of Tangmo's fingers is a long sturdy stick. For about five agonizing minutes, she moans, grunts and trembles her contorted fingers toward the stick until finally, she grabs it. This part, though, is a piece of cake compared to Tangmo's next goal.

The turtle snips his head and legs back in his shell and closes shop. He doesn't want anything to do with the prodding stick. Tangmo continues to poke, nudge and tap the shell with the stick and finally succeeds in flipping him over. He pops out of his shell and crawls under her chair. Tangmo groans, obviously exhausted. She smiles as best as she can at me.

I open a Narnia book to read but the Gulf of Siam today is quickly becoming much more interesting. It's growing agitated, upset, and looks like it's ready to throw a fit. Thickening, darkening and getting angrier by the minute. Clouds of purple velvet are crawling closer and eventually cover the sun with a deep fabric of darkness. The wind begins to bang about the tops of the trees, shaking the giant palm leaves. Tangmo's mother runs down to us, grabs her daughter in her arms, and screams frantically at me, "Go home! Go home! Susan, go home now!"

She dashes back toward her restaurant in a flash with Tangmo in her arms as the sky turns furious. The clouds are now black buffalos stampeding toward shore. The fishing boats and tugs on the horizon dissolve under their wild hooves.

The neighbor kids run over and grab my arm, pulling me out of the chair. I scoop up the turtle and we race back to our huts.

As I run across the road to my house, Tong yells "Hurry up! Shut your windows! Go home and stay inside!"

I keep running, nearly tripping over a dozen chickens that are blowing across the yard in messy balls, squawking and tumbling over and over again.

The first smack of lightning goes off like Satan's whip across the sky, and seconds later the deep belch of thunder breaks the heavens open.

Rain powers down as if out of a fire hose at full blast. I fight the door to get inside and have to lean against it to close it.

I place the turtle in my basket of clothes, hoping he can figure out how to snuggle down. He does. I change into dry clothes, then sit down on my bed, cross-legged.

As the storm kicks my hut like a depraved meth addict, I realize I'm not the only thing inside that is scared. A wet, gray snake, about three feet long, has crawled in to seek refuge. He sticks his tongue out at me, then slides behind my homemade bookcase, however, not before flaring his hood to remind me who's boss. It's a monocled cobra.

There is nothing I can do but leave him alone, because then he will leave alone. The electricity goes out, so I try to read by flashlight to keep my mind off the horrible and howling storm, and eventually fall asleep.

~~~

The morning is disturbingly quiet. No trilling insects. No birds in animate conversation amongst themselves. Nothing.

I check on the turtle. He's fine, so lift him out of the basket. The floor is pooled with water, but is quickly draining because of the spaces between the slats.

No electricity. I am missing a few small areas where my thatched roof has blown off, but considering the storm, not too much damage.

Turtle and I open the door to see what happened outside. When I crack it open, the cobra darts out and disappears.

I drag my sleeping mat outside to air out, throw all the windows open and spread my damp books in the sun to dry.

Surrounding my house is a tropical junkyard. Coconuts are thrown around like a fist full of marbles. Broken chairs, tubs, baskets, tools and branches are littered everywhere.

The road is swallowed in mud. Streams of water intertwine and drain back into the bay. They don't have far to travel because the ocean has pillaged the beach and is lapping at the cement road barrier. The waves don't make it over, almost as if they are exhausted from the night before.

Some of Tong's chickens are splattered on the side of my hut, flat as wet compressed feather pillows. The Sea is pretending she didn't have a drunken binge last night, having lashed and stumbled around in a violent rage. She has sobered up, back to sweet and blue. She can't remember anything.

Gradually all the neighbors begin to drift out of their huts. Everyone slowly wades around, surveying the damage. Tong, with her sarong pulled up to her knees, sloshes over to me on the porch. She looks around and shakes her head sadly.

As if trying hard to look on the bright side, she says, "We are okay. We are very lucky. I think other villages are worse than us. At least water here can go back to ocean quickly. It was just a little bit of typhoon."

She picks up a long stick and starts to poke and peel the chickens off the side of my hut. She then grabs all the lifeless, soggy chickens by their feet and sludges back to her house. Three flat chickens in one hand, two in the other.

I sit down on my porch, with the turtle next me, and slowly breathe in this mess. It's going to be days for this mud to dry. Where do we even start to clean this all up?

Nonetheless, we begin. I spend the next five hours picking up the yard, helping the neighbors gather up broken pottery bowls, toys and garbage. We throw hundreds of coconuts and squashed pineapples off our main road.

Around lunch time, Tong invites me over for a hot bowl of chicken and noodle soup. Yes, she has used one of the chickens from the side of my hut.

As we sit cross-legged on her porch, a drenched cat straggles up the steps. It lays on its side, limp and exhausted. I realize that this momma cat has a stillborn kitten stuck half way in and half way out of her body. The pale little baby is dangling between momma cat's legs. Tong grabs a plastic bag and gently tugs on the kitten.

"You do it," she says, her eyes starting to water, and hands me the plastic bag. With one hand on the momma cat and the other on the tiny body, I yank it out with a sickening suction sound. Blood and gooey internal globs follow.

Tong and I both immediately lose our appetites for noodles. I wrap the kitten in a towel, and Tong says she will make a fire later today and cremate it. Momma cat is too tired to move, and quickly goes to sleep in the corner of the porch.

For the next few days, all we do is pick up, clean up and wait for the water to drain off the road back into the ocean. No one can drive anywhere.

I want to call to my mom because I know she'd be worried. She'd be happy to hear I'm alive. Mothers tend to like to hear that, so I walk down to the post office to use the public phone located in the back room of the building.

Weasel isn't at the post office today, but has left the door open and unlocked for villagers to come in and use the phone to call who ever they needed to after the typhoon.

I call my mom and dad, and amazingly get through.

When my mom answers, I tell her I am okay, the typhoon wasn't that bad in Sichon.

"What typhoon?" she asks casually.

"The one a few days ago? Here? In the Gulf of Siam?"

"Really? We didn't hear about that on the news. I don't think it was in the paper."

"Oh. Well, there was a typhoon here."

"Were you in the typhoon?"

"A little. I heard the worst damage is further north. I'm okay though. Everything is still so very wet," I say, downplaying it all.

"Be sure to dry between your toes. You'll get athlete's foot if you don't dry between your toes. And write your Aunt Corinne. She always asks about you. I thought you said you wrote to her."

"Okay, I will. I mean, I did."

"Anything you need?"

"The usual, Cheese Whiz."

"Okay, Sue. Call again next week, love you!"

"Love you too, bye mom."

~~~

The next day, the roads are dry enough for the buses to run, so I walk to the Jet Sipette to go to Nakorn. The roadside shack had taken a beating, but is still standing. The old man and Scabby are sitting out front, open for business. I am relieved to see the pair made it through the storm, and things are getting back to normal.

"Sawatdee ca," I say to the old man.

"Sawatdee crop," he answers back. Then continues, "You go help typhoon people?"

"Yes, now that the roads are good, I'm going to my office today. I'm not sure what we'll do but I bet we will be busy."

He shakes his head and says softly, "Poor, poor people. Scabby no like typhoon either."

"Where did he go during the typhoon?" I ask.

"I took him home with me. To my house. But Scabby hates thunder. He hid under the blanket all night and cried like a baby."

"I'm glad you are both okay."

"Me too. I am glad you are okay too," he answers.

I buy a warm coke, the Bangkok Post and a bag of lobster flavored rice chips to share with Scabby. Scabby looks at me, looks at his butt, then looks at me again, then eats the chips.

I read in the newspaper that the dark and stormy night that flattened the chickens, caused the cat to miscarry and shook all the fruit off the trees was the bottom fringe of a devastating typhoon that stormed through a few hours north. The tosspot had a name, Typhoon Gay. The death toll was outrageous both on and off shore, and sadly adding up.

Later that morning, my coworkers and I go help at a disaster relief center the International Red Cross has set up along with the Thai Government in our neighboring province, Surat Thani. After a few hours riding in the back of Boonchu's baby blue truck, we arrive at the makeshift center. We work there everyday this week with the Red Cross delivering bags of rice and gallons of sanitary water for drinking and cooking.

Driving through the area, it looks as if God, with one mighty brush of his forearm, swept creation flat. The rubber trees lay on the ground in perfect rows. The coconut trees are uprooted and lay shredded and broken. Pineapple bushes and groves of vegetation are completely leveled by that giant steamroller of water. Bobbing in the overflowing ditch are soggy fruit, clothes, broken furniture, garbage and bloated, dead water buffalo. Homes and shops are crushed to nothing.

Streaming along the side of the road are wet people with large bundles on their heads and babies on their backs. They look like zombies, in shock, moving in slow motion. Standing around and moving around trying to do something in the face of overwhelming nothing. Trying to recover, clean up, salvage anything that can be saved. To go from next to nothing to nothing was not fair for these people. Yet, they carry on with no choice.

Back in the States, I remember reading about floods, famines and earthquakes in faraway, unpronounceable places. It disturbed me for a few seconds as I'd glance through the article, then turn the page. It is hard to see the devastation in real life.

Chapter Ten

The weekend back in Sichon, catching up on laundry, three neighbor boys run excitedly toward me.

"Susan! Susan! Telegram!" they scream in unison.

The post office had received telegram, which was intercepted by the kids because they want to deliver it to me instead. I wipe my hands as they eagerly give me the envelope.

Which, of course, the Weasel has already opened and taped back shut, and the kids have already tried to read also. Fine. It's good these kids practice their English, so I make them read it out loud to me.

It's a telegram from another PCV, Vim, that lives in my province, about two hours away but rarely see. Communicating with other volunteers is limited to postcards through snail mail and occasional telegrams.

Vim is an English teacher here, a young man my age with the posture of a very old one. The telegram informs me he is lining up an environmental field trip for twenty of his students. It's this weekend, which is my birthday. He is asking me and some other nearby southern volunteers to come help. I'm more than happy to go, because when there are two or more PCVs together, it's always a party/food/gossip fest.

I asked Vim many times before what Vim is short for. "What is your real name?"

He always smiles and answers, "Vim."

"So your parents just named you Vim?"

"Yep."

"No, really, tell me the truth," I would say.

"You can't handle the truth."

"I could handle the truth if you told me the truth."

Then, like always, he gives me his Joker smile where only one side of the mouth goes up and blushes.

"Vim, that's all it is," he repeats.

"Fine. Vim. That's fine," I say, not believing him.

Tomorrow, which also happens to be my birthday, we are to meet at a small village in Satun, a province hiding in the corner of southwest Thailand at a fishing port. From there, we would take a boat with the students to the National Park Island, Koh Tarutao, an hour by sea.

I take the next bus to my office in Nakorn to do one more day's work. I tell Nuang and my Supervisor I would leave tomorrow to celebrate my birthday.

"Happy Birthday!" they cheer.

"You eat cake!" my Supervisor says.

"Happy birthday to you!" Nuang screams and claps.

The entire office is thrilled I would be celebrating the day with my Americans friends. However for today, they want me to come with them.

"Where are we going?"

"*Tio!*" they all answer.

There is no direct translation of the Thai word, *tio*. Used a number of ways, it implies a pleasure trip, vacation or casual outing. Going to Malaysia is a *tio*. Going to visit a friend is a *tio*. Even when a man goes to see a prostitute, it's a *tio*.

By 10:00 a.m., I'm bouncing in the back of Boonchu's baby blue truck with two of my coworkers, Pee Poo and Pee Uaan.

All Thais have nicknames given to them at a young age, as Thai names are very long, sometimes five syllables. *Poo* means crab in Thai, and *Uaan* means chubby. (Pee Uaan, pronounced ooo-an, is not chubby by the way, she happens to be size four instead of the usual Thai woman size of zero or two.

Also, when addressing anyone in Thailand, if they are older, *Pee* is used, which loosely translates as elder sister or brother, and then their nickname. If they are younger, they are addressed as *Nong* which means, younger sister or brother. Nuang and I are about the same age and rank in the office, so I just use her nickname.

Pee Poo and Pee Uaan each have delicate lacy hankies covering their noses, attempting to keep the thick red dust at bay. In the front of the cab is Boonchu driving and my Supervisor, who is eating an orange and smoking at the same time.

"Where are we going?" I ask Pee Uaan again.

"*Tio!*" she shouts.

"I know! But where?" I ask again, just wishing someone would answer my damn question.

"*Tio!*" she answers again.

Argh, I give up.

She then continues, "Do you have dirt roads in America?"

"Yes, yes we do," I answer, but she doesn't believe me.

She puts the hankie back to her face as I cough into my elbow.

Boonchu stops the truck an hour later at a huge concrete slab scattered with short wooden benches and covered by a tin roof. This is the village's communal meeting place, their Town Hall.

Most of the villagers are already assembled. Colorful chickens of black with red and orange tail feathers are also in attendance. A sorry looking dog scoots by on his butt before someone kicks it out of sight.

The southern Thai dialect flies in one ear and falls out my other in a hopeless mess, failing to connect to anything inside my head. I understand it's a meeting, but what about, I have no clue.

My coworkers and I are received respectfully with many deep bows and the traditional *wai* because we are government employees. They are especially excited to see a *farang*. That would be me.

We are welcomed to our seats up front facing the villagers.

Gradually, the villagers take their seats and the talking stops. The meeting starts. My Supervisor stands up and begins talking and talking and talking. Boonchu rolls a cigarette, then wanders across the road to drink beer with some of the older male villagers who are too old to care about much.

Pee Poo becomes enthralled with peeling off her dead cuticles and eating them. Pee Uaan pulls out a bag of dried crickets and munches away. They are as bored as I am.

The villagers pretend to pay attention. At least they have me to stare at and whisper about to keep themselves occupied. I do manage to pick up a few words from my Supervisor's southern twanged speech: "development...cooperate...problems..." Then I catch a few more words: "*farang*...volunteer...American..."

Oh no. He's gonna make me get up there and talk. I should have known. Immediately, everyone is clapping, beaming, and Pee Poo pushes me roughly out of my seat. My Supervisor shoves the microphone into my hands, with the biggest fake grin I have ever seen.

"What is this meeting even about?" I hiss at him through a thinly forced smile.

"No problem, Susan! Say anything!" he says, nodding like his head is on a slow spring.

I want to hit him with the microphone.

I take a deep breath. I figured out a long time ago these rural villagers don't need anything from me, don't want anything from me, they are just happy I am here. An American. That is good enough for them.

I start with my little speech I always give when thrown into situations like this.

"I can speak Thai. I am from America. I am from Minnesota. It is cold in Minnesota. I am twenty-five years old. I have a mother, a father, and a brother. I love Thailand."

However, what really gets thunderous applause is when I say this, "I can eat spicy food!"

I turn and hand the microphone to my Supervisor. He pushes it back and says, "Sing a song! Sing a song!"

Everyone immediately joins in, "Sing a song! Sing a song! You sing Madonna! Madonna!"

Lord have mercy.

I want to tell my Supervisor that singing Madonna songs was not in the Peace Corps contract when I signed up. However, I gave up a long time ago trying to get out of singing Madonna songs for them. They always want me to, and something as simple as this makes their day. Actually, they will be talking about me for years.

I sing a few verses of *Holiday* and they love it. Good. I lay the microphone on Pee Uaan's lap and sit down. My part is now done, the *Farang* Show is over.

After another hour of the meeting, which I still have no idea is about, we mingle around before we go. I'm given a bag of star fruit, fingerling bananas and a sack of deep fried chicken feet. As I am putting the bags in the back of Boonchu's truck, a group of sparkling young teenaged girls grab my hand and start to pull me away.

"Where are we going?" I ask, smiling at their excitement.

"*Tio!*" they say in unison.

The girls lead me out toward the edge of the village to a small tangerine orchard. The trees are loaded with bright orange orbs, looking like bunches of grapes, clustered and heavy. They start picking fruit and begin to peel them for me to eat, filling up a large basket for me to take home also.

I decide to sing some more Madonna, *Vogue* this time. All the girls sing with me as we dance around the orchard.

I put two tangerines in my bra, which levels a few of the girls to the ground in laughter. At this moment, I wouldn't have traded places with Madonna for a million bucks.

~~~

That night back in Sichon, the rain slammed down in angry fists, a leftover beating from the typhoon storm system. The next morning, another inch of water is pooled on the floor. I don't care, I slop around the mess and start to pack. I'm going to Koh Tarutao to meet my buddies for my birthday no matter what.

The neighborhood kids are at my door, sent over by Tong to make sure I'm okay. The kids start helping place all my wet things out to dry, and sweep water out the door.

Later in the morning, the roads drain down, the village was only hampered for a few hours and everybody goes about their business as usual. The buses are running now, so I walk to the Jet Sipette to wait for mine.

Bong is laying in the middle of road, covered in mud.

"Bong! Get out of the street!" I yell.

"I'm not in the street! I'm in the mud!" he yells back.

"Then get out of the mud!"

"You are in the mud too!"

I look down and my legs are splattered in thick red paste.

"Fine, Bong! Lie in the mud if you want! I give up!"

He starts singing, *Never Gonna Give you Up* by Rick Astley.

Bong just punked me on that one.

Chapter Eleven

I'm not late. Well, I am, but everyone else is late too because of the rain that passed through the South last night. Eventually, five of us roll in and spend the afternoon wandering about the village of Ban Lao Pao, eating, smoking, talking with the villagers, drinking beer and waiting for Vim and his school kids to arrive.

It drizzles on and off, mostly on. The fresh air is fighting with the reek of fish and losing. When the sun decides to show its glorious face, we end up laying on the dock, waiting some more. Jose is making up rap songs about Thailand, Mick is singing Stone's songs, Allison is discussing her dreams, Nori is talking about what she wants to do after the Peace Corps, and I'm talking about Mike. All of us are talking at the same time. It's so much fun to speak in English freely that we simply can't shut up.

Finally, Vim ambles towards us with his backpack, his joker grin and two quarts of Singha beer.

"Guess what, guys? The school cancelled because of the rain. The kids aren't coming with us to Koh Tarutao," he says.

"Oh, that's too bad," Nori answers, trying not to smile.

"Bummer," I add, feigning disappointment.

Silence. Then laughter. Nobody admits it but everyone is more than happy the kids aren't coming. We still have a perfectly legitimate excuse to go party, swim and explore with no silly distractions like performing our Peace Corps mission.

We all run to the nearest shop and buy more alcohol.

Back at the dock, we pile into a shaky, wooden passenger boat that smells of oily rags and dead seaweed. The Thai crew consists of an eighteen-year-old captain and a few other assorted teenagers. They show off a little before proudly setting sail to the small and underdeveloped island of Koh Tarutao (Old Island).

Before World War II, Thai criminals and political prisoners were held there. During the war, food and medical supplies were cut off and the guards fled to the mainland, leaving the prisoners to fend for themselves. Most died of malaria, but the surviving prisoners became pirates in the Strait of Malacca. The rest became hermits and are said to still live deep in the dense jungle...or so the legend goes.

The sea is calm, dark blue, but starts to get stir crazy the further out we sail. At one point, the heavy clouds burst open up and we are quickly soaked with rain. We huddle together, laughing, and still drinking. About fifteen minutes later, the sun muscles back into the forefront and the rain stops just as suddenly as it started.

We are wet but happy, juggling along through the rough waters. Passing by jagged rock formations that jut up from the sea at random, twenty stories high, pure stone, capped with green mossy foliage and weaving brush covers their tops. They look like giant chia heads. Our boat zig zags in between these monuments, around sandbars and underneath crowds of gulls mixing and diving in the air. Flying fish shimmy across the surface, jump up, dart down and do it again.

Allison reaches into her backpack and pulls out a red canister. I see the logo. I would have spotted that one a mile away. It's the little Italian man with the handlebar mustache.

"You bitch," I say, staring at the Pringles can she is holding next to her face as if she's in a commercial herself.

"Big bitch," Nori says.

"You're going to get fat if you eat all those," I say.

"Real fat. Overweight. Obese. All pudgy if you eat all those yourself," Nori adds.

"No, Sue. No, Nori. I'm not sharing," she answers defensively.

"Please?" pleads Nori.

Allison pulls the ring top off the can and the smell of processed American food delights the air. Fried potato-y starch. Salty grease. Crisp empty calories. Delicious additives, preservatives, junk food. Ah...no place like home.

"Can I at least smell the can? It's my birthday!" I beg.

"No way, Sue, you'll steal them."

"Allison, I made a quart of homemade coffeelua for you," I answer, and pull out a large bottle I have I brought along. Coffeelua is the Thai version of Kahlua liquor. "The least you can do is give me some of your Pringles."

She laughs musically and hands me a two inch stack of the chips, Nori another two inches. After counting them to make sure we each have an even amount, we munch in silent euphoria.

Again, the sky reloads and begins to pound down bullets of rain. The boat swoops from one side to the other, scooping up water at each sway. Some tubs, bags and boxes fall off the boat from the unruly waves. We are taking in more water than I think a boat should.

"Where's the life jackets?" I yell at Allison, who thought she should finish eating the Pringles before being thrown overboard.

"Are none," she says slowly. "This. Is. Scary."

The world starts to reel. Jose begins singing "Don't rock the boat, bay bee..." I crawl to the railing, lean over and puke beer, Pringles and seasickness.

The Thai captain reassures us "No problem," just as the boat motor dies. Another Thai boy opens the door from below the deck and starts bailing out buckets of water, but not faster than the rate its splashing aboard.

We are drifting now, very close to Koh Tarutao, but not close enough to do anything about it.

Jose is now singing the *Gilligan's Island* tune. Allison, Nori and I start arguing over the loud noise of the windy ocean:

I wanna be Ginger.
No, I wanna be Ginger.
No, you be Mary Ann.
I wanna be Mary Ann.
I'd do the Professor.
I'd do Mr. Howell, he's rich.
Mary Ann is hotter than Ginger.
Ginger has fake boobs.
They didn't have fake boobs back then.
I bet Mary Ann knows how to cook.
My mom makes tuna casserole with Fritos on top.
No, man, you gotta use Lays classic.
How did Ginger keep that silver dress so clean?
I love her cat eye makeup.
You never wear makeup.
I wouldn't mind being Mrs. Howell.
Mrs. Howell was adorable.
What do you think she looked like when she was young?

One of the crew takes off the sarong wrapped around his head and starts swinging it around at another passing fishing boat. Thank God. The other boat churgles its way over, throws us a line, and begins to drag us to the island's dock.

We arrive ashore soaked, relieved and in dire need of more to drink.

The Thai captain was right after all. No problem.

On the island, there are about seven little bungalows for rent, so us women check into one and the men get their own. After we throw our bags in the door, Nori, Allison and I each grab a bottle of beer and set out exploring.

For about three hundred yards, we hike through the dark, thick, emerald green jungle. It must be heavy metal hour because the insects are deafening. We shout at each other to be heard. The bugs are pulsating, vicious, repetitive. Each bug head banger rockin' to their own rhythm.

When we break through the clearing, it's as if we discovered Easter-land. If giant Marshmallow bunnies roamed the earth, this would be their home.

Enchanting and surreal, the beach, the glorious beach, is layered with large, smooth, pastel-colored rocks. Pale pink, baby blue, spring green and soft yellow, egg-shaped rocks, each about a foot in diameter. We start talking all at once again:

Can we walk on them?
They look like they will break.
They are rocks, lets go.
Take a picture.
Where's my camera?
They look like eggs.
It's so beautiful.
How does nature do that?
Is this a Peace Corps moment?
I would definitely say this is a Peace Corp moment.
Looks like the Easter Bunny took a big dump.
Shut up.
Don't spoil this moment.
I have to take a dump.
Shut up you guys.
You're the one laughing.
Where is the camera?
I forgot to buy film.
Where did you find film?

I don't have any film.

Do you have film?

There's no film in my entire province.

Let's just take one of the rocks back.

A pink one.

I want a green one.

I don't think a camera could capture this.

Let's just look at them and remember.

Wow.

Allison, Nori and I sit on the edge of the jungle, looking out over the pastel, egg-shaped rocks lining the shore, edging the clear and calm turquoise sea.

It is the most beautiful place in the world.

~~~

An hour later, we go back to the bungalows to drink more and eat something. The family that owns the bungalows bring out plates and plates of food for us: curry, seafood, *som tom*, soup and spicy vegetables. Although we pay them, they are more than thrilled to have *farang*s that speak Thai on their island.

Later that night, Mick takes off his clothes and decides to go skinny dipping. He runs butt naked in the dark down the beach, falls face first into the sand, gets up and jumps into the ocean. Everyone is laughing, no one helps.

These men are like brothers to us, and we their sisters, with no attraction between us other than good-natured friendship.

Mick eventually finds his clothes and stumbles back to our bonfire and passes out. Everyone does eventually.

In the morning, Allison is sitting in our bungalow putting tiger balm on all the bug bites she got while sleeping out on the beach without a mosquito net.

"You little assholes. Why didn't you bring me inside last night?" she sneers, scratching her legs.

"We just came in a few hours ago too, so shut up already," Nori answers, and flips over to her back.

"If it makes you feel any better, I don't think you have lived until you pass out on a beach in southern Thailand," I add.

"Great, Susan. I'll just check that off my fucking bucket list and put it on my resume. What I don't understand is, I only had three drinks mixed with that coffeelua," she says.

"Yeah, you drank coffeelua, but also beer, Mekong whiskey and Sang Som rum," Nori answers.

"You did too," Allison counters.

Nori rolls over and covers her head with her sarong.

"What do you mean mixed with coffeelua?" I ask, not feeling too good myself.

"I only added a couple shots of Sang Som to my coffeelua. I can't believe I went skinny dipping."

"You guys drink too much and this is way too early," Nori mumbles from beneath her cover.

"Allison, the coffeelua *is* the alcohol. You don't have to mix anything to it, unless you're a drunk idiot," I say.

"What do you mean?"

"I took one bottle Sang Som, one cup sugar, one cup strong coffee, two vanilla bean stalks and put it all some empty booze bottles. Then, I let it sit for a few months."

"Really?"

"You deserve the best, Allison," I answer.

"So," she says, "in other words, I just added more alcohol to your nasty bootleg alcohol."

"Yeah, that's exactly what you did, genius," Nori says.

"Shut up both of you," Allison barks, and lies down for a nap.

Our stay on the island lasted for three days. Wonderful hikes each afternoon looking for hermits and laughing, drinking and swimming all night. It was soon time to go back to Sichon, sober up and get ready for work on Monday.

Chapter Twelve

Monday morning, back in Sichon, I walk through town and see Bong laying flat on his stomach in the middle of the road.

"Sawatdee ca, Bong," I say.

He turns his head towards me.

"Get out of the road!" I then yell.

Bong starts singing, *'Don't you forget about me'* by Simple Minds at the top of his lungs, ignoring me.

"Get out of the road, Bong!" I yell again.

"Don't you forget to get out of the road, Susan!" he yells back.

I shake my head and keep walking to the Jet Sipette.

When I first arrived at my village, I physically tried to pull Bong out of the road, but he wouldn't budge. No one seems to mind him there. He is like a monument in the village square, something to walk or drive around. The Fountain of Bong.

As I eventually started to understand a little about Buddhism, Thais believe Bong is in this state for something he did in his previous life. His condition is karma, neither good nor bad. They must let his life run it's course with no interruptions. Bong must do his time here, and exist the way he is. His condition is only temporary in this life, not the next. When he dies, hopefully he will come back to better circumstances than laying in the middle of the road singing pop songs.

I arrive at the Jet Sipette to wait for the bus. The old man is reading a Thai soap opera magazine and Scabby is itching his fleas. I buy a bag of BBQ prawn flavored chips to share with Scabby, and a warm Sprite for the ride to Nakorn.

I need to get back to work, or at least show up to my office and try to do something productive.

~~~

At my office in Nakorn, I sit at my desk for an hour and write a report for the Peace Corps office in Bangkok. My plan for tomorrow is to go to a little village west of Nakorn, Ban Tha Kwai, which means water buffalo village.

Ban Tha Kwai is my only project village. I had been there when I first arrived in country, fell in love with the residents and wanted to do something to help them. They are dirt poor, but the happiest bunch of people I have ever met. They have plenty of rice, but that is about it. No protein, no meat, no eggs, just rice and vegetables.

I had the bright idea of starting a duck egg project. My plan was to have the villagers raise the ducks for eggs. Then, they could take the eggs to the market to sell, and with profits, buy whatever they need; meat, education and clothes.

Capitalism, baby. Find something to sell, make money, and buy what you need with the profits. At least that's how it works in America.

I eventually received funding for the initial purchase of eighteen ducks, along with money to buy supplies to build the pens. The villagers made the pens and we bought the eighteen ducks.

Nuang walks over and sits on the corner of my desk. She is wearing a striped green and white skirt, black with red polka dotted blouse and pink pumps. She looks beautiful.

She drops a bag of jackfruit on my desk, and then takes a piece for herself.

"Eat *kanoon*, Susan," she says.

Kanoon, (jackfruit) is an enormous fruit, similar in size and shape to a durian, but the inside pale yellow fruit is much sweeter. It reminds me of Wrigley's Juicy Fruit gum in flavor.

"Go check on your project in Ban Tha Kwai," Nuang says.

"I'm planning to go tomorrow. I have a few things to do here today first."

"You go today," she insists.

"Why?" I ask, chewing on a piece of fruit.

"You go now. Go check. Now. Go," she says, then gets up and walks away.

Over her shoulder, she says again, "Just go. Go check on your ducks."

I don't have a good feeling about this.

I get on the next bus out to Ban Tha Kwai, which takes about an hour, and then another half hour on a motorcycle taxi through the jungle.

Once in the village, about a dozen kids surround me, thrilled I came back.

"Why aren't you in school?" I ask them.

"Rice harvest season," they answer.

As with many rural villages, absenteeism from school for farming and family obligations is high.

Nonetheless, I am excited to check on the ducks. My ducks. Their ducks. Our ducks.

We had received eighteen female ducks. Females lay eggs naturally. Like all species of females, same as humans, they ovulate. If the egg is not fertilized, it remains an egg, and the female duck pops it out. These are the eggs to eat. Just like chicken eggs.

If there is a male duck who does the ducky-doodle-doo with the female duck, then the egg will become fertilized. Then, when the female duck lays her egg, it will hatch into a duckling.

I want to turn these villagers into thriving duck farmers, re-nowned throughout the province as farmers of the freshest and tastiest eggs. They will have dozens of eggs to eat, dozen more to sell. Their income as well as their nutrition level would rise dramatically for the better.

When I walk out to the pens, there are no ducks.

The village chief, Pee Nut, who obviously just got up from a nap, comes strolling out proudly in a *pakima* (sarong) and a dirty white tank top.

"Sawatdee ca," I say.

"Sawatdee crop," he answers.

We *wai* to each other.

"Where are the ducks?" I ask.

"Delicious."

"No, the ducks. Where are they," I ask again.

"Very delicious. Can we have more?"

"Where are they? You know, the eighteen I gave to you?"

"We ate them," he answers, as if it's the most obvious answer in the world.

"What?"

"We ate them."

"Why would you eat them?"

"We were hungry."

I stand in silence. This poor man and his village ate the ducks. They ate all the fucking ducks.

No. Please no.

I failed. I failed to get my capitalism across, my money making idea across, my great American business plan across. Lost in translation, I don't know. All along, the villagers were probably wondering why I told them to make pens for a bunch of ducks that they thought they were going to eat. They probably built the pens to appease me, amused in some way at the *farang*. This wasn't their fault. They aren't stupid. I just failed to get my point across. My message. My idea. I failed helping them.

I turn around quietly, get back on the waiting motorcycle taxi and leave without saying another word.

I need to regroup, collect my thoughts, make a plan. I need to talk to my coworkers, figure out where I went wrong, what to do next. I needed a plan B. There has got to be a plan B.

That evening, I start to get depressed, so I go outside to sweep my porch for something to do. Even though I already swept it an hour ago, and an hour before that.

A Thai woman pulls up on her motor scooter. Nothing unusual, except she has a small monkey hanging on her back. Then again, that's not unusual here, so I go back to sweeping.

"Susan! Sawatdee ca! I found you!" she shouts, and stands at the bottom of my porch steps.

"Sawatdee ca," I answer, recognizing her as the mother from the childcare center. This is the monkey that was terrified up in the papaya tree, being screamed at by the pack of ornery children.

"Please, please come sit," I offer.

She declines, instead just kneels on the steps in front of me, looking up.

"Susan, will you buy my monkey?" she asks hesitantly, then puts her hands in a humble *wai* to her forehead.

Whoa. Not only is she kneeling in front of me, staying at a lower level than me, she *wai*'d as a sign of mercy, not just a simple greeting.

"What's wrong?" I ask, and sit down on the steps, not enjoying being on the receiving end of such respectful reverence.

"Please, Susan, give monkey a good home. Please buy my monkey."

The desperate woman is obviously in need of money. Maybe a family emergency, hospital bill, or just plain broke. She wouldn't be doing this for any other reason.

"Would you take three hundred baht?" I ask, because that is all I have extra this month.

She bows her head further and answers, "That is good, that is very good."

I go back into my hut, then return with the money, pressing it between her hands.

I realize she is *saving face* by offering to sell me something as opposed to begging. If I had said no, I would have caused her to *lose face.*

Thai people often go out of their way to help other people preserve their dignity, and often agree on things just to keep the social order of peace, which is the silent moral code in this country. This is called *greng jai*, similar to the word appease, or deference.

Superiors sometimes do it for subordinates, subordinates always for superiors. During my first few months in Thailand, whenever I complimented a coworker on their pretty earrings or cute blouse, the coworker would give them to me the next day, thinking I had wanted them. They did not want to hurt my feelings, or cause me to *lose face.* I quickly learned to compliment Thais on their overall appearance, not specific items.

Americans do this in ways also back in the U.S. How many times have I heard someone say, 'I felt like I had to,' or 'I didn't want to but I didn't want to hurt her feelings'?

"Do you want to keep the monkey, just in case you need to sell him again?" I ask sincerely.

She chuckles at that, but shakes her head no.

"You keep him here, he loves the beach," she answers, and hands me the monkey.

"What's his name?" I ask, as the monkey climbs from my arms to my back.

"Monkey," she answers, wondering if I forgot that I already asked her that question at the childcare center.

"I know it's a monkey, but what is his name?" I ask again, unable to shake off my American need to name pets.

"George Bush," she says with a smile, deciding to appease me as well. "His name is George Bush."

The woman isn't making a joke, or trying in anyway to insult my President. This is a suggestion made with deep respect to the United States of America. In her mind, it's an honor to the man and to me as an American to name the monkey George Bush.

"Perfect!" I say.

Delighted, she jumps on her motor scooter and whizzes away.

With a monkey on *my* back, I walk down to the beach where Tangmo is sitting. I stand in front of her with George Bush peeking over my shoulder. Tangmo squeals! She is delighted and jerks up a hand. George Bush jumps off me, lands in her lap and curls up comfortably. He gazes at me, contently.

"Do you want him?" I ask.

She nods her head once, and tries to smile.

"I suppose I better ask your parents," I say, and start to walk toward the restaurant. Her mother is just coming down towards us.

"I gave your daughter George Bush," I say, pointing to the little monkey as she approaches. "I hope that is okay."

Her mother *wai*'s, and thanks me. The mother may not have wanted George Bush, but if she had said, no, take it back, she would have caused me to *lose face.* So she *greng jai*s' and accepts the monkey as a gift.

I spend the rest of the evening sitting on the beach reading a Narnia book with Tangmo and George Bush before turning in early.

Chapter Thirteen

The Peace Corps will reimburse travel expenses and provide a generous per diem if there is a valid or at least believable excuse to travel to the Peace Corps office in Bangkok. A medical appointment with Dr. Toh, the PC doctor, or a meeting with my PC Community Development Program Manager, Kathy, are always my tickets.

One time I called Dr. Toh and told him I needed to come to Bangkok for a cheese sandwich and chocolate milk because I thought I had a calcium deficiency. He didn't think that was very funny, denied my request, but did send me a bottle of calcium vitamins.

I have two real excuses this time. I want to get some advice from Kathy on my failed duck project and what to do next about that. I also want to see Dr. Toh about my snail bitten lip. The swelling has gone down, but there is a persistent white sore that just isn't healing on the inside of my mouth. I don't think it's infected, but it won't go away.

Dr. Toh, a native Thai, is a Johns Hopkins top grad. His job now is managing me and one hundred sixty other volunteers, suffering from all sorts of ailments, illness and injuries, real, faked and imagined.

Last year he sent out a newsletter to all Peace Corps volunteers regarding a new policy handed down from the U.S. Government regarding Thailand volunteers.

The risk of rabies is huge, with the stray dogs, feral cats and
vermin. Although we all had our rabies vaccination, we were still
to do the following if bitten by a dog, according to the powers that
be in Washington D.C.

Catch the dog, cut it's head off and bring it to Bangkok for examination. The only way to tell if an animal has rabies, the policy
explained, is by examining the brain. It was suggested packing the
decapitated dog head on ice making sure the saliva glands are in-
tact and placing it in a leak-proof plastic bag.

If volunteers don't want to carry a dog head to Bangkok, the
policy further explained, we also had the option of sending it
through the mail.

I felt sorry for Dr. Toh that he was required by the U.S. Government to share this with us. I think if Dr. Toh had his way, he
would tell us if we got bit by a dog, we should simply get on the
next bus to Bangkok to his office and he'd take care of it.

I went to a doctor in Nakorn once. Only once. I had scratched
open a spider bite on my shin that soon became infected. It turned
into a swollen volcano of puss. I never knew my body could produce slime in such a variety of shades and textures. Pink, yellow,
green, white... For three days, the nasty lava seeped from my sore.
My leg quickly swelled up to resemble an elephant's leg. Gray,
oblong and huge. I gimped into the doctor's office using my umbrella as a cane. He looked at it for a second and asked me one,
and only one question.

"Does it hurt?"

"Yes," I answered.

He gave me a bottle of pills, a prescription for a refill at the
pharmacy and I gimped out.

I forgot to ask what they were, and although the bottle was
labeled, it was in tiny Thai lettering I couldn't read. At that point,

however, I didn't think twice about taking them. I was in too much pain. I figured they were antibiotics to kill the infection. What else would he prescribe me?

Before I went back to Sichon, I stopped by my office to tell them I was going to go home and get better. Nuang wanted to see my bottle of pills.

She opened the bottle and poured them out on my desk. Then she crinkled her nose.

"What's the matter," I asked, worried.

She shook her head pathetically and pulled out a few bottles of her own prescription pills.

"Yours are not pretty, not at all. Mine are prettier."

Yes, I had to agree. Nuang's pills were pink squares, blue triangles and yellow capsules. A fist full of lucky charms.

My pills were small, round and white. Boring.

"What does my bottle say? Please read it for me," I asked her.

Nuang read it to me, and I thought I understood what she said, but obviously didn't.

"Very good, you need these. These are very good," she said with approval, and scooped the pills back into the bottle. "Go home. Go home and take these now," she added.

I faithfully took my boring pills when I got home and fell asleep. At some point the next day, I rolled over, swallowed the next dosage, and fell back to sleep. I took some more during the night. Took pills, slept, repeat.

The third day, I woke up starving. I had been sleeping for seventy-two hours, waking up to pee and take pills, then going back to sleep.

Looking down at my leg, the open wound had begun to heal into a tight neat scab. The swelling was gone, and my leg was starting to look like a human leg again. It didn't hurt anymore. I felt surprising good, just hungry as heck.

I showered off, went to eat a plate of fried rice, and stopped by the pharmacy for a refill.

The pharmacist pushed twenty-one more pills toward me, except this time they were in a factory sealed pack and labeled in English. I asked him why he was giving me Percocet.

"Your prescription. This is your prescription," he said, and pushed up his glasses.

"Percocet?" I asked.

"You might not need this refill. But, you should save them just in case for later," he added with a wink.

I figured I took twenty-four Percocets in three days. I didn't eat for three days. I didn't move for three days. By doing nothing but sleeping, my body naturally healed itself. So, what the Thai doctor prescribed worked, just in a different way.

~~~

Nonetheless, today at the office, I receive a telegram from Beth, one of my best friends who is a volunteer in Chiang Mai. She is going to Bangkok on Saturday for an appointment and wants to meet me there. My other good friend Clare, who is stationed in the Northeast, should be joining us. This motivates me more to get to Bangkok this weekend.

I quickly ask Nuang if I can use my Supervisor's phone to call the Peace Corps office to request a doctor's appointment.

"No problem, Susan. Use the phone!" she says, and unlocks his office.

I call Dr. Toh. I want to make this sound really good. I have to get to Bangkok.

"Hi, Sir. This is Susan in Nakorn Sri Thammarat. Say, I think I got bit by an electric eel and my lip is about to fall off."

There's a silence.

"An electric eel?" he then asks.

"Yes sir. It's swollen, and painful. All my coworkers and friends here tell me I need to get it checked out."

"Uh, Susan, there are no electric eels in Thailand. I don't even know what that is. Maybe you were bitten by something else?"

"Yes, sir. I think it was a poisonous sea anemone," I say.

"I'm sure you would know if you were stung by a sea anemone because you would probably be dead," he answers calmly.

"Actually, it was a snail."

"A snail?" he asks.

"Yes, sir, it was a snail."

"A snail?"

"Yes, sir. It was vicious," I say.

"A vicious snail?"

"Yes, sir. I was attacked."

"By a snail?"

"Yes, sir. A vicious snail."

"You were attacked by a vicious snail?"

"Yes, sir. Viciously."

There is another long silence. I could tell he covered the receiver with his hand, spoke in Thai to someone else, shuffled some paper, then more silence.

I probably should have just told him the truth to begin with. I'm quite sure now that he wants me to come to the PC office in Bangkok to give me a drug test.

After about a minute, he finally says, "Okay, you come to Bangkok and I will take a look at it. I might test you, I mean it."

He approves my request and authorizes both travel and per diem for me. I feel like I won the lottery. I get to see Beth and Clare!

"Thank you very much, sir," I say and hang up before he changes his mind.

I almost cheer out loud.

I catch a bus back to Sichon, pack, grab all the twenty-dollar bills that my dad had sent me, and then catch another bus back to Nakorn to make the train. I make it to the station to get on the overnight sleeper to Bangkok. I am exhausted and wired.

I take a Halcion, which is what many PCVs do when traveling around on overnight travel to get some rest.

When myself and the rest of the volunteers first arrived in country, we spent three months in training. Once when Dr. Toh was presenting a class, I asked him what I should take because I had a hard time falling asleep. He scolded me, and told us not to take anything and let our bodies naturally adjust to our new environment. He then gave us a lecture on the dangers of taking sleeping pills that some shady Thais may offer for sale around the train and bus stations.

A volunteer named Henry, originally from Seattle who always quoted Jerry Garcia and Bob Marley, raised his hand.

"What are some of the names of the sleeping pills we are not supposed to buy?" Henry asked. "You know, just so I know what to stay away from?"

Half the volunteers in the room shot up and grabbed their pencils to take notes.

"Halcion is the main one. It's also called Triazolam. It treats insomnia. In Thailand, you can buy many drugs without a prescription from the pharmacies, but don't," Dr. Toh answered.

Duly noted, thanks Dr. Toh.

I now shut my eyes as the Halcion takes effect. I fall asleep to the pulsating pull of the train as we head north to Bangkok.

Chapter Fourteen

After the all night train ride, I arrive in Bangkok. The passengers are all rolled out of their bunks at 5:30 a.m. by the train *nong*s. The *nong*s are young men dressed in matching maroon uniforms that spend most of their time smoking cigarettes on the platforms between the train cars, but also do some work aboard.

All the sleepy-eyed passengers stand in the aisles until the train *nong*s fold the bed bunks back up into seats. A few minutes later, another train *nong* comes by with a tray of half filled, half warm, murky glasses of thick coffee.

"You, ten baht," he says, smiling too brightly at this hour.

"No, five baht," I answer.

"No, no, ten baht. You"

I give him ten baht, too tired to argue, while the rest of the Thais around me pay him the five baht.

At least the man across from me, who was incredibly smashed last night, looks more tired than I. He stares at some uncertain spot, his head bobbing like a cheap doll.

The air is tolerably cool and lightly damp before the city of Bangkok fully wakes. Eerie and hopeful. We chug slowly across an iron bridge just as the sun shows its first peachy glow. Lining the tracks live a world of squalid and chattering slum people. Too much in too little space, rammed together, tight as a brick wall. Laundry swings out every window, hairless dogs, grimy kids, noodle stands, boiling woks, garbage, garbage, garbage. The dwellers squat and stare as the train rumbles through their front yard.

I sit quietly and stare back at them. I wonder what they are thinking as they watch the train pass by.

We slowly wind between the dawning city and end up at the central station. The train lurches into the depot like a drunk stumbling home, fourteen hours after departing Nakorn. Once it comes to a shaky standstill, it dry heaves, gasps for breath, then pukes out the passengers stuffed inside.

When I step off the train, a stub of a man with no legs frog hops up to me, his knuckles looking like calloused elephant paws. He is level to my knees, with a greasy New York Yankees baseball cap, no shirt, and shorts tied with rubber bands at the bottom to hold in his stumps. He sits in front of me and holds his hands in a pathetic *wai*.

If I can spend ten baht on nasty coffee, I can surely give him ten baht also. So I give him twenty. He pockets the money, *wai*'s and scoots away.

I'm then harassed by taxi car drivers.

"Get away from me," I grouch, and head for a *tuk tuk* parked nearby.

*Tuk tuk*s are Bangkok's notorious three-wheeled motorized rickshaws. The driver is in front and about two or three people can sit in back. *Tuk tuk* translates as simply the sound it makes. The proper name for these are *sam law*s (three wheels).

They are really demon chariots. Acid trip carnival rides, racing through the mad circus traffic of Bangkok. They are Fun. Dangerous. Efficient.

I always smell like exhaust afterwards and my hair is a mess, but they are quicker than a city bus and cheaper than a taxi car.

After bargaining with the driver for a decent price to the area of town I want to go, we agree on something reasonable, which is still overpriced but not outrageous.

Feeling adventurous, I decide to stay in a part of the city I've never explored before, only passed through. It's an upscale shopping haven, drawing the wealthiest of tourists and foreigners. I wasn't meeting Beth and Clare until tomorrow on the other side of town, so have the day and night to myself.

I arrive at Sukamvit Road, and wander around looking for a place to stay. I decide on a little boutique hotel. I check in and plan to enjoy every inch of the heavenly carpet, sacred air conditioning and blessed real bed.

My dad always told me, "Sue, you are my favorite daughter." (I'm his only daughter.) I would always answer, "Dad, you are my favorite dad." So my favorite dad had sent me, his favorite daughter, twenty dollars a week for a very long time which I saved, and this room is where much of that money is going.

After a long, cool tub bath, the first bathtub bath I've had in almost a year, I lounge around my glorious hotel room, feeling like a queen.

The next indulgence is breakfast down the street at a fancy five star hotel a real bakery. I spend exactly twenty times the amount that I would normally spend in Nakorn for a meal. I order fresh bread rolls with real butter, caramel cheese cake, a toasted, buttered bagel with cream cheese and a kid's grilled cheese sandwich.

On the way back to my room, stuffed, I realize I left the bulk of my money in my fanny pack on the bed in the hotel.

How the hell could I forget that? How? I never take that thing off unless I shower. I don't have it, it's back at the room. I panic.

Oh, no. Oh, no, no...

An icky feeling crawls over me like ten thousand slow leeches.

Once in my room, I have a meltdown. The money belt is here, but the money is gone. I wail like a bereaved Muslim mother and run down to the reception desk. The maids and the desk clerk look at me cautiously, slyly, but not surprised or concerned. I blubber in broken Thai sobs that someone stole my money from my room. Then I run back to my room, search again desperately, and return to the desk. It's gone. I'm berserk. I know Thai hotel workers like to enter rooms of foreigners to snoop around out of curiosity, but usually they don't steal anything.

The clerk responds coldly and becomes defensive. She tells me specifically that I lost the money outside and no one stole it. She denies that anyone at the hotel stole it, that something must be wrong with me. Which is a weird response considering I never accused her or the maids of anything. I only said the money was stolen, could have been another guest.

Her vibes are negative and black. The anger inside me wads into a tightly packed knot. I tell her I need to check out because I have no money and want my room charge and deposit back. She shakes her head, no, and I start crying. She remains hard as a rock. I plead. I beg. I *wai*. She starts to curse at me. I resort to calling her nasty names in English. She calls me nasty names in Thai. I think briefly about calling the police, but know what little help that would do.

I have no proof. When it's a Thai against a foreigner in a situation such as this, nothing is done. Thais win. Foreigners are told to go home. Then again, I have no proof.

Within about one minute, I grab my backpack and am out on the street hailing a real taxi cab. I'm bawling, and even though I had already paid for the room, plus a deposit, there is no way I want to stay. I just want to leave.

I jump into the first car taxi without bargaining as I scrounge up enough words to get me to the other side of this massive city. Hopefully, the Peace Corps office is open and I can get my per diem money right away.

The driver never takes his eyes off me in the rear view mirror except to quickly glance at the road.

"Why are you sad? Why are you crying?" he asks.

"Because I hate Thailand. Fuck Thailand. I am so stupid," I mutter back.

"What happened?"

"That hotel is no good. They stole my money. I know they went into my room and took my money. Not good. I am so stupid. They knew I would be stupid."

The driver starts talking in a soft, fatherly monologue. I don't understand half the words he is saying, as I am too upset to process much of anything. He then switches to his simple English.

"Sometime Thai people good. Sometime Thai people no good. Sometime American people good. Sometime American people no good," he says in English.

I continue to stare at the broken door handle for the hour ride through traffic.

At the landmark where I told him I wanted to go, he pulls over. I get out, dig through my purse and find my last fifty baht to pay the fare. Definitely not enough to cover what it should really cost, but all I have left.

I hand it to him. He nods, smiles and pulls off, disappearing into the jam of cars and smog.

I am left still holding my fifty baht bill.

~~~

I take a bus to the Peace Corps office and am soon back in luck. With plenty of per diem money now in my pocket for the weekend, my mood quickly improves.

I take another bus to Kao San Road and walk into the Viengtai Hotel, our PCV meeting place. I ask if Clare or Beth have checked in, and Clare already has. Outside her room door, I knock excitedly.

"*Ni aria ca?*" answers the sweet voice from the other side.

"Clare, Why are you asking 'what is it' in the formal?" I ask in English. I'm dying to see my wonderful friend Clare who can barely speak Thai.

"*Ni aria ca, cob coon ca,*" the voice sings out again.

Now she just asked me 'what is it,' then said thank you.

"Clare, it's me, Susan."

"*Poot pasa Thai dai, my ca, cob coon ca.*"

Clare just asked me if I speak Thai and then thanked me again.

"Stop trying to speak Thai and open the damn door!" I say.

She starts to snicker and leans on her side of the door. Half the time I think she is pulling my leg, the other half I know she is pulling my leg.

Finally, she lets me in, and we hug and giggle. It's good to see my friend, and know we are going to speak IN ENGLISH all night.

We decide to leave a note on the door for any volunteers that are looking for us and go down to the little cafe across from the hotel. We pull up some chairs at the sidewalk table and talk until Beth arrives.

A big treat are french fries, which are very expensive, but are definitely worth it. Clare doesn't drink much, so we both order iced coffees.

About an hour later, Beth strolls toward the hotel and joins us, and we sit and talk for nearly four hours. It seems we just can't babble and complain enough, after weeks without speaking English, or even seeing another American.

We finally go back to the hotel room, and talk and talk more until midnight.

~~~

The next morning, Beth and Clare have errands around town, and I go to my appointment with Dr. Toh at the Peace Corps office. He writes a prescription for penicillin after examining the inside of my lip.

"You're lucky it was a small cone snail. The large ones have enough lethal venom to kill an adult human being. They use their venom to attack, paralyze and engulf their prey," he says.

"Somehow that doesn't make me feel any better, sir," I answer.

"You need to be careful what you suck, Susan," he advises.

"Uh, sure. Thank you sir," I answer.

Along with the prescription, he hands me a pamphlet on dangerous sea life and how to avoid them. I thank him, grab it and go.

Around the corner of the PC office is a small pharmacy where I fill my prescription and now I'm free for the rest of the weekend.

Hello, Bangkok.

Chapter Fifteen

Bangkok is a bowl of spicy vegetable curry. Thick, chunky and hot, swimming in color. Covered in dried chilies and rock sugar. Appealing when drunk, but sober, it's hard to gag down.

It is a city that shakes you awake. Surround sound with the bass turned up, head throbbing and bone deep.

Once described as the Venice of the East because of the palmed lined canals threading through the city, that description sadly no longer fits. There are still boat taxis and a floating market, but the throat squeezing stench from the garbage is almost physically painful to endure. The canals look like a college freshman's toilet after puking tequila and nachos with lumpy salsa and jalapeno chicken wings.

The streets are tunnels of hot steam. What tickles me is that there are old fashioned street sweepers. Men with wide brimmed hats walking around with a broom and trash container. They sweep up a bit here, then stop and smoke a cigarette, then sweep up their cigarette, then sweep up another piece of garbage. I have never seen a garbage truck ever.

Many Thais wear surgical masks to protect themselves from the fumes of belching traffic and unregulated factories. The sun is hazed by cobalt blue exhaust. Miles and miles of obese telephone cables and frayed electrical wires thread throughout the city like mating snakes. It's hard to see the sky.

No amount of wind or rain could cleanse this air. It's packed and putrid. Solid. Crammed with cars, whiny motorcycles and people, people, people. Coughing. Smoking. Honking. Blabbering. Puddles of gutter crud and swirly stench and thick gunk. My astringent pad over my face at the end of the day is always dirty. Not just black, but flecked with tiny globs of filth.

In the early 1970s, Bangkok had a population of 2.5 million. It now tops ten million. Many rural Thais came to Bangkok for employment, education and other opportunities. The city grew too fast, so the roads, buildings and housing are piecemeal in place; too many built too soon, too cheaply.

However, there is something about Bangkok.

There are vast chasms of extremes; holy temples and AIDS, succulent white crab over jasmine rice and fried bugs sold on skewers, European designer shops and cheap plastic pink sandals, exquisite wealth and beggars curled in corners, school children in proper matching uniforms and toothless heroin addicts, vendors ripping you off and vendors giving you something free to try. Loud. Peaceful. Crazy. Kind.

I love it, yet hate it.

Although it has no designated city center, there are three main hubs in Bangkok.

Silom and Sathorn Road area is the financial district, lined with banks, office headquarters and international corporations and businesses. Many embassies are also located there.

Siam Square is in the middle of Bangkok with four major shopping centers. Chulalongkorn University, Thailand's best university, is within walking distance.

The area around Rajadamri Road and Ploenchit Road has many luxury hotels; the Erawan Shrine, Bangkok Central World Plaza, Gaysorn Plaza and the huge Pratunam Market.

The Viengtai Hotel where I stay is located in the Banglapoo district, about a kilometer from the Grand Palace and the Emerald Buddha temple off Khao San Road. It's a favorite for backpacking tourists because of the cheap guest houses and *farang* food.

On the way back to the hotel after Dr. Toh, I buy one of my favorite treats. A fresh bag of boiled peanuts sold on the street. They are raw peanuts boiled in salt water, not roasted. The shells are wet and soggy. Inside, the peanuts are soft and warm, and taste like tiny bursts of warm peanut butter exploding in your mouth. I also buy a bag of boiled fingerling purple sweet potatoes. To eat, you rub the skin off and eat them like a french fry. Now don't get me wrong, I would die for some McDonald's french fries, but these are absolutely wonderful too.

I also need another iced coffee. There are no paper or plastic cups for to-go drinks here, everything is put in a little bag, tied with a rubber band for a handle and a straw. It's probably better this way, at least you know the bags are unused and somewhat clean. I first thought carrying around bags of drinks by a little rubber band would break, but it has never happened. It's true Thai ingenuity and works perfectly.

The deliciously thick and sweet iced coffee is as addicting as it is available. The cook boils water with the ground coffee and then strains it through a cloth bag into a metal cup. She then adds a long pour of Carnation sweetened condensed milk and stirs it up. Then, she puts the small plastic bag on her hand, sticks it in the ice, pulls out a glob, pulls the bag back over her hand so the ice is inside. Finally, she pours the coffee into it and ties it up.

As I walk back to Banglapoo with my bouncing bag of coffee, I see Jose, Mick and Mark sitting at the cafe across from the hotel. They are already drinking and well on their way to drunk.

Jose came up from Satun, and Mick from my province, and it's good to see them after our recent excursion to Koh Tarutao. Mark works in the Northeast on water projects.

Mick doesn't just live in a village like me, but moved to the middle of nowhere in the jungle with a Thai tribe. When we first arrived in Thailand, he was a handsome, well-built guy. After a year of hard jungle living, he's extremely thin and ragged. However, he is extremely successful with tons of great Peace Corps projects and speaks southern dialect flawlessly.

Mark is a sweet guy, came from an Ivy League in Massachusetts with an endearing Boston accent. Many PC women think he's a snob, but he's not, he's just brutally honest. I like that about him.

Waving me over, I join them for a few drinks. They are going to Patpong, the reddest of red light districts in Bangkok later this evening.

"To a disco!" Mick says.

"You're not going to a disco, you are going to a go-go bar, you fake," I laugh.

"No! Really, come with us, we are going to King's!"

King's was a very fun dance place I had been to a few times before and wanted to go again.

"Let me go get ready and I'll see if the others want to come with us," I say, and slap Mick across the back of the head.

"Where are they? Let's go get them!" Jose says, jumping up.

Jose, Mick and Mark are eager to try to talk Beth and Clare to go out dancing. We all return to the Viengtai Hotel and barge into the room. Two other PCVs, Tiffany and Nancy, also have arrived. Everyone is excited to see each other again, so we sit in the room smoking, drinking and talking until nine p.m.

Then Mick stands up, tilts to the left and screams, "Let's go party!"

"Aren't we already partying, Mick?" asks Clare.

"NOOO!" he bellows.

Beth throws a shoe at him.

None of the other women want to, but I say, "Let's go!"

I put on a short jean skirt, tight white shirt and black ballet flats. What can possibly go wrong in Patpong, said no one ever...

Chapter Sixteen

If Bangkok is a bowl of spicy vegetable curry, Patpong would be the insane diarrhea afterwards. Coming out in burning regret. The only thing positive about this place are the STDs.

Blaring techno music, neon, people oozing in and out and through the streets like wads of gummy worms. Most tourists think it's awesome and exciting, but some are wide eyed, rubber-necking as if passing an accident on the highway that involves a bloody casualty.

The *tuk tuk* lets us off at the end of Surawong Road and we start walking to the disco.

When we first arrived in Thailand, I had gone into one of the notorious go-go bars that line the street out of sheer curiosity. What is it about these places that a foreign man would fly thousands of miles to visit, this dildo Disneyland?

Once inside, it was a regular strip bar. The dancers for sale wore numbered tags, and took turns dancing on the stage or prowling the bar chatting up potential dates. There was a two drink minimum, one hundred baht each. (A soda pop on the street sells for eight baht.)

I was encouraged by two girls to go upstairs to see the show. It was another hundred baht for the cover charge upstairs, but the girls waved me through without having to pay. I have wondered why these prostitutes made such an effort to get me upstairs, as I wasn't there to hire anybody, drink or tip. They don't get many women in these places, obviously, so they treated me respectfully.

Upstairs was a sad, dark and smoky place, with neon lights and loud music. There was a long center stage with a narrow bar surrounding it. People sat on benches in front of the stage, or in booths around the walls. Bloated Arabs, fat Americans and freckled Scandinavian men filled the room.

All to watch the *Ping Pong Show*.

Young dancers gyrated around poles as one laid on her back and stuffed three ping balls up her vagina. She then shot them out, Pop! Pop! Pop!

Another girl stuffed hers with goldfish, then squirted them back into a fish bowl. Then she did the same with small turtles.

A skinny, adolescent-looking girl pulled multicolored streamers out of hers. Others popped out confetti bombs, gum balls and baby frogs. One even opened up a beer bottle by twisting around on it. She then shot the bottle cap out at a customer.

Many in the audience cheered, but there was an equal amount of men that look horrified and confused. The horrified and confused ones left, in shock. Unfortunately, there were plenty of men that loved to watch. And pay money, tons of money, to watch, thereby keeping them all in business.

The world's oldest profession has been everywhere, since the beginning of time. It's documented in the Bible and in all ancient civilizations.

In Thailand, prostitution exploded along with the Vietnam War. Pattaya, a town on the upper southeast shore, was approved as an authorized R & R destination. The troops serving in Vietnam were given a three day pass to Thailand during their hell year tour of duty.

It didn't take long for go-go bars to pop up along with prostitutes flocking to the city to make money off the desperate soldiers.

Daughters of the poor in Issan (the Northeast) were often pressured or victimized to go *work* to help their family financially. Some were outright sold to sex traffickers.

I felt sorry for what happened to and in Pattaya. Thais say it was once a beautiful, sleepy fishing village. Now, they warn me not even to go there.

"No good! No good really!" Nuang, my coworker once said about Pattaya, making a disgusted face. She added, "You no go there, really! Bad, bad, bad." She then looked at me with eyes that flashed an entire country's painful heartbreak.

The Vietnam War ended in 1975. However, instead of Pattaya going back to the sweet paradise it once was, male tourists from Europe, Asia and the U.S. came. Arab men from the Gulf are attracted to Thailand because prostitution is prohibited in muslim countries. This is why Hot Yai is so popular for Malaysian muslim men, since they can easily travel across the border. Men find a great release in the booze and sex in Thailand. And the beautiful Thai women in the land of smiles are made to welcome them.

They came in droves and still do.

The U.S. had picked a zit on the face of Thailand that the rest of the world squeezed open. It became infected and prostitution oozed into Bangkok, and drained down the peninsula, south to Phuket and then Hot Yai.

I don't blame the U.S., and certainly don't blame the military guys. Thailand itself is to blame for this. The culture and government allowed it to happen. Everybody made money. The Thais profited off the lonely soldiers, took advantage of their own daughters, and gave their country this bad reputation themselves.

Meanwhile, young Thai women squirt small turtles and ping pong balls out of their vaginas.

~~~

Once we get to Patpong, we grab some chicken satay from a street vendor and drink more. The Mekong is finally catching up to me. I'm in a dizzying swirl of lights, music and madness.

King's Disco is on the corner. Mick and Mark slip into a go-go bar but Jose and I go in. We slide through the crush of tourists and bar girls on the lower level patio and go upstairs to the dance floor. Jose is immediately swamped by girls and giddily drifts off. I'm pulled out on the floor by a bar girl, and then start dancing with some European backpacker hippies.

An Indian man steps in, and starts dancing with me. He is impeccably dressed, tall, dark and dashing. He doesn't know how to dance, but that doesn't matter. We dance and dance anyway. He then grabs my head and we start to kiss during a slow song. I just let him, too drunk to care.

It seems I fell into a trap. A trap of booze and available sex. I tell him I need to go outside to get some fresh air. If I had flicked a lighter in front of my mouth, it would have exploded into flames from the Mekong.

We kiss more outside, his hands up and down my head, through my hair, around my neck and ears. He doesn't grope anything more than my shoulders up. I am about to puke. I feel the vomit rise in my throat like lava. Rushing up and dense.

I have no idea where Jose went, no clue where Mick and Mark went either. I tell the Indian I have to go. Jumping in the first *tuk tuk* I see, I tell the driver to take me back to the hotel. An intoxicated Cinderella fleeing the ball.

About a block away from Patpong, I tap the driver on the shoulder to pull over, then begin to puke until my guts feel inside out. I'm never drinking again. The *tuk tuk* driver patiently waits until I finish. He then hands me a bottle of water and drives me back to the Kao San Road.

On the way through the humid night streets of Bangkok, I put a hand to an ear, and notice my gold hoop earring is gone.

Dang, must have fallen off.

Then I feel my other ear lobe. That earring is gone also.

I smack my neck, and my gold necklaces are gone.

Both of my Thai gold necklaces, at twenty karat each, are gone.

The thick Thai gold bangles on both wrists are gone.

That good looking Indian stole my jewelry.

While we were making out, he stole it all.

Or did he?

Hell if I know.

Serves me right for being so very drunk.

I arrive at the hotel, stumble in the room, and pass out on the floor. At some point during the night, or probably morning, my friends had put a pillow under my head and let me sleep until eleven the next day.

"Wake up sleepy head!" Clare says, in her sweet singsong voice.

"Get up you drunken wench!" Beth says and kicks me.

"Why do you go out with those guys?" Nancy asks.

"Seriously Sue, you and those other guys need to stay away from Patpong. Your spending money there only encourages that sleaze," Tiffany adds.

My head is hurting so badly I have no idea who says what next, just hear the women chattering:

She's perpetuating the problem by going to Patpong.

It's okay to go once to see what it's like.

Is she okay?

She's hung over.

Jose is the sweetest guy.

Mark can be an asshole sometimes.

Mick needs to gain weight. What happened to him?

Let's go have lunch.

That would be brunch.

You guys all drink too much.

You got mighty drunk yourself last night.

No, you're the one that went out and bought a jar of imported Kraft mayonnaise and ate it with a spoon.

You stuck your fingers in it.

Because you didn't share.

No wonder you puked.

I did not puke.

Where did you buy it?

I want a jar too.

You all smoke too much.

When did you start smoking?

I don't smoke.

You smoked all my cigarettes last night.

Let's go to the Dusit zoo after brunch.

I hate zoos. It's cruel to keep wild animals in cages.

Come on, I'm starving.

Around the corner there is a *farang* cafe that has pancakes.

No way, pancakes?

You can order them with shredded cheese in them. You put honey on them, which melts into the pancake, and it's awesome!

Cheese? They have cheese?

Cheese! In the frickin' pancake!

I hear the word cheese, and magically sit up.

"Fine, let's go eat!" I say, with my arms in the air.

"The goddess has awoken!" Beth yells, laughing.

I brush my teeth for about five minutes, trying to get the layers of Mekong out of my mouth, then splash my face. Quickly, I am ready to go. Leaving the hotel, we walk about seven blocks to the Happy Traveler Cafe.

There is nothing better to cure my hangover than a fluffy, big-as-the-plate pancake filled with shredded cheese, covered with honey, washed down with several glasses of iced tea with sweetened condensed milk.

Beth, Nancy and Tiffany refuse to go to the zoo with Clare, and instead want to get a traditional Thai massage. I agree to go to the zoo. Of course I agree. Nothing would be better than spending the afternoon with my sweet friend, Clare.

~~~

We pull out our Bangkok maps and bus schedules and catch the next one to the zoo.

An hour later, we find it. As we get off the bus, Clare says, "I just love the Big Mango, I wanna be a part of it."

Buying time to process her sense of humor, I shuffle around in my purse for my pack of cigarettes, pull one out, dig around for my lighter, light the cigarette, take a deep puff and exhale. This gives me enough time to understand she is referring to Bangkok as the Big Mango, as she is from New York City, the Big Apple.

As we walk to the entrance, we pass a beggar laying down, sleeping, next to his donation cup.

"Sleeping on the job again, I see," she says with a wink, and stops to drop in a few coins.

The first area we go to once inside the Dusit Zoo is touted as the highly revered and rare *White Elephant Exhibit*. In all honesty, I think because other countries have rare white rhinos or rare white tigers, and America has rare white buffalo, Thailand wanted something rare and white too.

Except, they aren't white at all. They are so very sick and malnourished they just look pale. Crepe paper thin, ghostly skin.

I hand one a boiled peanut. It obviously needs some protein.

"I think a lethal dose of sleeping pills would be better to feed him," Clare says in disgust. "I can't imagine their misery."

Most animals at the Dusit Zoo should be put out of their misery. The white elephants, however, are the saddest creatures I have ever seen in my life.

Five scrawny beasts in a row. Each has an iron shackle around a rear leg. There they stand. All day. On urine soaked, hot cement.

Twelve hours a day, the roar of Bangkok traffic behind them makes their frail ears twitch and the exhaust burns through their eyes.

The smallest, probably youngest elephant, keeps his rear leg straight out behind him, gently tugging, trying all day to be free.

The older ones look catatonic, their eyes covered in defeat. They have given up a long time ago. Every minute of every day of every month of every year must fester by for these poor animals.

A teenaged boy pelts the middle one with a banana. It ricochets off his shoulder and lands out of his reach. The elephant doesn't even flinch, just continues to loll side to side.

"Knock it off, punk!" I turn and scream at the teenager.

Him and his buddies just laugh at me.

"Let's go," Clare says. "I'm getting elephantiasis."

We leave and go have *pad thai* at a little stand on our way to the bus stop.

Pad thai (fried noodles, Thai style) is something I had eaten in the States but doesn't hold a candle to the real deal here. *Pad thai* is lightly fried rice noodles with green onions, bean sprouts, chilies, fish sauce and tiny dried shrimp, then sprinkled with finely ground peanuts. Usually with an egg, but chicken or whatever is available can be mixed in. The customer then adds the finishing touches from the condiments of fish sauce, palm sugar, sliced chilies or vinegar to suit their taste.

"Are you doing any projects in your province? What great and wondrous things are you doing down south?" Clare asks.

"Not much. My duck egg project failed," I answer.

"Why?"

"They ate the fucking ducks."

"Instead of raising them to sell the eggs?" she asks.

"Exactly."

She laughs and says, "Maybe they don't like duck eggs."

"They liked the ducks enough to eat them."

"Then why don't you just raise ducks?"

"I thought duck eggs would be easier," I answered.

"I think your coworkers and villagers are *greng jai*-ing you."

"I'm sure of it. I wish they would have said something sooner. My coworkers never told me that a duck egg project wouldn't work. The villagers certainly didn't say anything either. They let me plug ahead, thinking I was doing something to help them," I explain. "*Greng jai* is a beautiful thing, but in this situation, I would have preferred harsh honesty. Someone telling me, 'look, it ain't gonna happen. Here is why. Here is what you should try instead.' I wish someone would have called my plan bullshit, you know, American style."

"At least you tried," she says, reassuringly.

"Well, I don't know what to do now. I could either wash my hands of it and move on, or put more effort into the project and still try to make it work."

"Now you know what doesn't work and that's half the battle. I'd keep trying, if I was you," she says.

"Might as well," I answer.

She smiles at me, her kind eyes twinkling.

I smile back.

I'll keep at it. Because that is what Americans do.

Chapter Seventeen

Later that afternoon, I take a bus to the central station and catch the overnight train back to Nakorn. Clare, Beth and the others are also on their way home to their provinces also.

I sip a warm coke and eat another bag of boiled peanuts. Across from me, an old woman is trying to eat a white and purple cob of corn. I'm amazed, because she doesn't have any teeth. She is gumming the corn off, gnawing on it like a soft bone. She holds the cob toward me and offers me a bite.

"No, thank you," I answer sweetly. "Do you want some peanuts?"

She smiles, shakes her head no, so we both continue to snack as we roll out of the city.

I sleep through the night with no need to take a Halcion as I am exhausted.

Before sunrise the next morning, I get off the train at Nakorn and take the bus back to my village of Sichon. The air is a cool seventy-five degrees, with precious hours before the sun fires up her grill to over one hundred.

I do a few loads of laundry before going to work. Outside, I fill my tomato-red tub full of water along with a scoop of powdered soap. Then, I throw about four or five items in, stepping on them with my feet. Up, down and swish them around. I rinse each piece off then hang them up to dry on a small clothesline.

"Susan!" my neighbor Tong yells from across the yard. She has her hands on her hips, shaking her head.

"That is no good! That is not how you wash clothes!"

She always yells at me for washing my clothes by stepping on them with my feet, instead of using my hands.

"Sawatdee ca!" I answer, pretending I don't know what she is talking about.

"Susan! Dirty Feet! No good! No good at all!"

"How are you?" I answer.

"Susan! Hands! Use your hands!"

"You look pretty today!" I yell back, trying to change the subject.

"Susan! Wash clothes with your hands, not your feet!"

"Where are you going today?" I ask.

"No good, you wash no good!"

"How are the kids?"

I continue to ask her questions off topic and feign dumb until she gives up and leaves me alone so I can finish washing my clothes with my feet.

I leave for work, and pass by Bong who is lying in the middle of the road.

"Sawatdee ca, Bong, get out of the road!" I yell.

He looks at me like I am crazy, and starts to sing *Free Fallin'* by Tom Petty at the top of his lungs.

"I hate Tom Petty!" I yell again.

"Tom Petty hate you too!" he shouts.

I keep walking.

I buy a bag of wasabi roasted peas and my Bangkok Post from the Jet Sipette, sharing some of the snacks with Scabby before the bus arrives.

Once in Nakorn, I take a *song tao* to the market for breakfast.

In Thailand, *song tao*s are a common mode of transportation in cities other than Bangkok. In Thai, *song tao* means two rows. They are pickup trucks with a canopy over the bed, lined with two rows of benches.

I get off near the main market.

Walking through Nakorn requires full concentration, coordination and agility. The sidewalks are crooked cement blocks jutting up or disappearing into the ground at random. Running parallel to the ruptured walkways are deep gutters pooled with dark water that doesn't drain anywhere. The stratagem is to not fall in.

Like slides in a projector, one scene after another takes place in front of each storefront. Shop boys weld metal tubes and endless pipes together. Skeletal dogs shake for fleas. A young mother holds a naked baby above the sewer trench as urine trickles down it's peggy legs. There are clusters of teenagers reading comic books in front of a newspaper stand. Old men swill coffee at wobbly tables. Country women squat on the sidewalk vending trinkets and fruit.

There are plastic tubs filled with plastic shoes, plastic umbrellas and plastic purses for sale. Pushcarts and food stands offer fried rice, fried noodles, or fried bananas.

I knock my head on yet another awning. They are tarps wrapped at eye level on long heavy poles used to shield the open storefronts from the intense sun. It bounces off my head, swings back only to smash into me again.

Shooting straight towards me, however, is the most annoying obstacle ever. A drunk Thai man. He stumbles to a wavering pose. As I walk by, he jabs me in the ribs. He then slurs the word, *farang*.

Farang is not an insulting word, but annoying as heck. Thais often just yell that at me when I walk by.

Christine once told me to always carry a rolled up newspaper in case I need to smack a drunk man away, so I whack him with my Bangkok Post and it works like a charm.

My favorite produce woman is squatting in the shade of a faded awning, amid baskets full of rose apples, tangerines and lychees.

She waves me over, wiping betel nut dribble from her mouth with her sleeve. Her southern twanged Thai bombards me and only gets my smiles and nods as answers.

I have absolutely no idea what she says but our conversation lasts fifteen minutes. For the hundredth time, I ask her what her name is. She tells me again. I still can't understand.

My produce woman mothers over her array, fussing, rearranging, polishing. She grabs the pieces I choose and flings them aside. They are not good enough for her favorite *farang*. She begins to fill a bag with brighter and juicier fruit she pulls out of nowhere, babbling in approval.

"Ah! Ah! Ah!" she says.

"Oh! Oh! Oh!" I say.

"Ah!"

"Oh!"

"Ah!"

"Oh!"

She is especially excited about her basket of *gnaw*. *Gnaw* is a rambutan, a type of lychee fruit. (Like I even knew what a rambutan or lychee was before I got here.) Nonetheless, a gnaw looks like an alien golf ball from outer space. The skin is a thick red rind with soft pink bristles all over, tipped with green. The inside has the texture and taste of an excessively sweet pear, wrapped around an apricot sized pit. To open, you hold it firmly in the palm of one hand and twist with the other. Produce woman grabs five or six for me and drops them into my bag.

Theatrically, she refuses my money. She puts one hand over her heart, throws her head back and loudly laughs, while doing the universal sign of 'no' with the other. The other produce women next to her do the same, clucking and giggling. After much coaxing, she *reluctantly* accepts my money that she had every intention on taking in the first place.

I hand over twenty baht for about ten baht of fruit. While doing so, she latches on to my hand and starts to pet my arm hair. She then tries to pull a few hairs out. She tells me she wants them, I tell her she can have them. A passing elderly man stops next to me and points to my bag of fruit.

"You eat fruit, you," he says in English.

"Yes, I can eat fruit," I answer back in English.

"You eat fruit you!" he bellows with a grin too big for his face. He is proud to practice his English on me.

I step over a sleeping dog, a chicken, and a kid on a red tricycle with flat tires. A fat rat bounds out of the sewer with a shoelace. An old man leans over and blows his nose on the sidewalk.

I walk back to the main corner.

The intersection is invaded by a motley flock of motorcycle taxi men. They surround me and want to know where I am going and if I will hire one of them to take me there. As they rev their muffler-less cycles, I ignore them and go looking for a *song tao* to take me to the tailors. I'm having a skirt made of exquisite, beautiful Thai silk. I will probably never wear it here but will bring it back to America, and probably never wear it there, either.

"Madonna! Madonna! Sing a song!" are the taxi men's last request as I walk away.

I get in the first *song tao* I see at the corner. I usually sit in the cab with the driver to be more comfortable, but two people are already packed in, so crawl in the back. A few minutes later we are in front of the tailors and I bang my heavy five baht coin on the ceiling of the covered truck bed to let the driver know I want to get off. He screeches to a halt.

I get out and go to his window to pay, and he starts to take off again.

"I gave you five baht! It's two baht! Two baht!" I yell, with my arm still in the window of the already accelerating truck. I am running alongside the truck screaming at him to stop. He brakes twenty yards later, laughing hysterically, and gives me my proper change.

I snatch it from his hand, crunching and twisting his fingers in the process. I want to punch him in the face. I often over pay Thai people, but I want it to be my choice, not just taken from me. Sure, it's only three baht change, but it's the point of it.

The tailor's shop is closed.

Fine. I go back to the street to find another *song tao.*

There is one at the curb in front of me. No one is in the front seat except the driver, so I hop in the cab with him. I figure I lucked out.

I make myself comfortable and look straight ahead. The driver seems startled to see me. I feel him staring at me.

"Come on, I am a *farang*. I am white. Get over it and let's go," I mutter in English.

Seconds pass and turn into minutes. I still feel him staring at me. I casually pick my nails. Then my teeth. He continues to stare. I pick at my shirt. Then my arm.

"Go! Go! Go!" I yell, starting to get annoyed.

He doesn't move.

I slowly turn my head.

The driver looks terrorized and is gripping the steering wheel. His eyes are as big as a water buffalos. I continue to rotate my head so I am now looking out the back window into the rear of the truck.

Shit.

Are you kidding me?

Nothing but an open bed piled with pineapples.

I blink a few times and realize I'm not in a *song tao*. I'm sitting in some poor pineapple farmer's truck and he is certainly wondering why. Retaining my composure, I calmly get out of the truck.

"*Mai pen rai,*" I say.

Mai pen rai means 'never mind' or 'no problem.'

"*Mai pen rai,*" he answers back, and gives a soft nod.

I gently shut the door, grimacing, then jump on the first motorcycle taxi I see to go to my office.

~~~

"Look what the cat dragged in!" Nuang, the secretary yells in English when she sees me walking toward my desk.

"Sawatdee ca," I answer, regretting I taught her that phrase. When I first came to my province, I asked Nuang how her and the other office women always looked so perfect. Then in English, I said, "I look like what the cat dragged in." She quickly wanted to learn that phrase, and says it to me whenever I look especially haggard just to tease me.

"Where have you been?" she asks.

"To Bangkok, for a meeting."

"What kind of meeting?"

"A Peace Corps meeting," I answer, not wanting to go into details about my weekend.

I wasn't lying, but still feel I am a little.

Nuang sits on the corner of my desk and drops a bag sliced papaya next to me, and tells me to eat.

"Susan, we go help refugees today," she says.

"What refugees?"

"Vietnam refugees. They take boat here. We go help them."

About an hour later, Boonchu drives Pee Poo, Pee Uaan, my Supervisor and I in the baby blue truck to Pat Panang, a village on the coast where the refugees are being held.

There's a big problem with Vietnamese refugees arriving to Thailand. The government had adopted a new policy to turn them away, as they simply couldn't handle them all. However, they keep coming. Thailand received undeserved international flack for this policy, but in reality, they have never turned anyone away. The much publicized story of a few refugees pushed back and killed while at sea were at the hands of drunk and wayward pirates, not the Thai Government. Thais take the refugees in regardless of the policy, stuffing them into crowded camps until another country lets them immigrate, but they come in faster than they go out.

The Vietnamese Government has created a society where it's citizens want to flee on little boats risking death rather than live in their own country. Thailand responds the best that they can.

Eleven dead refugees washed up on the beach here last year when their little boat sank. Now, another refugee boat landed on shore in Pak Panang. This time they were sunburnt, hungry and scared, but still alive.

My coworkers moved them into a deserted meeting hall near the government office there, gave them woven mats to sleep on, new clothes and feed them daily bowls of rice and vegetables.

I wander over to the building where they are kept and peer through the open window. There are a few other gawkers looking in as well.

The refugees seem delighted to be here, not even bored. The women take turns combing each others hair, the men smoke donated cigarettes and a little girl is jumping around in a solo game of hopscotch.

There are several Thai soldiers guarding the building to keep them inside, although they certainly don't want to go anywhere.

My big white face catches the little girl's eye.

She radiates like most children, and skips over to have a closer look at me.

She doesn't know English or Thai, and I don't know French or Vietnamese. Nothing is said, so we communicate in the language of funny-face making.

I fish through my work bag and find a bag of crayons and an empty notebook and give them to her. She looks at them, unsure. I quickly show her what a crayon can do on a blank page, and she is delighted. I also give her a handful of barrettes from my purse, and a tube of cherry chap stick.

"Lipstick!" I say, and put some on my lips, and then hers.

Oh Lordy, how she can smile, not just with her mouth, but with her entire skinny fresh face. She loves her new belongings.

Just a small girl, in a small time of my life, with a name I can't pronounce even if I knew it. I wish I were in a position with power to do something more than just give her crap from the bottom of my purse.

Pee Poo later tells me the Vietnamese are going to be bussed to the refugee camp in the Northeast, and then hopefully, within a few years, be resettled in Europe or America.

I'm still not sure if these refugees are incredibly brave to risk their lives to leave Vietnam, or if they are ignorant. Probably both, with the third reason being hopeful.

At the end of the day, we return to the office, then I head home to Sichon. I'm sure I'll keep that little girl in my prayers forever.

Chapter Eighteen

The old man and Scabby are both snoring at the Jet Sipette. I don't disturb them when I get off the bus.

I walk to the post office to check for mail and enter quietly. I want to see if I can catch the Weasel stealing my mail.

Weasel is perched on a stool at the back counter, eating a bowl of noodles. I watch him reach into a drawer and pull out a green can of Kraft Parmesan Cheese...with the beloved red, plastic top, and shiny tin bottom. That Kraft Logo is a symbol of home to me, a reminder of all things American, a glorious brand that makes cheese in a can. I start to fume. It was sent to me, not him, I just know it.

Weasel then shakes some out on his noodles.

"Jerk!" I scream in English. Then in Thai, I scream louder, "That is my can of cheese! You stole it! I know you stole it! You opened one of my packages again!"

The Weasel looks calmly at me, almost annoyed.

"I don't know, Susan. I don't know. I don't understand what you mean," he answers.

I see a glimmer of mischief in his squinted eyes.

"That is my cheese! Someone sent it to me!" I yell.

"Who sent it to you?"

"I don't know! Someone did! To me! They sent it to me!"

"This is my cheese, I buy it," he smirks.

"No, you didn't!"

"Yes, I did."

"Thais don't eat cheese! Americans eat cheese! That is my cheese!"

I was out of my head, seeing someone eating an absolute rare and precious can of what I should be eating.

"Give it to me!" I yell again.

"*Greng jai*, Susan. Here you go. I don't like it anyway," he says with amusement and hands over the cheese.

Then, to rub salt into the wound, he pulls out a tube of cherry chap stick from his pocket, looks at it, smiles, and starts to coat his weasly lips with it.

"That's my cherry chap stick!" I scream.

He pauses, holds it up, "This?"

"Yes! That! Someone sent that to me! I just know it!"

"No, they didn't."

"Yes, they did. You don't have cherry chap stick in Thailand! That came from the States, to me!"

He replaces the lid back on the tube, and hands it over also.

"Stop pretending that you don't know! Stop opening my packages!" I yell and stomp out the door, not even checking for my mail.

I am so mad, I power walk all the way home, through the village, along the shore, livid.

By the time I reach my hut, I am drenched with sweat. I have my can of cheese and tube of cherry chap stick, so life is still good though.

Christine is sitting on my porch with the little neighbor girl, Nong Nok, painting the child's toenails.

Wearing a batik sarong and a fitted black tee shirt, Christine looks adorable. Her hair is in a loose ponytail on the top of her head. With her hair out of her face, minimal makeup and the plain shirt, I catch a glimpse of the young boy she once was. It startles me for a moment, because I often forget Christine was born male and still has a penis.

"Hi Yah!" she yells when she sees me clomping up the path, "Sawatdee Susan!" Then, she scolds Nong Nok for moving or she will mess up the pedicure.

I was planning on just locking myself in my house all night and reading, but it's good to see her, and the child's happy face.

"We cleaned your house for you," Christine says. "Susan, you have dirty house all the time."

"How did you get in?"

"Through the window!" Nong Nok pipes in.

I sit down next to both of them, exhausted. I gave up a long time ago trying to establish boundaries or have privacy around here. Even the Weasel opening my packages is just something that happens. No one but me seems to care.

"Come, Susan, go *tio*!"

"Christine, I don't want to go *tio*, I don't want to go anywhere. I just want to read and write letters tonight. No drinking either."

"Silly, silly, no, no, we go eat grilled shrimp."

Grilled shrimp sounds good, so I throw my work bag through the window without even opening the door.

I climb on the back of Christine's whiny little motor scooter, and off we zip to the Tangmo's restaurant.

~~~

Velveetah and Samantha meet us at the entrance.

"I'm not drinking any more alcohol," I say, and plop down in the chair. "I'm just drinking water tonight."

"Me too," Christine answers.

"Good."

Christine then orders a quart of beer for me, and one each for her, Velveetah and Sam.

"Susan, I love Captain. Army boy. Will you help me write a letter back to my Captain?" Velveetah gushes, pulling out a letter from her satchel.

It is postmarked from Fort Lewis, Washington.

I start to read it. Oh my goodness. He wrote that he had the best night ever, and misses her terribly. It's obvious from the letter that the Captain slept with Velveetah and is now in love with her.

"When did you go with the Captain?" I ask, not remembering too much after the snail on my lip part of that night.

"After you and Christine left with Mike. Captain is not captain in bed, he is a general!" she squeals.

I smile from ear to ear.

"Sure, Vel. I'll help you write one," I say, and start digging in my bag for a pen.

Velveetah pulls out a pink tablet with pandas on it and a neon green marker. She hands them to me.

"Here, write on this," she says excitedly.

As I am starting to take her dictation, three motorcycles, with two teenaged boys on each, roar up to the restaurant. They swagger in. Their attention is immediately drawn to us, three ladyboys and a white *farang*.

"You! You! Where you go!" one of them says in brittle English to me, and they all snicker.

Christine flips her hair. Velveetah picks her nails and Samantha just looks off at the ocean.

"You! You! You speak English you!" another guy says, followed by more laughter.

"What's so funny?" I ask.

"Shh, shut up Susan, don't talk to them," Christine says under her breath.

"You! You! Where you go?" he answers along with a sneer.

Christine stands up and snarls at them. Speaking in rapid southern Thai dialect that I can't understand, but she obviously is cussing them out.

The punks back off a few feet, but then seem to gain steam and talk back to her. Words zing back and forth.

Christine sits down and again flicks her hand.

She takes a long drink and lights a cigarette.

One of the boys walks up to her closely, stands right in front of her face, and pulls his penis out of his pants. His buddies roar with laughter.

Oh. My. God.

Her eyes blazing, Christine jumps back up and punches the guy in the face with a closed fist, sending him straight to the floor, bleeding. Thankfully, Tangmo's father along with her brother run over and make the guys leave before a brawl starts. They know, as well as I know, Christine, Velveetah and Samantha would have pummeled the teenagers to a pulp. One does not mess with a pack of ladyboys.

Getting back on their motorcycles, the punks tear off down the road.

"Not good, not good," Tangmo's father says, not so much to Christine, but to me.

Tangmo's mother brings over four more beers.

"Free, free," she says, opening the beers for us. She hangs her shoulders, feeling bad about what the boys did to Christine, and in front of me. She adds, "Muslim. Muslim boys..."

"Sorry Christine, sorry Velveetah, sorry Sam," I say sheepishly. "Sorry that happened to you."

"Susan. Some people do not like us. They do not accept us," Samantha says. Then she adds, "We are ostrich sized."

"What?" I ask.

"Ostrich sized," Christine says, putting her arms around her friends.

"What do you mean, ostrich sized?"

Christine flips her hand away like she is shooing flies, and wrinkles her nose.

"You mean *ostracized*?" I say slowly, trying not to laugh.

"Yes, some people still excrete us,'" she answers in English.

"Exclude," I say. "Dear God, the word is exclude. Ex clude."

"EX CLUDE," Christine, Vel and Samantha say together.

"Os tra size," I enunciate.

"OS TRA SIZE," they say back, slowly.

I am proud of my friends for using new English words.

"Where did you learn the word, ostracize?" I ask.

"We read gay American magazine," Velveetah says proudly.

Christine just gives me a wink.

"In magazine, America say ladyboys like us are sometimes ostrich sized, I mean, ostracized," Samantha adds.

I don't know how to say ostrich in Thai, and don't have my Thai-English dictionary.

"Do you know what a flamingo is?" I ask.

The ladies perk up, sit up and smile.

"You are more like pink flamingos, not ostriches" I say.

"Susan, do you like negro boys in America?" Christine asks.

My mouth drops open. Huh? Where the hell did that question come from?

"What are you talking about?" I ask incredulously.

"Do you like negroes in America?" Samantha asks, curious and almost childlike.

My mind is sifting through what was said before this, searching for a reason why they threw this question out there. Maybe the word ostracize? Exclude? Something about that?

Yep, I am sure now.

"Don't use that word, *negroes*. That is not the right word, not a good word to use in English. It's old fashioned, too. In America, we say, African-Americans," I answer.

"No, not Africans. Negroes," Velveetah adds, intently.

"Yes. Black people are African-Americans in America."

"Are they African or American?" Christine asks.

This is obviously a huge topic of interest to them. I am now not surprised by the question. Most Thais I know are absolutely obsessed with light skin tone. They stay out of the sun to avoid becoming tan, powder their faces thick with light foundation, and are infatuated with my pasty, white, hairy forearms.

I feel like taking off my shoes now because I am about to walk on eggshells here. Suddenly, I am the voice for all African-Americans in America so I need to get this right.

I say, "In America, all people are immigrants originally, so someone with ancestors from Ireland are sometimes called Irish-Americans, and in the case of black people, they were taken from Africa as slaves, so they are African-Americans."

"Why aren't they called Slave-Americans?" Velveetah asks.

"Because they aren't slaves anymore," I say, simply.

They are staring at me, unblinking, so I add, "Just say black. They are black. You have to be careful saying words in English. Labels, you know. One word can make a big difference, because sometimes one word can be powerful. Good or bad."

"Susan. Slavery is not good. Why you Americans do that to black people?" Christine asks, and furrows her brows.

Now I feel as if I represent all previous southern slave owners because I am white.

"No. No one likes this about our American history. It is a shameful past," I answer, shaking my head.

"Do you have sex with black boys in America?" Christine asks.

I slap my hand on the table and wail, "Gawd! Christine! Do you ever stop? I am trying to have a precious Peace Corps teaching moment with you!"

"What do Americans call you, then?" she says, slapping her hand on the table also.

"I don't know! I really don't know! Fine! If you want to know, sometimes men call me a dumb blonde, okay?"

Christine, Vel and Sam all burst out laughing.

"It's not funny! No one likes to be labeled! Blacks, Gays, me, no one!" I scream.

"But you *are* blonde, Susan! And sometimes you're not too bright!" Christine says, still laughing and puts her hand on mine.

"That's the point! That *is* the point! Don't use words that hurt people's feelings! Be careful what you call people!"

Christine then looks at me deadly serious. Her almond eyes are now slits of rage. She says in a low masculine voice, "Are you kidding me, Susan? You now lecture me about being called names? How many names do you think I am called every day?"

"That's what I mean!" I scream, and pull my hand out from under hers, and smack her hand back hard.

"Good!" she yells.

"Fine!"

"Good!" Christine yells again.

"I thought we were talking about African-Americans!" I scream back.

"Okay! I say black from now on!"

"Good!"

We both sit back in our chairs and take a deep breath.

Samantha raises her glass, and says, "Let's cheer to smart blondes and ladyboys!"

I start laughing, almost collapsing in relief that this conversation is now over. I raise my glass.

Just like that, we move on.

We have forgotten all about the teenagers before.

Chapter Nineteen

The next day, I spend a few hours in my office, writing a report to send to my Program Manager, Kathy, in Bangkok. There is not much accountability, but I do send her a report about once a month to let her know I am still alive, and what I am doing. Rather, trying to do, or not doing.

PCVs are mostly on their own once they get to their work sites. In the past year and a half, Kathy has come to conduct a site visit here only once.

My coworkers are ambivalent with my work here. They have done great things before I arrived, and will do great things after I leave. When I tell them I'm going on a *tio* for a few days to Hot Yai, or Koh Samui, or to visit my buddies in Satun province, they seem delighted. They are proud of their beautiful country and all it has to offer, and want to me to experience it. Going on a *tio* and enjoying oneself is just as important as working here in Thailand.

They also have a different sense of time. Their attitude is that it will get done when it gets done, so for now, let's enjoy ourselves.

Today is no different. Pee Poo, Pee Uaan, and Boonchu drive me out to a waterfall for a picnic during the work day. After the early picnic, they take me on a tour of a salt farm.

In Thailand, salt is harvested from sea brine. The fields are large, square, shallow plots near the seashore. They look like rice paddies surrounded by low embankments with footpaths.

To harvest the salt, the fields are flooded with sea water pumped in from the Gulf of Siam. Then, they are left alone to naturally dry. The water evaporates in about a month and the field is left covered in chunks of sea salt.

The salt farmers rake the salt into large neat piles, and begin the labor intensive task of shoveling it into wicker baskets. The men carry one basket on each end of a bamboo pole back to the main building where it's weighed, bagged up and sold around the country and overseas.

Thai salt is incredibly bright white, and contains other natural minerals from the sea, such as iron, magnesium, calcium, potassium, zinc, and iodine.

The salt farmers give me a ten pound bag before we leave, which I will give to my neighbor Tong when I get home.

~ ~ ~

About two p.m., I get on the bus to go back to Sichon. When I arrive at the Jet Sipette, the old man is sleeping again and Scabby is licking his paws.

"Hey, Scabs," I say to him as I pass.

The dog glances my way, and then starts to smell his butt.

I walk to the post office, hoping for mail, dreading to see the Weasel.

A horn honks behind me, so I turn around hoping it's Mike in the Ford F-150.

Dang it, no. It is a white Thai Government Toyota pickup truck delivering mail to the post office here.

The bed of the truck is full of blue nylon bags and a pile of boxes. Everyday, the driver drops off all the mail for the village at the post office, then continues driving around the area delivering to all the other little local post offices. I flag him down and he pulls over. I have a plan. I want to beat the Weasel to the punch and grab my mail right off the truck before he can get his curious hands on it.

"Sawatdee ca. I go with you to the post office," I say to the driver as I jump in the front cab.

He smiles back and says, "*Mai pen rai.*"

We arrive at the post office and park in back. The driver toots the horn and the Weasel comes out the door to help unload the bags of mail for the village. The driver pulls off two bags of letters and one small box.

Before the driver can give the box to the Weasel, I grab it.

Yes! It is addressed to me!

"Jerk!" I scream, and take off running around to the front of the building with my treasure. I have managed to intercept my package before the Weasel could get his grubby hands on it.

I rip open the box. It is from one of my best friends back in the States.

Pulling out the crumpled newspaper used for packing, lo and behold, there it is.

I could feel the heavens opening up above me and a choir of one thousand angels singing in exultation.

A bright orange bag of Cheetos cheese balls.

As I open the bag of cheese balls, the poof of powdered fake cheese sails out. I breathe in and start to eat them slowly and systematically while standing in the middle of the driveway.

Glorious. Crunch. Cheese. Processed. American.

One of my neighbors pulls in on his motor scooter and asks me what I am doing.

"Eating cheese balls," I say, and continue eating them one by one while staring off into the sunset like John Wayne.

He shakes his head in befuddlement and leaves.

Five minutes later, some middle schoolers walk by and ask me what I am doing.

"Eating cheese balls," I answer.

They cover their mouths, giggling at the *farang*.

For ten minutes, I robotically eat them until the bag is empty.

Then, I carefully tear the bag open so it's a flat sheet. I begin to methodically lick the inside silver lining of all the powdered cheese, in perfect rows, from bottom to top. By God, I am not going to let one microscopic red dye #40 cheese particle go to waste.

I am so focused on this, I don't hear the Ford F-150 pull in front of me.

"What the hell you doing?" someone yells.

"Licking cheese balls!" I yell back in English.

Wait, the voice was from an American male, in English.

It's Mike.

With his arms folded out the passenger side window, he stares in a mixture of amusement and horror.

He has on sunglasses and the cool Army guy black wristwatch with about every navigation gadget-timer-alarm-compass you can imagine. I look at his faded classic Boston spaceship tee shirt stuck to his chest with sweat.

I have more than a feeling.

I about have a damn near explosion.

I stop mid-lick and throw the bag down. I am too happy to be embarrassed.

"Mike! When did you get back!" I yell, and run over to the truck window.

The Captain is driving and Christine is sitting in the middle. She leans over Mike and yells, "Susan! Why you doing that? Why you lick bags like that? You crazier than Bong sometimes! Even Bong doesn't lick bags like that!"

"Shut up, Christine! Oh, hi Mike. What are you doing here?" I ask again excitedly.

"I'm looking for you," he says in that ever loving American accent of his.

"Stop doing weird things, Susan! Come now, Velveetah and Samantha are already at Tangmo's restaurant!" Christine says.

She puts one hand on the Captain's thigh, and the other on Mike's. She squeezes till both of them cringe in pain. Mike takes Christine's hand and puts it back on her leg.

"I knew you'd be hanging around the post office," Mike says.

"My friend sent me Cheetos today," I explain.

"I see that," Mike says, and reaches out to brush some cheese powder off my face.

"You crazy sometimes, Susan," Christine scolds.

"I'm starting to think all time," Mike teases me while opening the door.

I climb on his lap and all four of us in the cab drive to Tangmo's restaurant.

"Drop me off at my hut first, I gotta take a quick shower, please," I say to the Captain.

Mike has one arm out the window, one arm around my waist, and his face buried in my hair. I put my head back on his shoulder and couldn't wait to wrap my legs around him. I knew I was experiencing one of the best moments of my life. On Mike's lap, next to Christine, bouncing down a remote village road in Thailand, full of Cheetos. Could it get any better than this?

Oh yeah, it could.

~~~

The Captain and Christine drop us off at my hut. Mike stays on the porch while I go inside to shower off, brush my teeth and get ready for the night. He is immediately swarmed by the little neighbor kids. They rush over to view the big American man. Tong, my neighbor, brings over a plate of pineapple and bottle of water for him, and another neighbor brings a bag of green rose apples.

I quickly clean myself up, and stand by my bed looking for something to wear, dripping wet in my sarong.

I hear him come in and quietly shut the door.

Yeah.

I turn around, untuck my sarong and let it drop to the floor.

About an hour later, after burning off all those Cheeto calories with Mike, we walk hand in hand to Tangmo's restaurant.

The Captain, Christine, Samantha and Velveetah are on the beach with a table full of food and drink.

I don't know if Mike realizes the ladies are transgendered. I don't say anything, as it is none of my business to tell him.

If the Captain does know, he certainly doesn't care. He is head over in heels in love with Vel.

Mike and I sit down across from Christine, Sam and Vel. The Captain is sitting between Vel and Mike. I promise myself I am not going to get drunk tonight, but pour a little Mekong into my Coke.

"So, Mike, Susan told me she never have sex in the butt. Do you know she never have sex in the butt? You should have sex in the butt with Susan," Christine says, starting the conversation off.

Mortified, I thunk my forehead on the table. I thunk it again and a few times more. For the love of God, why does she do this to me...

I look up. Mike has his head back and is staring at the sky. The Captain folds his hands on the table and bites his lip, gazing off at some point unknown.

I grab the bottle of Mekong and add a lot more into my Coke.

Velveetah reaches over Sam and smacks Christine on the shoulder and says, "Shut up, Christine! Just let them be lovers!"

She then leans back and puts her arm around the Captain.

Samantha, meanwhile, is grinning like the Cheshire cat.

"Seriously, Christine. Can we talk about something other than this?" I hiss, and kick her in the shin. "Ask them if they can eat spicy food or durian, or something like that, for Christ's sake, ya know?"

Mike is still staring up at the sky. The Captain finally blinks.

"Sure, Susan," she says curtly. Then continues, "Do you have handsome brother for me, Mike?"

Thank goodness Mike comes out of his shock, takes a deep breath and good-naturedly says, "Why, as a matter of fact, I do!"

I take a big drink. Mike puts his arm around me and I relax a bit. At least this conversation is now going into another direction.

Later in the night, Mike and I end up going for an impromptu swim. A skinny dip. If rolling around in bed with him isn't lovely enough, hanging on him in the warm ocean is lovelier. In the moonlight. The clean soft waves. We don't talk much. Sometimes kissing, but mostly just holding each other.

When I look into his intense blue eyes, I have no fear of him. There is no commitment, no expectations, no plans. That makes me want those with him. I shake those feelings aside. For now, I only want the sweet now. I don't know what is wrong with me, but that is all I want. Just the sweet, beautiful now.

~ ~ ~

The honking horn of the F-150 rumbling in front of my hut in the morning is far too early. It must be the Captain and Velveetah. Almost immediately, Velveetah is knocking on the door, screaming at Mike and I to wake up.

"Susan! Mike! Get up! I have to tell you something" she yells excitedly.

"We'll be out in about fifteen minutes!" I yell back.

Velveetah doesn't wait and pushes the shutters open and stands in the window, beaming with a bright smile.

"We're getting married!" she gushes.

She shoves her left hand through the window, with a huge diamond dazzling on her ring finger.

I jump out of bed and grab her hand. The band is bright gold, twenty-two karat. The glistening marquise diamond is set between two smaller, glowing emeralds.

"Three karat diamond! Three karat!"

"When did you guys get this?" I ask in disbelief.

"Last night, we drive to Nakorn and pick it out. We are getting married! I'm going to America!"

I catch my breath, then lean through my window and give her a big hug.

"I go! I go tell Christine and Samantha, see you!" she squeals, and runs back to the truck.

After closing the shutters, I sit back down on the bed and stare at the wall, letting the news sink in. Mike rubs his eyes and shakes his head with a slight smile.

"Well, that was certainly quick," I mumble.

"Yeah, that was real quick," Mike says.

"I hope he means it."

"I think that ten-thousand dollar ring means it," he answers.

We sit in silence for a moment, trying to digest this.

"Did you know about it?" I ask.

"I told him to give it some time, but I guess he couldn't wait."

"Mike, say, uh, do you know about the ladies?"

"Christine, Vel and Sam?"

"Yes, you know. Do you know? You know...?"

"It's pretty obvious they are prostitutes."

"That too, but do you know about, you know, the other thing?"

"That they're trannies?"

I exhale fully, finally. He knows after all.

"Yep," I say. "Does that bother you?"

"Why should it?"

"I don't know, it bothers some men though."

Mike rolls over on his back, and puts his hands behind his head, and says, "There's a lot gays in the military, no one really cares as long as they do their job and keep their personal life personal. There's a flaming gay soldier at Lewis, no one gives him a hard time, though. He's a parachute rigger. Repacks parachutes all day. You can always tell when you are issued one that he packed, because it's perfect. Meticulous. Some chutes scare you to death by the way they are packed, hoping everything will work. Everyone wants one that he did because it opens flawlessly."

He then sits up against the wall and continues.

"There's a lesbian that works in Finance. Built like fire hydrant. But whenever someone has a pay problem, they go straight to her. She's the only one that seems to give a shit about soldiers. She will get on the phone, figure out what is wrong and fix it immediately. She's awesome. Specialist Jackson."

"How did you know they were ladyboys? Could you tell?"

"That's what we figured right away. You would have to be blind and stupid not to figure that one out."

"Who's we?"

"Captain and I."

"So he knows?"

"Yeah, didn't blink an eye. He thinks she is the greatest thing since sliced bread, or, fried rice, or just about anything" he says, and runs his hand through his hair. "I don't know, the Captain is kinda an interesting guy..."

"Obviously," I say, not sure how to feel about the situation.

"Captain comes from money, probably a billion. His dad owns an NBA team, that's how rich they are. He went to Princeton because that's his dad's alma mater. And, he only graduated because his dad donated a couple million to the school. Captain was a prick, spoiled, and his dad told him he can't take over the family money unless he does something with his life. So, Captain pissed and drunk goes down to the Army recruiters and wants to join. He gets in, and enlists for four years. He went to OBC (Officer Basic Course) then Infantry course, then airborne. He loved it so much, he signed up for another four years to go to the Special Forces Q course. He's a great officer, a great leader. But every single woman back in the States knows that he comes from money. Every single woman that he meets wants to marry him for his money."

"He hasn't told Vel about all that?"

"No, not about all his money. He always said he wants some-one to love him for who he is, not what he has. Vel doesn't know anything about it."

BANG BANG BANG

"Susan! You come eat rice! You hungry! Come now! Eat rice!" Tong screams through the shuttered window and then knocks a few more times on the door.

I lie back down on the bed and put my finger to my mouth, motioning Mike to be quiet. "Maybe she'll go away," I whisper.

"I know you in there, Susan! Is Army boy in there too? He come eat rice too!"

I whisper, "shhhhh," to Mike.

"You eat rice! Army boy come eat rice too!"

I shake my head. It's pointless to try to resist a Thai's warm and hospitable nature. If there is a *farang* or two in the area, it must be fed...a lot and constantly.

"You hungry! You come eat rice!" she yells again.

"Sawatdee, Tong! We will be out in a bit!" I yell back.

Mike and I throw on our clothes and I open the door. All five of Tong's children are sitting on my porch, eagerly awaiting the chance to see the male *farang* up close again.

When Mike walks out of my hut, the kids part like the Red Sea, totally in awe. They are afraid to get too close, so stand back, giggling and smiling.

Tong tells us to sit down on the eating mat outside on her front porch. She starts bringing out plates of food. Another neighbor woman, Pee Pong, comes over with two bowls of pungent curry, along with her four kids.

The adults sit on the mat, and the gaggle of kids stand in a half circle to watch Mike eat. They don't think I am all that great any-more, but the crowd of curious children are infatuated with the big American man.

Tong's oldest boy reaches out and touches Mike on the arm, then pulls his hand quickly away, laughing. Mike extends his hand, grabs the boy's hand, and shakes it. All the other kids now want to shake his hand, and nearly pull him off the porch while doing so.

Pee Pong screams at the kids in rapid southern Thai, wagging her finger. The kids revert to being quiet and just staring at Mike.

"Why you no marry Susan?" Pee Pong asks Mike.

I inhale deeply. This question isn't as bad as Christine's butt sex conversation starter, but I wish these Thais would stop being so, I don't know, Thai. Mike smiles, not sure what to say.

"Because she don't know how to wash clothes," Tong says.

"You don't know how to wash clothes, Susan?" Pee Pong asks.

"I wash my clothes just fine," I answer.

"But you don't know how to cook. Susan, you know how to cook? I never see you cook anything," Tong says.

"I don't need to, there is so much good Thai food here, I don't need to cook here. I just eat it."

"She eats cheese from a jar!" Tong's oldest boy says.

"With a spoon!" another child chimes in.

"Sometimes from a can!" some other child adds.

I hunch my shoulders and shake my head, hoping their attention will turn to Mike. And it does.

"How much you weigh, Mike?" Pee Pong asks.

"Uh, I haven't weighed myself lately," he answers.

"How many plates of rice you eat?" Tong asks, while scooping more rice on his plate, along with two grilled chicken legs. She then pinches his forearm.

"Just one, thanks, this smells delicious," he says.

"Do you have a fan in America?" she asks Mike.

"A fan? What?"

"A fan. Thai's call boyfriends or girlfriends, fans," I explain.

"Oh. Uh, no I don't."

"Susan is your fan now, Okay?" Pee Pong says, and puts another scoop of rice on his plate and pinches his other forearm.

"Please, let's not talk about all this. Ask him about durian or something," I say, and start eating.

"Can you eat durian, Mike? Susan will be your fan," she says.

"Yes, I can, but don't care for it. And yes, I wish Susan would be my fan," he answers.

I glance up at him, grin through gritted teeth, then stare at my plate.

"So, what are you two going to do today?" Pee Pong asks.

"Not sure. Probably go for a swim," I answer. I really just want to roll around in bed with Mike all day.

"We go *tio! Tio!*" both women exclaim.

"Uh, we will probably just hang around here," I answer.

"No! *Tio!*"

Mike looks at me smiling and says, "Sure, let's go. Why not."

I agree. Why not.

After we eat, I get on the back of Tong's motor scooter. Mike gets on the back with Pee Pong on hers, and off we go about twenty minutes away to visit a rubber tree plantation.

The plantation is acres and acres of thin, tall rubber trees, planted in meticulous rows. The rubber is tapped from the trees, much like tapping a maple tree for the syrup. Collected in buckets hanging from each tree, the latex is then poured into two by one foot pans, and left to dry.

Once formed, they are hung out on lines to dry further. The dried rubber mats are then loaded up on trucks, and hauled to Bangkok to be sold overseas.

The smell of the rubber sap is overwhelmingly sweet and chemically at the same time.

Tong, Pee Pong, Mike and I walk all afternoon through the rubber groves, chit chatting and enjoying the beauty of the amazing trees.

It turns out to be loads of fun, and we don't get home till five p.m that night.

The Ford F-150 is parked outside my hut, but no one is there. Mike and I walk down to Tangmo's Restaurant, sure that the Captain, Christine, Vel and Sam are waiting for us.

As we approach, I say to Mike, "You probably think all I do in the Peace Corps is eat spicy food, drink Mekong, and go on *tips.*"

"You mean you don't?" he says.

"Not always!" I say, laughing.

"You probably think all I do in the Army is sit on the beach in Thailand with a beautiful Peace Corps volunteer and drink Mekong with ladyboy prostitutes," he says.

"You mean you don't?"

With that, he puts his arm around my shoulder and I put mine around his waist. We see the gang at the restaurant, waiting for us. I wish he and I could walk like this forever.

~ ~ ~

The following morning, the Ford F-150 is honking again in front of my hut. Too soon. I suddenly become nearly immobilized in sadness. Mike kisses me on the forehead and tells me goodbye, and says he will see me soon.

I close my eyes, and he slips away.

Chapter Twenty

Mike and Captain are gone now, and Christine, Velveetah and Samantha go back to Hot Yai for work.

For the next week, I know my office in Nakorn will be closed. It is Songran, traditional Thai New Year, and the major holiday of the year. Many Thais return home for family reunions during this period. Officially, it's a three day holiday, but Thais turn it into a week long vacation. I know I need to go somewhere and do something. Otherwise, I worry I will fall into a deep depression.

I decide to go to Surat Thani, the province north of mine to try out a meditation retreat, Wat Suan Mokkh in Chaiya. Beth had gone there a few months ago, raved about it, so think I will give it a go.

The retreat is held monthly at a Buddhist monastery nestled at the bottom of a mountain range. I get on the next bus out of town.

About two hours later, and after asking around for directions for another hour, I join the forty other foreigners already gathered outside the walls of the monastery.

I check in, go to my sleeping room, and patiently wait for the next day, the first day on my road to Nirvana, God willing.

My room is a single wide cement cubicle containing two bamboo mats for beds with mosquito nets hanging over them and one barred window. The males are in another dormitory across the grounds, after all, the opposite sex is the number one disturbance in everyone's life, they tell me.

Bathing for women is outside at a communal water trough behind the squat toilet bathroom building. We are told no reading, no writing, no talking, no drinking, no smoking.

The only communication is to be *within* us, by ourselves. We are told not to leave the boundaries of the monastery. The only place to travel is inward.

While glancing over the daily schedule, I end up grinning more than I should. What the heck is this all about. The days are broken up into hour long chunks of meditating while sitting, standing and walking. Breakfast. Meditating while sitting, standing and walking. Lunch. The afternoon is similar, meditating while sitting, standing and walking. Bedtime is at eight p.m. because yoga is at four a.m.

I think I can handle this.

Except when my roommate moves in.

She is a skinny, beige haired American named Sylvia. Sylvia has a pointy chin, even pointier lips and the pointiest tongue. Wearing a trendy batik sundress she certainly paid too much for on her journey to spiritual enlightenment, she is furiously writing in a notebook.

"You really aren't supposed to be writing," I suggest helpfully.

"This is none of your God damned business," she sneers back.

Woah. If anyone needs a time out to meditate, that would be her. I decide to go wander around the temple grounds.

In the middle of the courtyard, there is a large sitting Buddha. He is about twenty feet high, solid gray stone and covered lightly in moss.

My favorite Buddha, however, is one of Thailand's largest reclining Buddhas located at Wat Hot Yai Nai in Hot Yai.

He is 35 meters long, not quite as big as the reclining Buddha in Bangkok at Wat Po, but I like him better. He has a sweet, almost goofy smile and his painted eyes appear to be looking directly at me. Behind the Buddha there is a mausoleum with hundreds of small doors with encased photos of people. Behind each door are the ashes of the deceased person. It almost looks like a wall of PO boxes at the post office in the States.

On one end of the mausoleum is a fortune telling machine from the 1960s. Insert a ten baht coin and the wheel spins around, stopping on a number. On the wall next to it are shelves with pieces of paper with hand written fortunes. The directions are to take the fortune that corresponds to the lucky number, and that is the person's future. I had spun the wheel many times, and always ended up with the number eight. One more than lucky seven, which probably means dumb luck. My fortune is always that I should not waste my time searching for something I already have.

This is probably true.

I walk back to the sleeping room and Sylvia is still writing in her notebook. She glares at me for a few seconds, then goes back to the notebook. I don't say anything to her, but grab my pocket knife out of my backpack, flip it open and cuddle with it all night just in case.

~~~

The schedule turns out to be no joke, especially the four a.m. rise and shine part. An ominous gong in the distance is the alarm clock. Sylvia is already outside against the wall, deep in meditation, with a cold Mona Lisa smile on her face.

Tonight, she is at it again, writing, writing, writing.

"Are you keeping a diary?" I ask.

"Shut up, I'm busy," she snarls.

The following night in our room, she is once again writing, writing, writing.

"You writing a book or what?" I ask.

"Yes, and I'm on deadline, so be quiet."

"About what?"

She glares at me again. I half expect her to slither out her tongue and snatch the mosquito buzzing around her head.

"About what?" I repeat.

She then, as if reading an outline, tells me about her life before coming here. She dumped her husband, then the next guy she went with dumped her, so she got a huge book advance to write all about *her journey.*

Except she doesn't say, *her journey.*

She says, "About my fucking spiritual journey, you fuckhead."

"For a writer, you're not very creative with your use of fucking adjectives," I say calmly.

"I'm on deadline! Leave me alone and stop talking!" she screams.

"Good luck with that," I say, and go outside for a cigarette. No one is supposed to smoke here, except me and about half the other women sneak behind the shower trough and light up. The monks know what is going on but don't say anything. I'm sure the men on the other side of the monastery are smoking too. The monks would simply lose too much business if they enforced the rule.

Later, I quietly go back into the room to sleep.

~~~

The next day, I make a little breakthrough with my meditation. Although I didn't come here to find the meaning of life or go on a spiritual journey, I realize I'm an old fashioned sinner clinging to my faith in Jesus. Nothing philosophical, esoteric, mystical or even explainable, just a good old forgiving Jesus.

The next day, I grow amazed at the parallels of the words of Buddha and the wisdom of Christ. Similar, timeless messages that run along together but fork when it comes to the end. Buddhists are recycled back. No, not me. Call me boring, but I want to go to heaven and look forward to spending eternity there. One time around on this earth is enough and all I have, so I'll keep trying not to mess it up too badly until then.

That night, Sylvia starts boasting about how enlightened she became when she soaked her butt in the River Ganges in India.

She brags how she looked into the eyes of an elephant (in hideous circus paint, chained to the ground for life because of metaphysical, navel-gazing tourists like her) and claims she found her soul mate and the meaning of life. Blah blah blah. She keeps a "happiness list," recording everything that makes her happy, one of which is *photosynthesis*.

"What?" I ask in awe of her arrogance.

"Photosynthesis, you idiot. The sun. You know, the sunshine?"

"What are you talking about?" I ask, just to wind her up a bit.

"Sunshine on my shoulders is like a photosynthesis to me. It makes me feel alive, inside and out. It helps me grow. It's on my happiness list. Sunshine on my shoulders makes me happy."

"John Denver wrote a song about that."

"Who?" she asks, throwing down her pen.

"That guy with the granny glasses and the Tupperware bowl haircut."

"What are you talking about?" she asks.

"What?" I ask back.

"Excuse me, but are you high?"

"He wrote a song about that too."

She cringes and goes back to her notebook.

"Did you know I am a follower of Scabby?" I ask later.

"Is that Hindu Mysticism? Egyptian Druse?" she asks.

"No. It's Scabbyism."

"What's that?" she asks, confused.

"Scabbyism is unconditional love, pure gratitude and peaceful contentment."

"Is that in India? I was just in India," she says, alarmed she may have missed something trendy.

"No, he's a dog at the bus stop," I say.

"Would you just get out of here and leave me the hell alone?" she yaps, staring indignant daggers at me.

So I do. Nothing against Buddha and Eastern religion, but I have grown fed up with this smug 'monkette' roommate of mine and her pompous ego.

God isn't hiding in some cave in India or monastery in Thailand. He's not something that someone has to go searching for to find. He's everywhere, all the time, already. The sad part is her book will probably be a best seller.

I pack and walk out of the monastery as fast as I can, realizing what I said about Scabby is absolutely true.

I catch a bus on the main road back to Sichon. There is drunk guy across the aisle that looks like Charles Manson with a burlap bag full of dozens of chicken feet. The other drunk man behind me keeps pulling my hair, but only a few strands at a time. Whenever I reach back to rearrange my ponytail, he waits a few minutes, and gently tugs again. Another drunk man in the seat next to me gets sick and barfs on the floor.

I eventually make it back to my village at midnight. Scabby walks around to watch me get off the bus, then goes back to his hole behind the Jet Sipette. I take a deep breath full of the ocean breeze wafting down the long dark road and walk home, elated.

~~~

In the morning after a quick shower, I pass through town on my way to work. Bong is lying in the middle of the road on his side, twirling a finger in the dirt.

"Bong! Get out of the road!" I yell.

He looks at me and starts to sing *Wake me up before you Go-Go* by Wham.

"How about you go-go out of the road?" I yell again.

He just sings louder.

I stop by the post office to check for mail. When I walk in, I smell it. I about drift to heaven on the scent. I smell Aveda. The

Weasel has intercepted an Aveda product sent to me, I just know it. I could smell that stuff a mile away.

The Weasel is sitting at the back table, with a little mirror propped up, combing his hair.

"Sawatdee ca," I say loudly.

Sawatdee ca, Susan."

"Give it to me," I say.

"Give you what?" he asks.

"The Aveda, give it to me."

He goes back to looking in the mirror, combing his hair.

"The bottle," I say.

"No bottle here."

"The spray."

"No spray."

"The gel!"

"No gel."

"The shampoo!"

"No shampoo."

"Lotion?"

"No lotion."

"Foot exfoliant?"

"I don't know what that is," he answers.

Exasperated, I scream, "Just give it to me! Give me the Aveda and no one gets hurt!"

I slam my hands on the counter, livid.

"Give what to you?"

"That aromatherapy! That Horst! That Aveda!"

He stands up and pulls out a letter from under the counter. It's from my dad. He then goes back to the table to look at his hair in the mirror.

I snatch the letter and storm out the door. I am so frustrated, I want to pull my *own* hair out. I rub my eyes until they are red, and stomp down to the bus stop.

At the Jet Sipette, I buy a bottle of water and bag of shrimp flavored chips. I splash some of the water on my face to try to cool down as Scabby gimps over to see what I'm doing. He seems to sense I am still mad. He licks his butt, then lies down, his tongue lolling in the dirt, still looking at me.

The old man nudges him with his foot.

"Scabby smart. He knows trick," he says, smiling slyly.

"Really? Let's see!" I say, relaxing a bit.

"Scabby!" the old man yells, and the dog scoots over closer to his feet. "Scabby, shake!"

The old man holds out his withered hand.

Scabby just sits there and smells his palm.

"Scabby, shake!"

Scabby looks at me, then at the old man.

"Shake, Scabby, shake!" he repeats again.

The dog slowly leans on his right front paw, and with great effort, lifts up his left paw. He then places it softly in the old man's hand, who shakes it up and down.

"You did it! Good job Scabs! Who's a good boy?" I squeal.

The old man is proud as a peacock, and gives him a cracker. I want to pet Scabby but he never lets anyone touch him except his trusted owner.

"Today we work on new trick. I surprise you tomorrow, with new trick too," he says, laughing a little.

A few minutes later, the bus to Nakorn screeches to a stop, and I jump on, leaving the old man and the dog in the dust.

Chapter Twenty-one

"Susan, you eat *mangkhud*," Nuang says, and drops a large bag on my desk. They are called mangosteen in English, and are the most cutest fruit ever. The size of a peach, they have thick, reddish-purple skin and four waxy, green leaves on top. They look like something Dr. Seuss would draw, because they are just that adorable.

The inside flesh is segmented like an orange, snow white and tastes of a sweet and sour mix of apple and pear. To open, I put my thumb on the bottom core and push up and twist.

Nuang sits on the corner of my desk, crossing her legs in a checkered silk pencil skirt, emerald green fitted blouse and red pumps with yellow bows. Not one glossy, black hair is out of place, perfectly slicked back into an elaborate bun.

Higher class Thai men dress up also, but usually in polyester or linen pants and pull over smock tops. They grease their hair down to the point that they look like skull fitting helmets.

Thailand, in 1990, is classified as a developing nation, and receives used clothing from organizations in the States. Common villagers wear sarongs or shorts and often donated tee shirts. A boy in Sichon once was wearing a shirt that read, 'Stop Staring at my Tits.' Young girls, so angelic looking that the only thing missing are their wings, often can be seen wearing Motley Crew or Black Sabbath concert shirts.

A volunteer in Issan, Karla, swears that she recognized her very own college dorm room shirt she donated to a church clothing drive several years ago. The odds of that being the one were out of this world, but there were only thirty of them made for her and her dorm mates. Stranger things have happened.

~~~

I grab a mangosteen and start to eat one as Pee Uaan walks out of the Supervisor's office with a letter and a magazine.

"You have mail, Susan," she says, grabbing a mangosteen also.

She hands me the envelope and the latest edition of the *Diarrhea Dialogues*. On the cover is a close up photo of a PCV, smiling broadly, with one finger to his chin and looking up, as if he is thinking. The headline reads, *Let's explore tapeworms and parasites!*

"Oh dear God, lets not," I whisper to myself. "Seriously, Peace Corps. Why do you do this to me?" I drop the magazine immediately into the trash can.

The letter is addressed to me from Honeywell Corporation, Pacific Division, postmarked Hong Kong.

I open it up with my sticky mangosteen fingers, and pull out a letter and a check for one thousand dollars.

Nuang shoves another gob of fruit in her mouth and grabs the check.

"Susan!" she yells, spitting pulp all over me. "We got money!"

I sit dumbfounded. I can't believe Honeywell sent us a check. With the exchange rate, one thousand bucks is almost twenty-five thousand baht.

When I first arrived in Thailand, I asked my mom to send me the addresses of all the Minneapolis based corporations; 3M, General Mills, Dayton Hudson, Target, Cargill and Honeywell. I sent handwritten letters to all of them, enclosed some photos of especially cute kids, and mailed them off to the 'PRESIDENT' of each corporation. I had no idea there was a lengthy grant writing process involving proposals, budgets, timelines and interviews to receive money from these companies and their foundations. I was clueless. I am sure we went over this in technical training, but I was probably daydreaming and not paying attention.

Lo and behold, my letter somehow made it to where it needed to be, and a year later, we receive this check. It is made out to me, so Nuang and I go to the bank right away. I endorse it over and we deposit into our office's bank account.

The whole office shuts down when Nuang and I return. We go across the street and eat, drink, and celebrate, happy as can be.

The money in my Supervisor's good hands will be used for a bathroom at the childcare center I visited awhile ago. There is still plenty left over to be used for other centers in the province. I am relieved more than anything. At least I got that much for them.

It's all thanks to a man named Mr. Knoblauch, President of Honeywell Asia Pacific Division, who generously and quietly signed a check from his own personal account, bypassing the formal grant application. By doing it this way, he, a complete stranger yet fellow American, allowed me, a complete stranger yet fellow American, to save face. We are eternally grateful.

Chapter Twenty-two

When I get off the bus at the Jet Sipette, the old man is sleeping in his chair with Scabby snoozing at his feet. The dog opens one eye, wags his stumpy tail, then goes back to sleep. I pick out a bag of tamarind flavored rice crackers, leave money on the table and continue to the post office to check for mail.

The Weasel is sleeping too, with both his hands tucked inside his crotch. He is wearing a crisp white tee shirt that reads 'I ♥ Minnesota.'

"Sawatdee ca! That is my tee shirt!" I scream. I can't believe he did it again.

He awakes with a jerk, fumbling to get his hands out of his pants.

"Susan!" he says, jumping up and smiling sincerely for once. "Come! Come! I want to show you something!" and motions for me to follow him to the back room.

There in the middle of the floor is a brand new Xerox copier machine. The box it came in is next to the wall along with an instruction manual.

"Look! Look at this!" he says, excitedly. He lifts the cover and lays his entire chest on the glass. He pushes the button.

There is a whirl and a whiz and out slides a piece of paper into the tray. 'I ♥ Minnesota' is clear as day.

He then puts the side of his face on the glass, pushes the button, and out slides his smudgy profile.

I am beyond excited. I have been looking all over my province for a copy machine. My office in Nakorn only has a mimeograph machine. I have wanted to make coloring books in simple English for the kids at the elementary school for a long time, but never have been able to find a copy machine.

"Where did you get this?" I ask, delighted

"I don't know. I borrow it," he answers, smirking and shrugging his shoulders.

He must have intercepted it being shipped to someplace. I am fairly sure he will box it back up and send it on it's way eventually, but just wants to play with it for a day or two.

I have to act fast if I want to get my English books done. Grabbing a ream of paper from the table, I hurry home to start my project. I have to finish them and make as many copies as I can before he packs it up again once someone realizes it's missing.

I stay busy until two in the morning, drawing, writing and arranging. I make four different books, one for the elementary school aged kids, and one for the older kids. I create a simple coloring book for the preschoolers. All in English.

When Weasel arrives at the post office in the morning, I'm waiting by the door. He smells like Victoria's Secret Raspberry Passion body spray, obviously that someone had sent me, but I don't care at this point. His pilfering and conniving ways are beneficial to me now.

For the rest of the morning, Weasel and I copy, collate and staple hundreds of books, using the entire case of paper that also came with the machine. He is going to have to lie through his teeth with a straight face to explain what happened to the case of paper and toner. However, I am not worried, he is good at that.

When we are done, Weasel shuts down the post office for a few minutes to run me back home to store the heavy boxes of books.

I grab a stack and can't wait to go to the nearest childcare center and school to pass them out.

Walking through the village on my way out, I see Bong sitting in the middle of the road. He has a stick and is drawing in the dirt, then rubbing over the ground to erase it. Then doing it again, and again.

"Sawatdee ca, Bong," I say, cheerfully.

"Sawatdee crop, *farang* Susan," he answers.

Squatting next to him, I give him a few coloring books and crayons from my bag.

He lights up like a neon sign above a Patpong strip club. Immediately sitting up with the books in his lap, he starts coloring. Scribbling all over the page.

"No, in the lines. Bong, in the lines," I say, and show him how to do it.

He then focuses, biting his tongue, and colors neatly and methodically.

Feeling good about the progress I just made with him, I say, "Bong, get out of the road. Go sit on the sidewalk."

He shakes his head and ignores me now. He obviously is too busy coloring.

Well, one out of two suggestions work. That ain't bad. I keep walking to the Jet Sipette to catch a bus to the school.

I spend the rest of the day traveling around to the little villages in the area, delivering what the Weasel made possible. I still am not ready to admit he isn't a total jerk, but he did come through for me this time.

When I get home and after a quick shower, I walk down the beach to a rickety rice stand and ordered *kao pad goong* (fried rice with shrimp).

Kao pad is fried rice with just about anything I want or whatever the cook has: chicken, beef, pork, shrimp, squid or just vegetables. If I am really hungry, I ask for it with an egg. Only the cooks don't stir fry the egg with the other ingredients like back in the States. They add a sunny side up egg on top.

The *kao pad* vendor slides my spicy, steaming order into a plastic bag so I can take it to go.

Tangmo is sitting in her chair by the shore in the shade. George Bush is on her lap, spinning the bracelet on her wrist around and around.

I pull over another chair and sit next to them. She gurgles as a greeting to me and lobs her head a little. I offer her some rice but she flings her hand in the air to signify she has already ate.

Spending the rest of the night on the beach reading a Narnia book, I wonder how I got so lucky to be stationed in this paradise. I go to bed early, tired and happy.

~~~

BANG BANG BANG

I look at my pink plastic alarm clock. It's 7:00 a.m. on Saturday morning. I had wanted to sleep in late, but that obviously isn't going to happen.

"Susan! Susan!" and more banging on my door.

It's Christine.

The shutters fly open and there stands Christine in the window with the glowing sun behind her. She looks like an angel. A big, raven-haired transvestite angel with fake boobs. She doesn't wait for me to get out of bed to open the door to let her in, she just steps over the window sill.

"Susan! *Tio*! *Tio*! Let's go *Tio*!"

"*Tio* where?" I say, rubbing my eyes.

"Koh Samui! Come on, I help you pack!" she says excitedly.

"Now? Do we have to go now?"

"Yes, now. The *song tao* to the dock to catch the ferry leaves in fifteen minutes."

"Why are we going to Koh Samui now?"

"I have a work date, I have to go meet him there! You come with, it will be fun!"

Koh Samui is the second largest island in Thailand after Koh Phuket. From my village, it takes an hour to get to the dock to catch the ferry, and another hour to the island.

It is becoming an extremely popular tourist destination, with five star hotels as well as little bungalow huts with ceiling fans for the budget backpackers. Many of the backpackers stay for months at a time.

The island has an uninhabitable jungle covered mountain in the middle, but all around the edges are pristine beaches. The sea is turquoise, clear and calm. There is one road that goes around the edge, with small villages along the way. The main port is in the biggest town, Cheweng.

Christine grabs my backpack off the floor and starts shoving clothes into it. She stops only once to hold up a sundress, wrinkles her nose, and says, "Susan, you dress like a Peace Corps volunteer."

"Uh, because that's what I am?"

"You dress unsexy. Those sandals are old man sandals," Christine says, pointing at my feet.

"I told you before to leave my hiking sandals alone."

"They are like Frankenstein shoes."

"You just don't stop, do you," I answer.

"No problem, Susan, we buy you new sandals on the island."

With that, we jump on her motor scooter and buzz down to the Jet Sipette, just in time for the *song tao*. The old man tells Christine to park her scooter behind the shack, and Scabby will guard it for her. Scabby just grunts and goes back to sleep.

We get on the *song tao* and head to the dock.

Once on the ferry to Koh Samui, we sit on a bench in the rear of the top deck with our dark sunglasses on so we can gossip about the tourists onboard.

"Why do white women have hair in corn row braids?" Christine asks, motioning to a chubby woman wearing a stretched out tank top and batik wrap skirt. "Blacks look good with them. She look stupid."

"I don't know, it doesn't look right," I agree.

"Those hippies over there stink," Christine says. "The hippies love Thailand. They buy drugs in Chiang Mai. Cheap up there."

"All that makes me sick," I mutter.

We watch as a group of three Israeli backpackers sit down on benches not far from us. Many come to Thailand after they finish their two year conscripted military service. I can tell they are Israeli because they are confident, clean, and drop dead gorgeous. Seriously, I have not seen a male or female Israeli tourist who isn't good looking.

I nudge Christine to look at them.

"Susan, those guys are cute!" she whispers.

"Way too cute," I whisper back.

One of them stands up, removes his shirt and I about choke. I do start to choke, so Christine hits me in the back.

"Listen, Christine, they are speaking Hebrew, doesn't that sound cool?" I whisper.

"Jewboys?"

"Shhh! Don't say Jewboys. Americans don't use that word. It's not good. They are Jewish," I answer quietly.

"Jewboys are cruelly handsome," she says.

"I just told you not to use that word!"

"Fine," she says.

"Where did you learn that phrase, cruelly handsome?"

"In a porno magazine. My boyfriend read it to me," she answers as a matter of fact.

"Cruelly handsome? No, don't say that."

"Then what are they?" she asks.

I gaze at the man for a moment, and then say, "Okay, cruelly handsome."

"Jewish boys are sweet. I had one for customer once. An old one though," she whispers. "Where's his little hat?"

"What?" I ask.

"His little black hat," she answers.

"You mean a yarmulke?"

"What's a yarmulke?"

"It's a little black hat," I say.

"That's what I said in the first place, Susan. I said, where is his little black hat?"

"It's called a yarmulke. The little black hat is called a yarmulke."

"Do you think they wear them to cover up their bald spots?"

"No, it's a religious thing. I think it's an Old Testament thing. Jewish men are supposed to cover their heads," I answer.

"That little black hat doesn't cover anything except the bald spots."

"I don't think those guys right there are going bald anytime soon," I say.

"I bet he has a hairy ball sack," she says, leaning against me.

"Oh my gawd, Christine, just shut up," I murmur under my breath, trying to act normal.

Christine smirks, thinking it's funny to embarrass me.

The young man is a masterpiece, sculpted like the statue of David. How the hell does one tiny country produce such exquisite men?

He looks at me, and grins a little. I try to grin back.

L'chaim.

"Go talk to him," Christine says.

"No! I can't just do that!" I exclaim. I'm nervous just looking at him, the Masterpiece.

"Why not?"

"He will think I like him!"

"But you do!"

"No, he will think I am desperate."

"You are," she says.

"He probably has a girlfriend."

"If he did, she would be here with him."

"No, I'll just follow him once we get to the island and see what bungalows he checks into, and check into the same ones."

Christine nods her head in approval and says, "Good plan."

~ ~ ~

About a half hour later, with me staring at the Masterpiece the entire time, we disembark at the port of Cheweng. Everyone wanders around the main strip for a while, buying beer, clothes and souvenirs.

Christine pulls me into a small shop, makes me try on some kitten-heeled slip on sandals, then buys them for me.

"Susan, I have to go. I have to go meet my date," she says with a big smile, happy I now have shoes which she approves.

"Okay, how can I find you later? Will you stop by? I am going to follow the Masterpiece and check into the same bungalows he does," I whisper.

"I come see you!"

"How? How will you find me?"

"It's a small island. I know everybody. I ask around,' she says. "And Susan," she adds.

"What?"

"Don't be silly! Wrap that willy!"

I laugh and tell her thanks. She hugs me, grabs a handful of my hair, smells it for a few seconds before disappearing into the crowd.

Chapter Twenty-three

Then I see him. There he goes. The Masterpiece and his buddies are getting on a *song tao*, probably headed to their bungalows.

I run across the road and hop in too, accidently banging my backpack on his beautiful head.

"Hello," he says. Smiling, he grabs my bag and places it on the floor for me.

That curly auburn hair, those hazel eyes, those hairy legs, his good posture...

"Sorry, hello," I answer, trying to act uninterested, and take a seat opposite from him.

I slowly pull my feet out of my hiking sandals and slip into the kitten heels.

I am too flustered to talk, much less move.

He smiles again at me.

Those eyebrows. There's no movie star salon in Hollywood that could create eyebrows as perfect as his.

I sit and stare at him through my dark sunglasses. Turning my head to the right, while staring at him. Looking down, while staring at him, looking up, while staring at him. That is all I do. Stare at him.

About twenty minutes later, the Israelis get off at a bungalow stop. *Oh, what a coincidence, this is where I am staying...*

I get off also.

They check in, and head toward their assigned hut.

Look back, I scream in my thoughts, standing at the outdoor desk to check in too.

He looks back and smiles.

I about collapse. I'm in the same vicinity as the Masterpiece. I need a beer, so order one to bring back to my hut. I need to calm down and drink some courage. I don't come out of my bungalow for a few hours. I am too nervous to see him again, then become worried he might leave to go somewhere else.

Most bungalow complexes on Koh Samui consists of a main house where the workers live, and an outdoor reception desk to check in and out. Nearby, there are usually twenty small thatched roof huts to rent for the night or by the month. They have a main room with the bed, mirror and sitting chairs with a table. The bathrooms have a squat toilet and shower. There is always a large open restaurant on the beach with a bar, with tables inside and out along a boardwalk. On the sand, there are lounge chairs and tables also.

I walk out of my bungalow, down the path and to the beach-side restaurant.

I see him.

Oh my, the Masterpiece is sitting at a table all by himself on the boardwalk. He is wearing aviator glasses and a turquoise tank top, reading a book, drinking a beer.

His two friends walk by, each with an arm wrapped around a Thai bar girl. On their way to the bar, of course.

I walk over to his table in my new kitten heels and say, "Oh, hi. Excuse me, but do you have a stamp? I want to mail a letter."

Gawd, that's the lamest pick up line ever. However, it seems to work.

"No, but do you want a beer?" he answers with a grin.

"Sure!" I sit down and gaze at his twirly ringlets of copper brown hair. I want to ask him how his hair does that, but then I think that would be something my silly Thai coworkers would ask a *farang*.

"How does your hair do that?" I ask.

"Excuse me?" he asks confused, and self consciously runs his hand through his hair.

"It's really hairy down there. I mean, nice down here on the beach. It's nice hair, I mean here." I say. "You have nice hair."

He stares at me and says a little uncertainly, "Thanks?"

"I mean, here. All over. You too. It's really nice."

I can tell he is second guessing his English comprehension skills.

"Yes. It's very nice here," he says, cautiously.

I need to calm down, regain, or rather gain my composure and just shut up. So, I absentmindedly reach for his beer and take a big chug, nearly finishing it.

A look similar to constipation flashes across his face.

"When I asked if you wanted a beer, I meant I would buy one for you. *My* beer you're drinking might be a little warm," he says, and raises his perfect eyebrows.

"Uh, sorry. Of course! Sure! That would be great!" I answer, grinning like a fool.

He bolts out of his seat, says he'll be right back, he's just going to the bar, and walks quickly out of sight.

Dammit. I really muffed this one up. I won't ever see this guy again. I managed to scare him off in about ten-seconds flat. He probably ran away to see if he can catch up with his friends and the bar girls.

Mad at myself, I guzzle down the rest of his beer and then throw the empty bottle as far as I can down toward the shore.

A few minutes later, he returns and places a cold Singha in front of me, and one for himself. He takes his seat again, looks at me, then glances at the table.

"Where's the other beer?" he asks.

"What beer?"

"The one I was drinking, and then you drank?"

"Oh, that one. Uh, there was a huge gust of wind and it blew off the table. I see it down there by the water. I was just about to go get it. I don't like litterbugs," I answer as I jump up and sprint down to the shore to grab the empty bottle.

I run back up to our table, slam the bottle down, and take a deep breath. I am going to try this again.

"Hi. My name is Susan. Pleasure to meet you. What's your name?" I say with a smile, finally with some confidence, and stick out my hand.

"Hi. My name is Elad. Good to meet you too," he says, smiling also.

Whew.

We start talking, flirting a little, and laughing a lot. I had no idea why I was so nervous, because he immediately made me feel as if I was the center of his universe. He asks all kinds of questions about me, and then it is my turn.

"What did you do in the army?" I ask.

"Just a dumb tanker. I drove tanks."

"What are you going to do when you return to Israel?"

"I am going to college, of course. I want to study music. I play the cello."

"Really?"

He continues, "I want to move to Europe and join the Vienna Philharmonic Orchestra. I have an audition there in three months, so maybe I can study music there and play my cello soon."

"That is so amazing. Maybe I'll come see you," I say.

"I wish you will," he answers, putting his hand on top of mine.

We talk and drink beer for another hour, then go meet his friends at the next bungalow over for dancing and dinner.

About midnight, we walk on the soft beach back to our own bungalows. In nothing but the blue glow of the moon, he puts one hand on my forearm, slowly up over my shoulder, squeezing it tight and pulls me forward for a kiss.

Oy vey

When I awake in the morning, I can't believe he is in the bed beside me, snoring and naked. The Masterpiece.

We don't talk much, but stay in bed rolling around on each other until about eleven a.m. We then put on our swimsuits, run down to the beach and jump into the waves for a quick swim before breakfast.

His friends are already at a table on the boardwalk, eating breakfast with their Thai bar girlfriends. We join them, wet and refreshed.

Just about every guest at this bungalow is eating breakfast at noon with some serious cases of tangled and uncombed bed heads. Some people have already started to drink, getting ready to do it all again today. Drink, rinse, repeat.

The bar girls are named Whitney and Madonna. Beautiful and petite, but a little rough around the edges. They look at me in guarded fascination as we sit down.

I order a mango smoothie.

They don't know I speak Thai, so start talking about me.

"She's pretty," says Whitney.

"She's too big," says Madonna.

"Look at the hair on her arms. Why do *farang* women have hair on their arms?"

"They have hair on their legs, too. They have to shave their legs to get it off," Whitney answers.

"Why don't they shave their arms too?"

Whitney then reaches over and starts pulling the blonde hair on my forearm, snickering.

She continues to whisper loudly to Madonna. "Why she sleep with men for no money?"

"*Farang* women don't charge men to sleep with them," Whitney says.

"Some *farang* women do," I say in Thai.

"Oh! You speak Thai!" Whitney says, embarrassed. Madonna giggles into her hands.

"Yes, I speak a little" I answer.

"No! You speak very well!" they both say at the same time, now thrilled to talk with me in Thai.

A barrage of questions follow: where are you from, where do you live in Thailand, can you eat spicy food, how many plates of rice can you eat?

About an hour later, Elad and his friends announce they are taking a ferry to Koh Phangan, the smaller island next to Samui for a scuba expedition. The trip is sold out, so I can't go, though. Elad says he will meet me back here for dinner.

I'm not that disappointed that I can't go. Quite honestly, I am just exhausted after being played like a cello all last night, and want to nap on the beach all day.

He gives me a slow, intense kiss and leaves. Looking back on the way to the ferry, he waves goodbye.

My stomach now growls because I haven't eaten since last night. I head to the bar and order a plate of *kao pad goong* and *som tom* with two iced coffees.

The food is over priced, tamed down in spice for foreigners, but I don't care. I eat like a pig to slop, shoveling it all in.

"Hello! Hello beautiful!" someone screams into my ear about five minutes into my meal.

It's Christine. She is a vision, large and in charge, wearing a red bandeau bikini top, yellow and purple flowered sarong, floppy straw beach hat and silver stiletto heels.

"Sawatdee ca! How did you find me?" I say, rice sputtering out of my mouth as I am thrilled she found me.

"Because you are always at the bar drinking," she answers, and sits down next to me.

She lights a cigarette and elegantly crosses her legs.

"No, Christine, I am at the bar because I am eating. I'm hungry," I say, and start eating again.

"You have sex with cute Jewish boy? Is that why you're so hungry?"

"I am not going to answer until you ask me appropriately. You say, 'Did you make love to the beautiful Israeli man last night?' Just try it, ask me that."

"Okay. Did you do that?"

"Maybe," I say between bites, getting hot thinking about him.

Christine orders herself an iced coffee.

"Jewish boys have circumcised wieners. Americans too," she says out of the blue.

"Yes. Fine. Now please, I am trying to eat," I say, cooling down.

"Indians are not circumcised."

"Really, Christine, I am eating."

"Thai men too. Not circumcised."

I put my spoon down and turn myself toward her, totally disgusted and say, "Seriously. I don't want to talk about this."

"Wieners not circumcised look like dirty little elephant trunks," she says, and bats her eyes sweetly.

"Okay. Whatever. Now stop it," I say taking a deep breath.

"Circumcised wieners look healthy, like big enoki mushrooms."

"Hush!" I say loudly.

"Was Jewish boy good in bed?"

"Yes. Now stop talking about this."

"Stop talking about what? Enoki mushrooms?" she asks.

"No! Wieners!"

"Big wieners?"

"Yes! No! I'm trying to eat here! What the heck, Christine? Do you keep a list of nationalities you sleep with or what?" I say, getting flustered.

"I should make a list, Susan."

"Don't make a list, and stop talking about wieners!" I say, exasperated.

There is a few minutes of silence as I try to eat again, with her grinning at me and smoking.

"Did he like the kitten heels?"

"Yes. Thank you," I answer.

"Told you," she teases.

"I am going to stay another night with him. When are you going back?" I ask.

"My boyfriend wants to fly to Koh Phuket, maybe tomorrow."

Phuket is another tourist island on the opposite side of the southern peninsula. Bigger, louder, and more crowded with expats and tourists.

Suddenly, Christine becomes deathly silent. With a smooth quick motion, she puts on her sunglasses and pulls down her straw hat. She then spins around on her stool and faces the back of the restaurant.

"Shhh," she says quietly. "Don't look."

I take another bite and whisper, "Why?"

"I think he followed me," she says under her breath.

"Who?"

"Don't look."

I look. I see him.

Walking down the boardwalk, he's slowly surveying the beach and all the guests at the bungalows.

I dang near choke. I had forgotten about him, but now remember him all too well. His fat burrito body, his bloated face, his rolly poly neck flabs. It's the German tourist from Hot Yai. I am paralyzed with fear. His silver briefcase that Christine stole is still under my bed back in Sichon.

"He recognized me last night," she whispers.

"We need to leave, Christine," I say quietly and put my sunglasses back on too.

"Ya think?" she whispers back. She then drops down and squats on the floor behind the bar, pretending to do something to her sandal.

When he walks by the front of the bar, he looks at me. Thankfully, he turns his head back to the beach. He obviously doesn't even know I was in the room that night. He doesn't see Christine hiding under the bar either, but I can tell he has a feeling she is near. He looks back at me again before leaving.

I pay my bill and then Christine and I walk quickly back to my bungalow. I shut the door, lean against it as Christine looks at the unmade bed.

"You have sexy sex, Susan," she says and sits down on the mess.

"What are you going to do?" I plea, ignoring her comment.

"No problem, I leave now with my boyfriend to Phuket."

"What about that briefcase? You gotta get that briefcase out from under my bed!"

"I did a long time ago, dummy."

I put my hands to my cheeks and plop down in the wicker chair facing her.

"You did?"

"Yes, of course."

"When?"

"When you were gone, I went in and took it out of there," she explains as if it's the most obvious thing in the world.

"You climbed through my window again?"

"Of course. I don't want you involved with this."

I rub my eyes in relief.

"So?" I ask.

"So, what?"

"What was in it?"

"What was in what?" she asks in return.

"Christine! Stop talking in circles! What was in the briefcase?"

"I'm not telling you. That would make you more involved."

"I'm already involved!"

"I'm not telling you."

"Was it drugs?"

Christine makes a disgusted face and shakes her head.

I continue, "Was it spy papers, or diplomatic papers, or something like that?"

She looks at me like I am being ridiculous.

"Money." I state.

She doesn't say anything, just puckers her lips, raises her eyebrows and gazes at me.

I get the message. It was money. It must have been a lot since it was locked up in that type of briefcase. Must have been a whole lot if this man would try to track her down around Thailand to get it back.

"I'm going with you," I say. "I'm going with you to Phuket."

"Don't be silly, Susan. I'll be okay. I leave now with my boyfriend. Fat man will never know to follow me there."

"Why don't you go back to Sichon and stay with your mom for a while? Disguise yourself as a boy? He'd never find you there," I beg. "He might go to Phuket to look for you."

"You didn't notice?"

"Notice what?"

"He was wearing a Phuket tee shirt. He must have just came from there," she said.

I think back and she was right. He was wearing a new "I got Phuked in Phuket" tee shirt.

After a moment, I nod and agree.

"Okay, good. Good. You better go now," I say.

I open the bungalow door, and look around to make sure the coast is clear. Then, we slip out and power walk to the main road. She flags down the first motor cycle taxi that whizzes by.

I watch as she sits sideways on the back, crosses her legs and hangs on to her hat. Her black hair streams behind her as she disappears around the first bend.

I am left a nervous wreck. I don't think all the beer in the world and another romp with Elad could calm me down. I have to go. I want to get out of here too. I don't want to be on the same island as the German burrito.

Seriously, who carries around a briefcase full of cash? A drug lord? The mafia? A sex trafficker? This German is as shady as the Black Forest, no doubt about it.

I run back to my bungalow and write Elad a note, telling him I have to leave suddenly...I am so sorry...I had the best time last night...and to please stay in touch. I give him my address in the Sichon, Nakorn and Minnesota.

Last night, he had mentioned that he and his friends had originally flew to Indonesia, stayed in Bali for a while, flew to Singapore, took the train up through Malaysia, and then to Koh Samui. He had said that after here, they are going all the way north to Chiang Mai, then back to Bangkok for a flight to India.

I hesitate before leaving. I will probably never see this man again. No, not probably not, but never not. I take a deep breath and realize I am grateful for the pleasure of even meeting him. One night with him, maybe that's what made it so magical. I'll always have the delicious memory.

Chapter Twenty-four

After the incredible high and low with Elad and Christine on Koh Samui, I return to Sichon and dive head first into a thick soupy depression. Elad is gone. Mike is long gone and Christine is in Phuket. I become so melancholy I feel as if I am dissolving into vapors. In training, they warned us we would have bad days. Really bad days. It's just sometimes, the bad days here for me are beyond just bad.

For the next five days, I only leave my hut to sit by Tangmo and George Bush on the beach, or walk down to the post office to check for mail.

"Sorry, Susan. No mail for you," the Weasel at the post office says every morning, and I know he is telling me the truth.

"*Mai pen rai*," he says. "There's always tomorrow."

"If I make it to tomorrow," I mutter, and sulk out the door.

I still manage to yell at Bong to get out of the road. Bong must have bought some new cassette tapes, because he is singing songs from the *Stayin' Alive* soundtrack and *Disco Divas Greatest Hits* the whole week.

"How about *you* stay alive, Bong, and get out of the middle of the road!" I scream.

"Ahh! Ahh! Ahh! Ahh!" he sings back in high falsetto.

"How about you get out of the road so you don't get hit by a truck!?"

He switches to Donna Summer and starts singing *Hot Stuff*.

"Fine! Go ahead, Bong, you crazy fuck! Get hit by a truck! How hot is that?" I scream, and stomp back to my hut.

Pee Poo, Pee Uaan and Boonchu drive out to check on me one afternoon, but I just tell them I am not well.

"I'm sick," I say.

"Are you missing home, Susan?" Pee Uaan asks, standing at the bottom of my porch steps.

"Yes. No. I am sick. I have a headache."

"We miss you too. Here, eat papaya," Pee Poo adds sweetly, and places a bag of fruit on my porch.

"Do you want some beer? I have some in the truck," Boonchu offers helpfully.

"No, thank you, I'm good."

They all *wai*, and hesitantly walk back to the truck to leave.

Now I feel guilty. These loving people are worried about me, but right now I am too depressed to deal with them, or anything.

This has happened a few times before, withdrawing to the point of immobility. Barely able to talk. Moving in slow motion, with nowhere to go anyway, so it doesn't matter.

I read. I don't dare drink, fearing I will just drink myself into oblivion. I stare at the geckos having sex on the ceiling for hours. I write madly in my diary about nothing in particular. Pages and pages of barely coherent scribbles. I want to talk to someone, any-one, but can't. I should get on the bus and go find Mick, the other PCV in my province, but can't even get the energy to do that. I should call my best friend Karry back in the States, but that would make me miss home more.

I don't want to go back to America, but I don't want to be here. I don't want to work, but I don't want to be worthless. I don't want to drink, but I don't want to be sober.

Where did the past two years go? I only have about six months left here. Although some days drag by, the months fly past. I start to worry. Will I go to grad school? Join the military again? Get a job or start a career? Travel some more? How could I hold a regular job in the States after Thailand? Living on Thai time? Could I settle down and get married? How am I going to tolerate a friend back in the States that complains about something menial when it's really nothing in the big picture?

Remembering about a week before I left for the Peace Corps, I had moved back home from college, a minty new graduate ready to take on the world. I was sitting at the kitchen bar watching TV.

My mother was at the kitchen table balancing her checkbook with her big clunky calculator. I stared at her for a long time as she peered through her bifocals, raising her eyebrows, slightly adjusting her head, punching the keys on the calculator with those old fingers that used to wipe my bottom, wipe my tears, wipe off food from around my mouth, wipe my nose. I realized she would cut off her own legs with a chain saw if she had to for me. I walked over to her, leaned down and started bawling as I wrapped my arms awkwardly around her.

She snuffled, guided me to the couch and we sat there for about an hour. She had on a dark green velour sweater and I soaked it with tears.

I blubbered about being accepted into the Peace Corps, as it had been my dream throughout most of my college years. It was about to happen. I was leaving for twenty-seven months, going half way around the world. My mom just held me. That was so long ago, it seems now. Seems like a lifetime ago...so much has happened.

I realize now I need to pray. So on my knees in my little hut in Thailand, I do.

tap tap tap

tap

It's the scruffy neighbor kids at my door.

I pull myself off the floor, wipe my tears, open the door, and three of Tong's boys are holding a rattan ball.

"Can you come out and play?" they chirp.

No one has knocked on my door and asked if I can come out to play since I was ten years old. Their eager faces, their gaped-tooth smiles. The simplicity and innocence of playing without a care...I want to play too.

"Sure," I answer wearily.

Then I switch to English and say, "It's better than washing down a bottle of Halcion with a pint of Mekong and slitting my wrists with my pocket knife."

The kids just smile, yell, "Hurry, Pee Susan, let's go!" and excitedly run into the yard.

We play for about an hour as the universal yin and yang pull me out of the horrid deepness and onto safe shore. Everything is going to be okay. Thanks, Jesus. And you too, Buddha.

Chapter Twenty-five

I take a good, cool shower, the first in a week. Refreshed, I get ready to go to my office in Nakorn, and get back to saving the world as a Peace Corps Volunteer.

"Sawatdee ca, Bong! Get out of the road!" I yell as I pass him in the village.

He doesn't look up, but starts singing *Jive Talkin'*.

I keep walking, and stop off at the post office.

The Weasel is standing at the back table, with a Monopoly board laid out in front of him. He has the green hotels and red houses lined up perfectly, all the colorful money in neat piles, and is sorting through the title deeds.

He did it again.

That is my Monopoly game. I asked my mom to send me one last month.

"Sawatdee ca!" I scream.

He calmly turns and looks at me, almost annoyed.

"Oh, I'm sorry. Am I disturbing you as you steal my Monopoly game?" I say sarcastically.

He turns back around.

"That is my Monopoly game," I state.

"Moh noh poh lee," he answers, holding up the lid, trying to read it in English.

"No, it's pronounced Ma na poh lee," I sneer, "and it's mine so give it to me."

"No, this is mine. You buy your own game."

"What? Where did you get it then? That's mine!"

"No, it's mine," he says, and takes the little car token and starts pushing it around the board, making vroom vroom noises.

"I don't believe you!"

"Susan. What is my name?" he says quietly.

"What?"

"What is my name?"

I stand dumbfounded. He is the Weasel. Weasel man. Weasel post office guy. Weasly Weasel. And he knows everything about me, reads my letter, wears my clothes, eats my food, opens my packages, but I don't know his name.

"What is your name?" I ask, caught off guard and feeling like a schmuck.

He walks toward the counter, reaches down and gives me a letter. He then goes back to the board game. Taking the little shoe token, he starts tapping it around the avenues.

"You have got to be kidding me," I say, snatch my letter, and stomp toward the Jet Sipette.

Scabby is licking his butt and the old man is sleeping in his chair. I leave some money on the table and grab a pack of cigarettes and a warm Sprite. The bus comes and I jump on.

On the bus I read my letter. It's from Gaurang, the Indian man I made out with in Bangkok. The one that I think stole my jewelry. I don't remember giving him my address, though.

He writes lovely, formal English; *What a pleasure it was to meet you, I can hardly wait to see you again,* and *Do call me next time in town.* I have his number now.

The letter is in direct contradiction of him stealing the jewelry. Did he do it? I wonder. How could he have possibly have done that, and then write this romantic letter also? Maybe the jewelry just fell off when I was dancing as the dance floor was packed, or some Thai scam artist somehow got it off me? I was really drunk. Thinking about it, as far as I can remember, I could have taken it off and put it in a beggar's cup.

I reread the letter about twenty times, then put it back in my bag. It would be interesting to meet up with him again, but sober this time.

~~~

"Look what the cat dragged in!" Nuang says when I shuffle into the office and plop my work bag down.

"Sawatdee, ca," I answer, very happy to see her after a week holed up in my hut.

"Susan, did you eat rice yet or not?"

I sit down at my desk and Nuang follows me with her heels clicking. She sits on the corner and hands me a bag of juicy, yellow mango slices.

"Eat mango, Susan."

I realize how hungry I am. I haven''t eaten much all week, if at all. I start devouring the sweet, delicious fruit.

"Susan, eat rice, lets go eat rice," she says, noticing I have quite an appetite. I'm sure she is relieved to see me show up for work after a week absence. I probably look a bit thinner and more hag-gard than usual.

Nuang says something in rapid southern Thai dialect to the rest of my coworkers.

"Come, eat rice," she says again, grabbing my hand, pulling me down the steps and out the door before I can protest.

Sometimes I feel as if I am their pet. Their pet *farang*, someone to care for, feed, and make sure is happy. In a way, I am. I am *their* American, and by God they want to take care of me.

We walk a few blocks from the back of the building to an area I have never been to before, although it is very close. It's a Muslim area near a small mosque. We sit at the first outdoor rice stand. She orders for me a plate of *massaman* curry.

I am not sure what *massaman* means, as it's not a Thai word, but since I live in the South with a large majority Muslims, it reminds me of 'Muslim man' curry.

The fragrant stew is made of coconut milk, potatoes, powdered peanuts, bay leaves, cinnamon, curry and tamarind. The beef chunks are tender and amazing. All is served on top of rice, sprinkled with cashews.

My whole week of depression slips away. This is the ultimate comfort food. No one will ever tell me not to eat my worries. With every spoon full of this curry, I eat the frustration, guilt, loneliness, shame and anxiety. I taste them, savor them, swallow them, and can't wait for Mother Nature to process those bad feelings out into the toilet.

Nuang doesn't eat anything, but just sips an iced coffee and chit chats about what I missed. She makes sure I eat every bite, which isn't hard to do.

When we arrive back to the office, there's a telegram for me.

"Susan! You have telegram!" Nuang says as she rushes to pick it up. Pee Poo and Pee Uaan walk over also to see what it says.

All four of us gather around it like it could be a marriage proposal from George Clooney. I open the yellow envelope.

It's from the Peace Corps office. It is a reminder that I have my annual meeting with my Program Manager, Kathy. I have to be there tomorrow and it's already late afternoon. I forgot all about this appointment in my haze of sad hibernation. I need to leave in a few hours to make it.

"Go! Go to meeting!" Nuang says, and claps her hands a few times.

"Go! Go now! Go to meeting!" Pee Poo adds.

"I won't make it!" I say, panicking. "I still have to take the bus back to Sichon, pack, then return here to Nakorn to catch the train!"

"Boonchu drive you now!" Pee Uaan screams.

My Supervisor comes out of his private office, folds his arms, and leans in the doorway. "Go, Susan. Boonchu drive. He drive fast. Good luck."

I'm not sure if he is telling me good luck with the meeting, or good luck with Boonchu driving fast.

Now that my Supervisor got involved, in about two minutes Boonchu is waiting for me in the baby blue truck at the front of the building. I jump in and hang on for dear life.

We speed down the main street in Nakorn on our way out of town.

In Thailand, there are only three basic rules when it comes to traffic lights.

Green light means go very fast.

Yellow light means go faster.

Red light means go not as fast.

Once we are on the main road to Sichon, Boonchu lights a cigarette and cracks open a beer.

"How much do you get paid?" he asks.

"I don't get paid, I am a volunteer," I answer.

"How much do you get paid?" he asks again.

"Not much, just enough to live on."

"How much do you get paid?"

"All volunteers in Thailand receive a four thousand baht monthly living allowance. That's for food, clothing, rent, transportation, for everything," I finally say.

With the exchange rate, that is less than $200 a month, but plenty to live on here in Thailand.

He seems to consider this a moment, then asks, "In America, do you have poor people?"

"Yes, many are poor. Many Americans are extremely poor."

"As poor as some Thai people?"

"Maybe not as many, or as bad, but still poor."

He thinks about this also, then asks, "Why don't you help poor American people in America instead?"

"Uh, well, that's a good question."

"Do you eat bread in America?"

"Yes, we eat bread in America. Bread, rice, and noodles."

Boonchu shoves the empy beer bottle under his seat and says, "I don't like bread."

We continue talking and before I know it, I have grabbed my backpack from my hut and we are now racing back to Nakorn. Boonchu drops me off at the train station in record time.

I make the night train and drop into my seat, exhausted and dripping in sweat. I am feeling blessed to have these Thai coworkers that made this happen.

I buy a bag of pineapple, take a Halcion, and sleep the best eight hours straight in a long time.

Chapter Twenty-six

I arrive in Bangkok about seven a.m. After buying an iced coffee at the station, I decide to spend the morning shopping. A while ago, I read in the Bangkok Post that the United Colors of Benetton had opened their first store in Bangkok. So, I plot out on the map and catch a bus to find it.

About an hour later and three bus transfers, I see the store. It's a glorious, a two story glass building right on the corner near Central Bangna Plaza. When I walk in, it feels as if I am in a department store back in downtown Minneapolis.

I start rummaging through the racks, thrilled with anticipation. However, my euphoria doesn't last long.

Dang. There are no clothes over the size of six. I try to squeeze into a few things, but cannot zip, button or snap anything, even after not eating for a week during my great depression.

I try. I try. I try. I suck it in, move boobs around, tuck in butt cheeks, but to no avail. I can't fit into any of this.

Sure, I understand I am in Thailand, with Thai sized women, but other people live here too, I mutter under my breath.

Dear Bennetton, you can kiss my fat, white ass.

I walk out frustrated and angry.

Across the street is another department store. I go inside and wander around for an hour, but can't find anything that fits either. Nothing. Nothing at all. There is a plus-sized section, but it's only full of muumuus. As in MOO MOOs.

I'm deflated and pissed off. Do I really have to go back to Banglapoo, the hippy tourist section near the Viengtai Hotel, and buy a tie dyed tee shirt and batik elastic skirt for something new to wear?

Disappointed and about to walk out of the store, a young shop girls comes around a rack of clothes and gives me a sweet *wai*.

"Sawatdee ca! You are big, you are beautiful!" she says in English, infatuated with me.

"Thank you, but I am too big," I say, and *wai* in return.

"You need new clothes!"

"Yes, I do. I want a beautiful dress, but can't find anything here," I answer.

"You sometimes too big," she says.

"Yes. I am too big. I want a big beautiful dress."

"*Mai pen rai!*" she gushes, and takes me by the hand, leads me down a flight of steps to a rack in the corner of the basement.

By this time, two other shop girls have also latched on to me and are chirping and chatting in Thai about my big size, my white skin, and blonde hair.

The shop girl pulls out a lovely, silky blue, wrap dress with rich cream trim. They then push me into the dressing room. I walk out wearing the dress, feeling fabulous. It fits perfectly.

"Shoes! You need shoes!" they all shout.

There is no way they will have a size shoe to fit me.

A minute later, one of them brings out a box of size ten, creamy open toe heels. They coordinate with the dress perfectly.

"Size ten shoe?" I ask incredulously.

"Ladyboys shop here," one of them says. "They big too, just like you."

I buy my outfit and take the bus to Banglapoo to check into the Viengtai Hotel. And although it cost me a couple hundred baht, I'm thrilled I found something stylish that fits.

After a plate of fried rice and iced coffee on the corner, I head to the Peace Corps office on Rajvithi Road. I don't want to be late for my meeting with Kathy.

I am nervous because she thinks I'm batshit crazy.

~~~

A year and a half ago, I had run into her office wearing a black wig in disguise, screaming hysterically that the Thai police were coming to arrest me. I collapsed in a chair, bawling and twitching barely consolable.

During PC training, we were constantly told that no matter what we do, never make disparaging remarks toward the King or the Thai royal family. They are revered to the elevation of Buddha. The royal family doesn't do anything politically, but are loved, respected and beyond reproach.

So, what did I do? I wrote a postcard to my PC friend, Beth, up in Chiang Mai, the usual small talk, how you doing, etc. I then wrote something like, 'What is up with the King's hat on the front of this postcard? He looks like a giant Q-tip! Ha ha!'

A few days later, Beth wrote back, telling me the police had been questioning her about the postcard, where did it come from, and who insulted the King. I didn't realize she was joking around. Instead, I panicked. I thought the police would come arrest me and it would be a huge international scandal: PEACE CORPS VOLUNTEER INSULTS KING OF HOST COUNTRY! I then would rot my life away in a horrible Thai prison.

I bought a black wig, a hat, shades, and got on the next train to Bangkok from Nakorn, and ran to the Peace Corps office. I crumbled in front of Kathy, took off my disguise, and told her what I did. It was a horrible stupid mistake, supposed to be a joke, and I wanted diplomatic immunity or something or anything to keep me from going to jail, I sobbed.

Kathy calmly called Beth at her office, spoke a bit, then hung up with a hesitant smile on her face.

"Beth was just joking too," she said.

"What?" I whined.

"Don't worry about it. Go back to Nakorn, and don't write anything stupid on a postcard again, okay?"

I cried more in relief.

So, this is the woman I have to meet with today. Except she isn't here. She had been called late last night to go to a volunteer's site who got in some sort of trouble. Kathy spends most of her time getting PCVs out of trouble. No wonder I rarely see her.

"You will need to reschedule," the PC secretary tells me. "Can you come back here next Friday morning? I am so sorry to make you travel back and forth like this."

I am trying hard not to throw my arms up in the air and fist pump in joy over the fact I get another expense paid trip to Bangkok next weekend.

"Well, I am so swamped with all my projects down in my province, so busy, you know, but I possibly could squeeze it in," I say with a straight face.

"Okay, Susan, see you next week. Don't forget to pick up your per diem," she says.

I go into the library room to see if there are any new books to read. PCVs take books, read, and return them here. Most are very worn out, but very good.

"What happened? Where's Kathy?" I ask a volunteer I don't know, who is in the library room too, looking for books to bring back to his site.

He pulls a book off the shelf, looks through it, then puts it back in it's place, nonchalantly.

"Rumor has it some volunteer got drunk and tried to screw a water buffalo," he answers.

"No way, really? Why? Seriously? We are in Thailand, for God's sake. Who needs to screw a water buffalo?" I ask.

Another volunteer I don't know walks in, drops his backpack, and says, "No, that was last week. You know that weird guy, Steve, who got funding to buy a pizza oven for his village? Him. They sent him back to the States. *This* dude is in the hospital because he got drunk last night and tried to shoot a bottle rocket out of his ass. Has second degree burns. Ended up setting a rice paddy on fire. The U.S. Government has to pay the farmer for it now. They want to put him on a plane and send him home, but he can't sit, if you know what I mean."

Nodding my head, I say, "Yeah, I met Steve before, something was definitely off about him."

The other volunteer agrees. "I can see how someone might try the firework thing, but the water buffalo thing is too weird, man."

"Yep," I mutter.

I pick up my per diem money and travel pay from the secretary, go buy some beer, and head back to the hotel.

~~~

After a shower and a plate of *som tom* ordered from room service, I pull out Gaurang's letter. I read and reread it. Gaurang. He's so very handsome but I don't like his name. What strange thing to dislike about him. However, his writing is polite, beautiful and eloquent. He dots his 'i's with upward dashes.

I start to get nervous, then decide just to go for it.

I pick up the phone and dial.

"Hello?" someone answers.

"Hello?" I answer back.

"Blahblahdeeblahblahdeeblah," someone says in Urdu.

"Hello?" I say again.

"Hello?"

"Gaurang?"

"Yes?"

"Hi, this is Susan. Remember me?"

"Susan?"

"Hi."

"Susan!"

"Hi."

"Susan! Are you in Bangkok?"

"Yes, are you?"

"Of course, you called me here."

"Okay, that's great," I say.

"Where are you?"

"In Bangkok," I answer.

"I know that, but where?"

"Here, in Bangkok."

"I know that, but where are you in Bangkok?" he asks again.

...okay, this conversation isn't going anywhere, I need to take a deep breath and regroup...

"Uh, do you want to meet later?" I ask.

"Love to, where?"

"Anywhere."

"Meet me at King's Disco. Can you meet me there about nine p.m.?" he suggests.

"Sure, bye, see you."

"Great, Susan, see you soon."

Okay. I just made a date. With an Indian man that may or may not have stolen my jewelry. A total stranger I made out with once. What the hell am I doing? I wasn't thrilled about meeting in Patpong at King's again, but maybe he just suggested that because he knows I know where it is. But dang, he is so dashing and well dressed I'd meet him just about anywhere.

He would be my third man here, the third in two years.

In my old circle of single college girlfriends back in the States, three guys in that time would be considered conservative, maybe even a dry spell. But, to pick a man up for the sole purpose of a roll in the hay? To be held? Kissed? To be ravished at least for a while? Am I looking at them like sex objects? The way the sexpat tourists I hate so badly look at Thai women?

When I see that rare, attractive man here, it drives me crazy. What really drives me crazy is that I know they won't be around here for long. Only passing through. I am here and they will not be tomorrow. But I will be. I have one chance, or it will be gone.

Would I behave this way back in the States? Absolutely not.

I realize how lonely I get here in Thailand. And how sex is so uncomplicated here. Easy. I mean, seriously easy and not connected to love in anyway, just pure lust.

Oh, where are you from? Israel. Wanna go back to my bungalow and screw all night? Absolutely.

Okay, it didn't go quite like that, but then again, that's how easy it is.

Well, my options at this point are: Don't go to Patpong to meet Gaurang, return to my village, stare at the geckos on my ceiling for the next month and drink myself into a coma.

Or, I go out with Gaurang and have a good time. If we get along, and because he lives in Bangkok, I could possibly even date him like a normal young woman. I could come here to see him every few weeks, develop a relationship with him, he could come visit me in Sichon, or we could meet on Koh Samui, laugh and make plans together, work out issues together...wow...I would like that.

I run outside and buy another beer, then start to get ready. I can't wait to wear my new dress.

~~~

I jump in a *tuk tuk* which wildly speeds me through the purple haze of Bangkok traffic to Patpong. The throbbing music, neon signs, flashing lights and fried street food pull me in like a net. Careless indiscretion, spurred on by beer, propel me into the middle of it all. I pass the Pussy Lounge, the Kit Kat Saloon, and take a seat at the bar outside of King's Disco. I order a beer and wait for my tall, dark and dashing stranger.

A few bar girls come over and ask if I want a ladyboy for the evening. A few ladyboys come over and ask if I want a tomboy (a woman who dresses and acts like a man). A few tomboys come over and ask if I want a bar girl.

"No, I am waiting for my boyfriend," I answer to all.

To keep them at bay, I buy drinks for the bar girls so they will leave me alone.

He arrives right on time. Our eyes meet the moment he passes by the front of the open bar on the street.

"Susan! Good to see you!" he says, and walks quickly over to give me a big bear hug.

I am over being nervous thanks to the alcohol, and am delighted to see him also. All my doubts, hesitations and suspicions of this guy fall away, this lovely man.

"How long are you in town for?" he asks, and gives me a kiss on the cheek.

"Just tonight," I say, dreamily.

He smells of the right amount of Armani cologne. His polo and pants are pressed. His nails are buffed and manicured.

"I like your dress!" he says with a charming smile.

"Really? Thanks!"

"You look great, Susan. Do you want a beer?" he asks as he orders himself one and sits down next to me.

After a few, we run upstairs to the disco. It is too loud to talk, so we spend about three hours drinking, dancing and flirting.

About midnight, I am exhausted so tell him I want to go.

"Can I come home with you?" he asks, batting his thick black eyelashes and looks at me with those dreamy beyond black eyes.

I had made up my mind a long time ago

"I'd like that," I answer with no hesitation.

Back in my room at the Viengtai Hotel, we immediately start to kiss again. He then abruptly excuses himself and goes into the bathroom. I can hear him brushing his teeth with my tooth brush, flushing the toilet, then he comes out, naked.

In the light from the bathroom, I see it.

I see his wiener.

Christine is right. It looks like a dirty little elephant trunk. A teeny, weeny, dirty elephant trunk.

I sit on the edge of the bed, cross my legs, and say, "No. You are not touching me with that," and reach for a cigarette.

"Excuse me?" he says, standing right in front of me.

"I, that, uh," I stammer.

He takes the cigarette from my hand and grabs my wrist firmly. He doesn't appear offended, but obviously wants to make himself clear.

Still holding my wrist, he says softly, "Susan, I am Hindi, I am not circumcised."

"Oh," is all I can answer.

"Look, if you pull up the skin, there ya go."

He lets go of me, then pulls up the skin with two fingers revealing a regular wiener.

I just sit there. He's right. It does.

"We don't circumcise for religious reasons, but it also protects and keeps everything clean. It's like a wrapper."

He then pulls the foreskin back down and twists the end, as if indeed a wrapper. The tip looks like a wrapper of a Hershey kiss chocolate drop.

"Can I try?" I ask, hesitant but curious.

"Sure, of course."

With reluctant acquiescence, I reach out and pull the foreskin up, and then back down, and give the end skin a little twist.

"That's kinda cool, can I do it again?"

"Absolutely."

So I do.

"Can I one more time?"

"Yes."

"Again?"

"Again."

By this time, his dirty little elephant trunk has grown into a full sized tusk. He takes me into his arms and we spend the rest of the night doing just about everything that dirty little elephant trunk can do.

At noon the next day, after room service for breakfast and some new kama sutra positions, the Thai maid knocks on the door and tells us we have to leave, or pay for another night.

I have to catch the train home, so I pack and we leave together.

"Please call again, Susan, I want to see you again," he says into my ear while we are saying goodbye on the street corner.

"Sounds great because I'll be here next Friday too. I'll call you when I get in town." I answer.

"I would love that," he says, and looks at me with those dreamy beyond black eyes.

We kiss goodbye.

I jump on the bus to the train station as he hails a cab back to wherever he came from. I can still smell his cologne in my hair.

Chapter Twenty-seven

The next morning, my train arrives in Nakorn. I take a bus to my village of Sichon, and get off at the Jet Sipette.

The old man is dusting his table and Scabby is staring at the ground, entranced by a small rock.

"Susan. Scabby learned a new trick," the old man says.

"Good! Good! I want to see the new trick!" I answer, thrilled.

The old man walks over to Scabby and holds a shrimp flavored cracker above his nose.

"Scabby! *Wai! Wai!*" he says eagerly.

Scabby smells his paw.

"*Wai!*" the old man yells again.

Scabby smells his other paw.

"*Wai!*"

Slowly, almost bored, Scabby pushes himself up on his flabby butt. His two rear legs balance him perfectly at a ninety degree angle with his tail jutting out in back as a solid base. Then, he puts his front paws up in front of his nose, and drops back down.

"Scabby! You did it!" I scream. I want to pet him, but know that would freak him out. The old man gives him a cracker, then offers me one.

"Good boy, Scabby, who's a good boy!" I coo. The dog just gimps under the table and closes his eyes, exhausted. He's probably thinking that was way too much work for one measly cracker.

I start walking home, not stopping at the post office because it is closed. I eat a plate of shrimp fried rice in the village and end up taking a nap all afternoon.

~~~

I am back at my office in Nakorn the next day to check in with my coworkers. Nuang glides over in white high heels, a black skirt and a pink and red striped blouse.

"Eat *frang*, Susan," she instructs, dropping a bag of sliced, peeled guava on my desk with a bag of rock sugar to dip it in.

She then sits on the edge and says, "Why you go up to Bangkok? Your supervisor Kathy called here the next morning to say don't come."

"Uh, because I didn't find that out until I was already in Bangkok?" I answer.

"Well, she say you have to go again. This Friday. You go again this Friday."

"Yes, that is what she said. I go again Friday. Before I go again, this week I will teach English in Sichon, so probably won't be back here till next Monday," I answer.

"Okay, Susan, I tell Supervisor. Eat guava! Good luck!" she says with a big smile, and squeezes my arm.

I leave and spend the rest of the week at three different schools, teaching English, making peanut butter and singing Madonna songs.

~~~

The weekend finally arrives, so I return to Bangkok. I check into the Viengtai Hotel, and immediately call Gaurang. He says he will come by the hotel around six tonight. Hooray! I can hardly wait to see this gorgeous man again.

I take the bus to the Peace Corps office for my meeting with Kathy. She is here this time and all goes well.

I can tell she thinks I'm still nuts and is trying to handle me with care so I don't lose my mind again.

Explaining to her I don't really do many projects like most of the other PCVs who accomplish great and wondrous things in their provinces, I tell her I mostly teach English, pick up men and drink Mekong with transgendered prostitutes. (Okay, I don't say the last part, but she is more than satisfied with me going to schools and teaching English.)

She informs me that whenever she calls my Supervisor, he reports how much the Thais love me and how amusing I am to have around.

"He thinks you're nifty!" she says, excessively cheerful.

"I think he's nifty, too. But, I've been here for almost two years and still can't pronounce his name. I'm not even sure what it is."

"That's okay. Thai names can be difficult. He also tells me you are really good at eating spicy food and singing Madonna songs!" she gushes, pushing up her bifocals with an eager smile.

"Yes, ma'am," I answer sheepishly.

"Susan, that is the second goal of the Peace Corps! Helping promote a better understanding of Americans on the part of the peoples served!" she says, reciting word for word the second Peace Corps goal.

I can tell she thinks I am still absolutely nuts.

"His only concern is that you can't eat durian," she says. "Is that true, Susan? You can't eat durian?"

"No. Yes. I can't eat durian," I admit.

She taps her pencil on the paper.

"Have you tried, Susan? Have you tried to eat durian?"

"Yes. No. But I can't."

She looks down at her paper.

"But I can suck snails. Just not very good," I add.

She perks up.

"You suck snails? Susan! That is fantastic!"

"Yes, just not very good," I mumble, touching my lip.

"See, Susan? You are good at something!'

"Well, but not really," I answer.

"You just keep sucking those snails. And don't you worry, your Supervisor did say that the unfortunate fact you can't eat durian should not reflect negatively on your performance review," she says, and goes back to looking at her paper.

"Okay, I just try my best."

"You just try your best, and only do what you think you can handle! Every PCV is different!" she reassures me, obviously relieved the appointment is almost over.

She pushes up her bifocals, shuffles some more paper on her desk, then sits back in her chair.

On her encouraging note, I *wai*, grab my per diem money and go back to the Viengtai Hotel.

~~~

I begin to get ready for my second date with my tall, dark and dashing stranger. I shave my legs, wash my hair and even put on makeup for the big date.

Except by six p.m., he is not here.

Not by seven p.m. either.

I walk down to the corner and buy a bottle of Mekong. If he is going to stand me up, I might as well get drunk, I mutter.

There is finally a knock on my hotel room door at eight p.m.

I throw my Narnia book down and rush to the door.

"Gaurang?" I ask through the crack.

"Hi, sweetie, it's me. Sorry I am late," he says.

I swing open the door, so very happy to see him, I can hardly be upset anymore. God, he looks good in his tailored pants, white shirt and expensive shoes. Those beyond black dreamy eyes.

We embrace warmly, then he holds me at arms length and says, "Why are you wearing this dress?"

"What?"

"You wore this blue dress last week," he answers, dropping his hands from my waist.

"Uh, well, in my village down south, we don't have a Neiman Marcus," I answer, trying to make a joke. Besides, this dress cost me a fortune and can't afford another new one even if I wanted.

"Don't you have anything else to wear?" he answers curtly, walking into the room and pours himself a straight shot of my Mekong.

Okay, fine. He is late. He disses my dress. He doesn't get my sense of humor. He helps himself to my booze without asking.

In America, this would be four strikes. He should be out. However, I am so desperate and downright infatuated with his looks, I decide to count all four as only quarter strikes, so they equal just one.

Way to rationalize, genius.

He takes a seat on the bed, and I sit across from him in a wicker chair.

"So, how have you been? Gosh, I missed you!" I say, excitedly.

He downs his drink and puts the glass back on the table.

"Well, let's go. Come on," he answers.

"All right! Where are you taking me?" I ask, smiling.

"We are going to a new bar in Patpong," he answers, now fixing his hair in the mirror.

"Gaurang, I was hoping we could go out to eat somewhere nice, maybe one of the fancy hotels. The Sheraton? I heard they have steak and salad with blue cheese dressing. They always have great cabaret shows too. I have never been there and am dying to go," I say, still upbeat.

"I'm not hungry. Let's go to the bar, hurry up" he replies.

"Why don't we do something just you and I, go somewhere different? I don't really want to go to Patpong again. It's fun occasionally, but I was hoping we could do something else tonight."

"I want to go to Patpong," he says without looking at me.

"Gaurang, please. I was hoping, you know, I was thinking..."

Without a word, he grabs the hotel key that is laying on the table, shoves it in his pocket, and walks out the door.

What just happened here? I say out loud.

Maybe he just went outside to get some fresh air. Maybe he went outside for a smoke, or to buy me flowers, or make dinner reservations at the hotel reception desk just to surprise me.

He doesn't come back.

I sit in the chair in my blue dress until midnight.

I don't even want to drink.

I sit and wait.

He doesn't come back.

I wait an hour more.

He doesn't come back.

I finally take off my blue dress, crawl into bed and go to sleep.

~~~

I can't breathe.

What, oh, what?

What is going on?

It's a dream.

Suffocating.

Please God.

What is on me?

After a minute, I realize Gaurang is on top of me, naked.

I turn my head toward my pink, plastic alarm clock.

It's three a.m.

"Get off me I can't breathe what are you doing..." I gasp.

He starts to fumble around down there.

"You're heavy please get off me..." I say breathless.

"You didn't mind this last week," he says slowly and quietly.

"Please what are you talking about..."

"You like this," he whispers in my ear.

I realize he is not drunk. Not at all. I know he had a few, but he is not drunk by any means. I wish he was, so he would at least have an excuse, a reason, something other than what he is doing to me now.

"Stop. Please stop that, no, get off me, please..."

"You didn't complain last time."

"Because you weren't a mean fucking pig last time."

I immediately realize I shouldn't have said that because now he is even more aggressive.

I want to run out of the room screaming no! After calling him, asking him to meet me, and bumping and grinding on him all that night at the disco, then meeting him last week. I want to run and beg the hotel receptionist to please please please call Kathy. How did he get the key, Susan? What did you expect? What were you thinking? I can hardly move. No. Why is he doing this?

I can't move. He's got my arms in an awkward position with his strong forearm pushing my head to the side, painfully. His other hand is rude. It hurts. He's pulling my leg up, squeezing it behind my knee. I hate him. I don't know what to do. I go limp. There is nothing I can do. I just want to get this over with so he will get done, get off and pass out.

In a few hours, Bangkok will wake up. I will then sneak out and go to the bus station for the first morning bus down south because I don't want to wait for the next night train to Nakorn.

I close my eyes tight.

Chapter Twenty-eight

It takes me about eighteen hours to get back to Sichon by bus. I don't care, as long as I am heading south. Every minute is one more mile further away from him.

At midnight, I get off the bus at the Jet Sipette. It's closed down for the night. Scabby gimps around to the front of the shack, looks at me, looks at his butt, looks at me again, shakes his head, then goes back to his sleeping hole.

I inhale the fresh air. I can smell the ocean. My village.

It is good to be home.

The next morning, Sunday, I wake up scratching myself between the legs. Dang. I am itchy. I take a cold shower, but it still itches. Probably heat rash from the long, hot bus ride.

By Monday, I am on fire down there. Burning, I douse myself with cold water, itch, scratch, take another shower, powder myself, put on lotion, then another shower, more powder, take another shower. Nothing I do relieves the burn. I was planning on going to Nakorn to my office, but there is no way I can go out in public and work in this condition. I am hurting. It is painful.

I sit on the bed, pull my shorts down and take my hand mirror to look down there. Geez, not good. I have more than a rash. I must have an infection.

Holy Mary, mother of God, I don't want to think about it.

I take a deep breath.

Gaurang. If I could possibly hate his guts any more than I already do, I do. Times one hundred. Times one thousand. I know I got it from him, whatever it is.

I am such a slut. A whore. A whore slut. A slutty whore slut whore, I say out loud to myself.

As I start to cry, there is a knock on my door.

"Susan!"

It's Christine. I'm not in the mood for her or anybody right now, and only want to be left alone.

"Susan! You sexy girl! I know you in there!" she screams through the shutters.

I throw the hand mirror across the hut. It shatters into tiny, sharp pieces.

"Don't call me sexy!" I scream hysterically. "I hate sex! I hate it! I hate Thailand and all the sex in Thailand! I hate Hindi sex! I hate Kosher sex! I hate American sex! I hate it!"

I hate myself. I am so stupid, naive, careless. I just want to run home crying to my momma. I want to sit in her warm kitchen and eat her tator tot hotdish with canned green beans. I have never missed her so badly as I do right now. I want my mom.

Christine pushes open the shutters and stands quietly in the window.

"Susan?" she asks softly, eyebrows furrowed with concern. "What happened?"

"I'm a hypocrite!" I scream like a banshee.

"No, Susan, you are not fat," she says emphatically, but confused.

"What? What the hell are you talking about?"

"You not fat, no, you no hippo," she answers.

"What? What are you talking about, Christine?"

"You no hippo," she says again, calmly.

I take a breath, and then figure it out.

"Gawd no, Christine, not a big hippopotamus. A hypocrite! HYPO-CRITE!"

The tears begin to run down my face.

Christine steps through the window. I am sitting on my bed with my shorts down around my ankles, the sunlight reflecting off the broken mirror against the wall.

"Susan," she says again.

I pull up my shorts.

She sits next to me.

"You have problem down there?" she asks gently.

I take a deep breath and say, "I think so."

"Why you no use condom, stupid?"

"I do."

"All the time?"

I hesitate. I don't remember if Gaurang did. Of course that asshole didn't use one.

"Maybe in Bangkok I forgot," I answer.

"You must insist, Susan. Don't be dumb."

"I don't think we did."

"I told you, Susan, don't be silly, wrap that willy. Remember when I tell you that?"

"Yes. But, he was a little drunk," I answer, oddly making an excuse for him.

"No, no excuse. He drunk. You dumb," she says sharply.

"I know, I was dumb."

"Very dumb."

"Yes, very dumb," I agree.

"Very, very dumb."

"Christine, yes. I was very, very dumb."

She puts one arm firmly around me and holds my hand with her other hand.

"Susan, you know what STD stand for?" she asks, her almond eyes intense.

"Yes. I know."

She suddenly jumps up, faces me and screams, "It stands for SUSAN TOO DUMB!"

"Shut up!" I scream back.

"It stands for SUSAN TOO DRUNK!"

"Gawd! I get that!

"You get that?" she scolds.

"I get it! Okay? I get that! But it wasn't like that, Christine! I didn't want to!"

"You have sex with him before, why you no want to now?"

"I didn't want to, not this time," I say quietly.

"Why?"

I take a deep breath.

"He was mean," I answer.

"What you mean, mean?"

"I mean, mean."

"Mean?"

"Yes. Really mean."

"What kind of mean?"

"Awful mean."

"You mean, that kind of mean?" she asks, her concerned face dissolving into anger.

"Yes. That kind of mean. It was awful."

I then put my head in my hands, convulsing with tears, fear and anger.

She sits back down and puts her arm around me again.

"Susan. Eastern men think woman only two ways. Wifey woman and fucky woman. No in between," she says quietly.

This makes me cry harder.

I can feel her hand tightening around my shoulder.

She then asks in a low masculine voice, "What is his last name? What is hadji's last name?"

"You mean Gaurang's?"

"Yes, what is his last name?"

"Why?" I ask hesitantly.

She then says very softly, yet very distinctly, "Because me, Velveetah and Samantha are going to Patpong to cut off his willy and shove it up his ass hoe. I know Patpong. I know my sisters there. No one likes this."

I start smiling, almost laughing. Then start crying again.

Oh, Lord have mercy. No. No, no, no.

Hell hath no fury as a ladyboy scorned. No, I couldn't imagine unleashing a pack of them on my worst enemy, not even Gaurang. They have a deep sense of street justice.

Christine once told me that Samantha put out a lit cigarette in a man's cheek because he tried to short change her for a blow job. A bar girl in Hot Yai once called Velveetah a faggot, so Vel pulled out a fistful of the bar girl's hair, along with a piece of her scalp. I have seen Christine punch someone off his feet.

As much as I would love to see someone stomp on Gaurang with a sharp stiletto heel, I don't want to be responsible for him becoming maimed, permanently disfigured, and yes, possibly killed. No.

I bury my face in her shoulder, sobbing, and her long black hair covers my face. She is perfect, this transgendered friend of mine. Strong and protective, yet soft and understanding.

I did indeed know his last name. I had asked him, and he told me. It was confirmed later when I saw it on his ID as he pulled out his wallet to pay for drinks the second time I met him.

"What is his last name? We find him," she says decisively.

"Honestly, Christine, I don't know," I say.

"What is it?"

"No clue," I answer.

"What is it?"

"No idea. I just want to learn my lesson and move on."

"What is his last name?" she asks again.

"I was kinda drunk when he told me, uh, you know, I don't know."

"What is it?"

"I can't remember." I say.

"What is it?"

"I can barely pronounce it," I answer.

"What is it?"

"Something Kadashian. I seriously don't know."

Christine grips me tighter, then lets go.

"Okay, dummy, you will be okay," she finally says.

She then adds, "*Mai pen rai*, we go fix your itch now. We go take care of this itch now. We take care of other things later."

I finally exhale. Grateful, regretful, hopeful and full of shame.

She continues, "Come. Lets go to Nakorn, I know a doctor. He will check you out."

I just sit there, trying to catch my breathe.

"Come, now. We go and take care of this, dummy," she says, and pulls me off the bed, through the door and into the sunshine.

With that, I get on her motor scooter and we ride all the way to Nakorn as I sob quietly into her Love's Baby Soft scented hair.

Chapter Twenty-nine

I thought Christine would take me to some dark alley, coat hanger, illegitimate women's clinic. Instead, we pull up to a professional looking health office not far from the main street in Nakorn.

The lobby is clean and smells of bleach, and several female nurses in starched white uniforms are busy about. A sweet receptionist checks me in. The nurses all chat with Christine, friendly as they obviously know her. I don't know if that is good or bad.

Christine holds my hand as we wait. She speaks in rapid southern Thai dialect back and forth with the receptionist until I am called to see the doctor.

In the examination room, one of the nurses tells me to disrobe and put on a white gown, which I do. Patting the exam table, she tells me to lay down. She immediately puts a white sheet over my face and torso, so that I can't see.

I hear the door open and the doctor walk in.

In Thailand, it is not polite for a male doctor to see the face of a female patient while doing intimate exams. He does not talk. Only the nurses do, telling me its okay, this is what is happening, it will be over soon.

After a minute of gentle scraping and poking around down there, he is done. I hear him leave. After the door shuts, the nurses pull the sheet off my face.

"Susan. You are okay. You have to take antibiotics. Then it go away. No problem. You are lucky, you only have a yeast infection," she says with a smile, but did give my hand an extremely tight squeeze when she says the word, *problem.*

On my way out, Christine has already paid for the bottle of prescription antibiotics for me. She gives me two and a cup of water to wash them down.

"Take these. And stay away from that hadji in Bangkok," she says with a sneer.

"Yes," I mutter.

"Susan. Do you know Kenny Rogers?" she asks.

"Who?"

"Kenny Rogers, the gambler."

I rub my blood shot eyes and ask, "You mean the country singer?"

"Yes, Kenny Rogers the handsome man singer."

"Yeah, I know of him," I answer.

"He say you have to know when to walk, know when to run."

Exasperated, I ask, "What the hell does Kenny Rogers have to do with my itchy twat, Christine?"

"Your hadji boyfriend in Bangkok. You need to run from him. Don't take no apology from him. He not worth the gamble. He might look good, but he is bad."

I take another swallow of water.

She continues, "He dumb too, he should know better, too. He's dumb and bad."

"Yep," I say defeated.

I just want to go back to my hut, smoke cigarettes and stare at the geckos on my ceiling and forget all of this. I want to sit by Tangmo. I want to see Scabby. I want to yell at Bong. I want to argue with the Weasel at the post office, and things to be back to normal and boring. I am so very tired.

In silence, we get on her motor scooter and ride back to Sichon with my face in her Love's Baby Soft scented hair.

Christine drops me off at the Jet Sipette. She is in a hurry to catch a bus to Hot Yai for a few days work.

"Christine?" I say, before she leaves. "What about Mike?"

"What about him?"

"I don't know. None of this would have, oh, never mind. I don't know what I'm doing...I miss him."

She turns off her scooter and looks at me.

"Be careful with him, too. He might be married," she says.

The thought never crossed my mind.

"What?"

"Handsome Army boy like that, sexy, sexy, he probably has a wifey in America."

I catch my breath.

Scabby gimps over to the motor scooter and takes a piss on the back tire.

I never thought about it. I could handle him having a girl-friend back in the States, but not a wife. Heck, something would be wrong with him if he didn't have a girlfriend. And there is certainly nothing wrong with him.

"Ewe, no, Christine. I can't think about him being married," I say, cringing.

"He's not married. Not married," she says.

"What the hell, Christine? Then why did you tell me he was?"

I light a cigarette, now upset, as Scabby bumps his head against Christine's leg as he tries to flop down. She nudges him away.

"I never said he was," Christine answers, taking my cigarette and starts smoking it.

"You said he might be! Implying that he was!"

"I said might be. But, he's not. Not might be not. But not."

"What does that even mean, Christine?" I scoff.

"You're dumb and need to be careful. Be careful with men."

"What are you talking about?" I ask.

"You know what I'm talking about, dummy."

"Stop talking in circles!" I say louder.

"Stop listening in circles!"

"Fine!" I say, and grab my cigarette back.

We are yelling at each other at this point. Scabby grunts and puts his paws over his ears. The old man watches us, amused, and starts eating a bag of chips like he's munching popcorn at the matinee.

Christine snatches the cigarette back, takes a puff and blows the smoke in my face.

"Why don't you just ask him?" she says.

"I'll do that!"

"Do that, Susan. Just ask him," she says snidely.

"I might never see him again!"

"Then it doesn't matter, does it!" she screams back.

"I want one of these guys to matter!"

"They all matter, but it's different in Thailand!" she retorts.

I grab the cigarette back.

"Fine. Okay," I say in a softer tone of voice.

"Besides," Christine says, smiling and grabbing the cigarette again from me. "I looked in Mike's wallet. He's not married."

"Then why did you tell me he was?"

"I didn't, dummy!"

"When did you steal his wallet?"

"I didn't steal his wallet. I looked in it!"

"When did you not steal his wallet but look in it?"

"Doesn't matter when. No photos of children, no photos of wifey. No numbers or business cards from bar girls or Thai bars. Just your address."

"Really?" I ask, taking a deep breath.

"He did have a photo of a black dog, though," she says.

Mike had talked about his dog, a black lab named Ranger. I had teased him and asked why do all Army guys have a black lab named Ranger.

"Christine, I think I love Mike," I say as I exhale.

"No, you don't. You love idea of Mike. Handsome Army guy meets lonely Peace Corps volunteer in Thailand. They fuck on beach. How romantic. Maybe you should write a book about it, Susan. I can be in your book too. Nice story. But, you don't love him. If you did, you don't fuck Jewboys and Hadjis."

"Just shut up. Shut the hell up. I don't want to hear this."

"Fine. You hear it anyway. You want me to say it again?"

"Who are you to give dating advice, anyway?"

"I give very good dating advice, Susan. Here is my advice. Marry for money."

"Seriously? That's your advice?" I ask incredulously.

"Yes, dummy. It is. Now go be good," she says, starting her scooter.

I push Scabby out of her way.

"And don't be silly! Wrap that willy!" she yells over her shoulder and takes off down the road.

The old man stands up, and with a feather duster, slowly flicks it back and forth across his rows of goods as he stares at me. Although not understanding English, he understood the entire conversation.

I continue to stare down the road, trying to process what Christine has just said. After a few minutes, the old man says,

"Susan, come look."

He sits back down in his plastic chair.

He continues, "Scabby learn new trick today."

"No way, really? Let's see!" I say, very relieved that I can now focus on something else. I'm thankful to be back in Sichon. I want the monotony and safe, familiar routine of my own village.

Scabby straggles over and sits in front of the old man. The dog glances at me, as if to say, "Watch this, girlfriend."

The old man makes the universal sign of a gun with his hand.

"Bang! Bang!" he hollers.

Scabby looks at me, then back at the man, before collapsing to the dirt, panting.

He then pushes himself back up, and the old man gives him a cracker.

"You taught him how to play dead!" I say, laughing.

"Scabby not dead," the man answers defensively. "It's a trick."

"I know that, but the trick is to play dead," I explain.

The man smiles, and then pats Scabby gently on the head.

I buy a Bangkok Post, a bottle of Pepsi and walk to the post office.

~~~

I brace myself before going through the door. I am prepared to be pissed off, like I always am with the Weasel.

Sure enough.

The Weasel is standing at the counter, chomping away at something, and sorting letters. He looks up, sees me, and blows the biggest pink bubble I have ever seen. My God, he must have three pieces in his mouth.

I catch a whiff of the bubble gum when it explodes.

"Bubble Yum!" I scream at him. "That is Bubble Yum! I just know it! You have my Bubble Yum!"

He shakes his head and blows another bubble.

"No, it's mine," he says, and goes back to what he is doing.

"That is my Bubble Yum! Look!" I yell, pointing at the red and pink wrappers on the counter. I grab one and nearly stuff it up my nose, inhaling the wonderful, sweet scent.

"No, it's mine," he says, ignoring me.

"Someone sent me Bubble Yum and you stole it! Like you always steal my stuff!"

He blows another bubble.

"Do you want a piece?" he calmly says, and hands me the last piece in the package.

I snatch it from him and shove it in my mouth, chewing and chomping away my anger.

He then pushes a few letters toward me, all taped shut after being opened. I grab those also and storm out the door.

~~~

That evening, I sit on the beach with Tangmo and George Bush. I'm still itching myself like Scabby on a bad day but at least Tangmo doesn't notice.

Tango's mother walks down to our chairs and pulls another chair next to us. I cross my legs tightly, hoping I don't have to scratch any time soon.

"Tangmo leave tomorrow," her mother says quietly.

"What?" I ask, confused.

"She leave tomorrow. The government has a place for her. A school for her. She is going to school."

"Where?"

"Songkla. Not far, but not here. She won't be here."

I see her mother is starting to tear up, but with pensive, absolute joy on her face.

"She is going to school?" I ask again.

"Yes, tomorrow."

"That is good news! That is good luck! That is good for her!" I say and pop up out of my chair in excitement.

"I will not love it. I miss her already," her mother says. "But, this is a small boarding school for children like her. We visit there last weekend, and it is very helpful for her. They have special teachers for her. Tangmo smart, she needs to learn how to be smart at school, too."

Tangmo jerks her head toward us, and slowly raises both hands. She then collides them together in a kind of clap.

George Bush, who is hanging around her neck, grabs one of her fingers and starts to nibble on it.

"She is a good girl, smart," her mother says, putting a hand on the child's knee.

Her mother then gets up and leaves because I don't think she wants to cry in front of me.

Tangmo, George Bush and I sit on the beach one last evening. For the next few hours, I scratch myself and stare at the ocean. Tangmo gurgles a bit and stares at the ocean, too. George Bush plays with her hair, twirling pieces in his little hands. Then, about seven p.m., Tangmo's brother comes down to carry her back home and I go home also.

Chapter Thirty

As I walk back to my hut, I see a glorious yellow envelope taped to my door. It's a telegram. Bounding up the steps, I grab it and read. It's from Jose, telling me to come to his house in Satun province this weekend. It is another *tio*, with four other volunteers from the South also invited.

The plan is to go to Namtok Wang Sai Thong, a beautiful waterfall with limestone tiers shaped in a multilayered lotus flowers, and drink ourselves silly. I can't wait to forget about Gaurang.

So I do. I arrive to Satun late Saturday afternoon, undoubtedly the right place but at the wrong time. The gang has already left without me, thinking I am unable to make it. What they did leave is a note on the door with the directions to the waterfall party just in case.

Jose lives in a closely packed community, several tight blocks of row houses. All the neighbors emerge to stand around and watch the sweaty *farang*, me, pound on the door, snatch the note, curse and sweat some more. I turn around and start to walk back down the road to see if I can't find some way to get to the waterfall on my own.

Before I turn the corner, I'm accosted by three bouncing teenaged girls. One grabs my backpack, the others each claim an arm and lead me to a nearby house. They know my name and what province I'm from, apparently forewarned by Jose that I might come straggling through.

"*Tio!*" they say excitedly.

"You are beautiful!" they tell me.

"Where are we going?" I ask.

They don't tell me.

The only reply I receive is another ringing chorus of "*Tio!*"

I feel captured by the friendly natives and now at their mercy. They won't take their happy hands off me. When we reach their house, they throw my bag inside as the mother rushes out.

"Sawatdee ca, Susan!" she gushes, "*Tio!*"

The next thing I know, the girls and I are in the back of a pickup truck filled with wicker baskets of limes. Mom speeds off down the road with the girls holding my hands and begging me to sing Madonna songs.

Every PCV has their own collection of '*Tio* from Hell' stories...made to go somewhere by a well meaning Thai, whether it be a close friend or friendly stranger, and whisked away to destinations uncertain. Sometimes promised to be back by five p.m., I am, but two days later. Sometimes ending up at a wedding or a funeral, and the only way back is by a drunk with an empty bottle of Mekong in his lap.

It's the Thai's warmhearted, welcoming nature that prompts them to take me places and show me things. It's best just to let go and let Thailand happen, rather than try to control it. That can't be done, anyway.

On this *tio*, we arrive at a shanty neighborhood along the coast of the Andaman Sea. The reek of fish is dense and the poverty even more thick. I'm given a basket of limes and each of the girls and mom grab one also.

We then walk from one wobbly hut to the next, selling them to the villagers. It feels odd selling limes to people as poor as this, but they pull out their one baht coins and are happy to pay for them. Limes must be hard to find in this area of Thailand.

The kids along the dock are clad in dirty shorts or in soiled tee shirts. Never both, though, obvious too poor to have both a shirt and shorts. Shoes are nonexistent, so are most of their toenails, eaten away long ago by fungus.

The fishermen are baked nearly black with heavily creviced faces. The women eye me in disbelief. Some smile, some feel my arms, all stare. What is a *farang* doing in their village selling limes, they must be thinking. Hell if I know either.

After a few hours, we return to the family's home. They insist I eat supper with them and spend the night.

Knowing I can't catch a bus so late back to my province, and Jose and the rest of my buddies won't be back for another day, I appreciate the invitation.

Soon, the cooking area comes alive with mother and daughters busily slicing, stirring, boiling, and frying.

Thai food historically traces its roots back to China and India. Long ago, the Silk Route was a set of well traveled roads that brought merchants, traders, monks, soldiers and nomads to and throughout Thailand. They brought their spices and cooking styles with them. Then, each region in Thailand added whatever local ingredients they had on hand.

This mix of foreign and local influences ends up creating deliciously distinctive dishes.

Issan, the extremely dry area that includes the landlocked provinces of the Northeast, are the poorest in Thailand. The people of *Issan* have learned to eat just about anything, and do. Bugs, lizards, snakes, chicken beaks, nothing is wasted. Any plant that grows, they will sizzle it up in a wok, throw in some hot peppers and call it dinner.

The provinces of northern Thailand, which borders Burma and Laos, is known for *lanna* food, influenced by their northern neighbors. There is, of course, no seafood but much pork (which is

almost non existent in the Muslim south). They also don't use coconut milk as in the South, simply because there are no coconut
trees in the mountains.

Pak Dai, the southern peninsula where I live, has abundant
seafood and tropical fruit. The influence of the Silk Road is here
too, with the use of cardamon, cinnamon, turmeric and other
spices from the Middle East. Street vendors also sell roties, which
is Muslim flat bread fired on a griddle and filled with spicy beef or
sweetened condensed milk.

The food from the central provinces is referred to as *Royal
Cuisine* because it's from the area of both the former Thai capital,
Ayutthaya and the current capital, Bangkok.

True Royal Cuisine is lauded as meals fit for a king. There are
no pits, peels, seeds or bones in the dishes. Nothing is too spicy or
too salty. White breast meat chicken is used, not the hearts, feet or
heads. However, many restaurants advertising Royal Cuisine just
charge more and serve the same thing the street vendors do, just
in a fancier place.

Thais use all five tastes in one dish: savory, salty, sour, spicy,
and sweet. This agrees with the Buddhist philosophical thought
that each taste sensation relates to each of the five elements: metal,
water, wood, fire and earth.

Savory is also referred to as umami, the Japanese word for
delicious. This is why monosodium glutamate (MSG) is added to
so much food. It simply brings out the rich, hearty, savory flavor.
Thais use MSG by the bucketful. Some PCVs ask for their food
prepared without MSG, but the cook usually dumps some in
anyway.

~~~

After cooking and eating for nearly two hours, the mother rolls
out a woven bamboo sleeping mat in the front living area for me
and the three girls to share. I sleep well, tired and full from their
hospitality.

In the morning, the mother again is cooking for me. Four fried eggs on top of a giant plate of rice smothered in fish sauce, and plates of papaya, mangos and jackfruit. They beg me to stay another day but this *tio* is over for me. Not having a lot to begin with, I don't want them to cook and feed me all of their food.

After using three different excuses, they accept the fourth as good enough and I can leave with no hurt feelings. There's one condition they make. I have to come back and take them all to America with me. I wish I could

"Okay, no problem. We can sell limes in America," I assure them. They make me promise, so I do. We exchange addresses and I give the girls each a pack of Big Red gum. I wish I had more to leave with them.

The mother drops me off at the bus station in town, just in time for me to grab one back to Sichon.

My *tio* to Satun turned out to be amazingly fun, despite nothing going as planned. This happens a lot in Thailand. Sometimes things turn out for the better. Sometimes for the worse. Sometimes they just turn out...Thailand style.

Chapter Thirty-one

The next day is August 3, 1990. At the Jet Sipette, the old man is reading a newspaper. There are three other men standing around reading newspapers too. Scabby is licking his butt.

The old man sees me, stands up, and hands to me the latest Bangkok Post.

In about a 200 point sized headline, across almost the entire top of the page, reads, "IRAQ INVADES KUWAIT."

I wasn't fully aware of the monstrosity of this event, but knew the U.S. would get involved, like we always do. Right or wrong, America will be front and center.

I realize I have no idea what is going on in the outside world. The only news I have is this thin English language newspaper once every few days.

I jump on the bus and go to my office in Nakorn.

Nuang comes over and sits on the corner of my desk, dropping a bag of dried red berries in front of me.

"Eat, Susan, eat. Goji berries," she orders.

"Nuang, do you know anyone with a satellite TV? I want to watch CNN today," I ask, sucking on a sour leathery berry.

"Susan, you should watch the news," she says, concerned.

"Yes, I know, I should. I want to. Do you know where I can watch English news? I want to see some news from America about what is happening."

"Come," she says and pulls me by the hand.

We walk down to the main floor to a closed door. She pulls out a set of keys and unlocks it. It must be some sort of conference room. She flips on the big boxy TV, adjusts some antennas, wiggles a few cords and eventually finds CNN Headline News for me. Wolf Blitzer comes into focus.

"Shhh," she whispers. "You keep volume low. You watch this news. This is not good news."

I sit in the conference for most of the morning, in shock and worried sick. Around lunch time, Nuang opens the door and hands me a telegram.

Oh no. It's from Elad. Although it originated in Bangkok, he writes that he is returning to Israel early, that there is 'trouble at home.' I take that to mean he is expecting to be called up for Army Reserve duty. He tells me he had a great time with me, gives me his home return address on the telegram, then the words, 'bye-bye, Dear.'

Then I think about Mike. I bet he's on his way to Iraq.

I pray. There is absolutely nothing I can do except pray.

~~~

A few days later, I am sitting on the beach by myself, staring at the ocean with no Tangmo. George Bush runs over to Tangmo's chair, crawls on, bares his teeth at me, then scurries off. Ever since she left for school, the monkey acts like he hates me.

I am reading my mail that I had picked up earlier, and open a letter from Beth. She writes four pages, front and back.

Beth will be the first PCV from my group to return to the States. Our time here is nearing an end. She is leaving in two weeks, and I'll probably leave in four. Clare, Allison, Nori, Jose,

Mick, Mark and everyone will eventually trickle out of here back home within the next few months. Back to Reality.

Peace Corps volunteers arrive in groups of about fifty, every six months. When the new group arrives, the old timers that have been here two years rotate back to the U.S.

When I first arrived to Nakorn Sri Thammarat, a PCV named Jim was leaving soon after completing his two years of service.

Jim lived near my office, so before he left, for about a month I would stop by and say 'hi' on my way in or way out of town.

He was in a program called Filariasis & Malaria control. Part of his job entailed sitting in swamps all night and catching mosquitos. Then, the next day he and his Thai coworkers analyzed and dissected them, checking to see which ones carried malaria.

He also had tales to tell of villagers with lymphatic elephantiasis, penises swollen to watermelon size, breasts infected and so engorged that they hung down to the woman's hip bones, and necks that looked like there was softball lodged in the throat.

Jim was incredibly intelligent, but did have an edge to him. He was usually an easy going fellow, but sometimes would snap and swear fluently in perfect southern Thai to anyone who happened to make him mad.

He was my hero. I wanted to be as fluent as him, and be able to swear in Thai too. He taught me some dirty words to say.

One time I stopped by and he was in one of his broken moods. His body was bristled, and his face pulled in a clench. He must have had a bad day in Thailand, which was understandable.

He was squatting outside his house next to his motorcycle, tinkering around, trying to fix it.

I was about to leave because I could tell he didn't want company. A fourteen or fifteen year old boy walked by, and squatted near him, and started watching Jim fix his bike. Jim asked him to hand him a tool, so he did, and they started talking. And talked and talked. I walked over, sat against the house and listened to them.

They talked about the planets. They talked about the prices of chicken in New York City. They talked about the school system in the States. I couldn't wait to be as cool as Jim and be able to speak the language and communicate to Thais like he did that day.

Now, I was the old timer leaving.

I start to think too much.

If someone were to ask me, which they undoubtedly will when I return, 'What did you do in the Peace Corps?' I would look at them like a deer in the headlights, and say, well, I did grow my hair long and all one length. I read the Narnia series five times. And I learned how to make a mean coffeelua.

Oh, and always insist on condoms. I learned that too.

Great.

I'm such a loser, I whisper, and light a cigarette.

A few fishing boats bob on the horizon. The neighbor kids run by, wave, and keep going.

How could Beth leave? How could I leave? How could Clare leave? I shake my head and think about a time a year ago we were all at the Viengtai hotel together.

The conversation veered towards men, like it always did. Lack of, the wrong kind, the indifferent ones, the smothering.

Clare said she was once married, but claims she was an unhappy wife, and eventually divorced.

"Why were you unhappy?" Beth asked.

"Well," she said, with a slight smile, "did I tell you about the time I painted all the furniture in the house black?"

"What do you mean you painted all the furniture black?" I asked, and leaned back on the bed, preparing for another Clare story.

"That's what I did. Ya know how when you first get married, all these older relatives or whoever want to give you furniture? Next time, just say no. Say no, no, no."

"Okay," Beth said, waiting for the rest, trying to make a connection.

Clare continued.

"I woke up one day, shook my head at everything, frowned at my life so went to the store and bought a couple cans of black spray paint. I had decided to paint the living room coffee table. So, I am out on the side of the lawn painting away, wander back into the house, and drag out the end table. I start painting that also. Then I run out of paint, so drive back to the hardware store again and buy about eight more cans. I drive home, and finish the table. Then, I'm thinking, why not just do a few more pieces?"

She then says, "The nosy neighbor woman of mine, snoopy, always nosin' around, came over to see what I was doing. She was asking too many questions, so I go inside and continue there. I spread newspaper on the floor, and start to paint the kitchen table. Plus all the chairs."

"My husband is busy watching the games, baseball or some game on TV downstairs, and eventually appears in the doorway with a concerned expression on his face. He asked me what I was doing. I said, "A little redecorating." He just looked at me for a second and returned to the sports show. He couldn't care less."

She continued, "A bit later I'm scanning obsessively. I had painted the book shelf, the side tables, and drove back to the hardware store for more paint. I wanted to start painting the kitchen cupboards black."

Beth and I sat for a moment digesting this.

"Highly symbolic, Clare. An unhappy wife in an unhappy home," Beth answered.

Clare nodded.

"Yep. When you start painting everything black, it's time to move on," she answered.

Clare and her husband divorced a short time later, and she joined the Peace Corps.

I look down at my lap again. I don't know why I thought about Clare's story. Then I knew. I am still holding an unopened letter. It's from Gaurang.

Chapter Thirty-two

Mike is comfortable blue heaven. Elad is exotic purple. Gaurang is painted black.

I hold up his letter so I can see it better through the sun. His beautiful, elaborate hand writing on the envelope. It's thick, maybe three or four pages.

What do you want, I mutter. What could you have to say to me? How is it possible that you even have the nerve to write to me? How *dare* you write to me?

Then I look closer at the return address. The address is Room 401, Samitivej Sukhumvit Hospital, Bangkok.

Oh no, they didn't. But, they did. I should've known. I'm positive the ladyboys kicked the shit out of Gaurang and put him in intensive care.

"Susan!" someone yells, nearly knocking me out of my chair with a slap on back.

Speak of the devil in the blue dress, it's Christine.

"Hi yah, Susan!"

"Sawatdee ca!" I jump up, wanting to hug her, but instead sort of hop around in the sand a bit, so very happy to see her. I'm relieved she made it back from Phuket and away from the German burrito man.

She is wearing a nautical inspired blue and white stripped mini dress with red wedge-heeled espadrilles. She has a white scarf around her head, knotted on the top, old Hollywood style.

"Hello! Hello!" she says, and sits in Tangmo's chair.

George Bush runs over, jumps in her lap, and starts to play with her gold hoop earrings.

"God, it is good to see you," I say, and sit back down.

Tangmo's brother brings out two beers for us, and Christine orders chicken satay with spicy peanut sauce and a plate of fruit.

I throw Gaurang's letter in her lap, forgetting she can't read English.

"Who's this from?" she asks, picking it up.

"Gaurang," I answer.

"Ewe! Get it off me!" she screams, throwing it back on my lap with a vengeance.

"I haven't opened it."

"Good! He ass hoe, Susan, he ASS HOE!" she screams again, grabbing the letter back, enraged.

"He is in the hospital," I say, shaking my head.

"Really? In hospital? He sick?" she asks, a little too innocently.

I knew it. I just knew it. I should have never told her his last name. Then again, she probably would have found him easily in Patpong anyway.

Still angry, she continues, "You know what I do with this ASS HOE letter? I wipe my ass with this ASS HOE letter!"

"I think you wiped your ass with *him*, that is why he is in the hospital," I say.

"I no speak Engwhish, wha?" she says with a smirk.

"Shut up, Christine. Stop talking in circles. I just want to know, when did you guys go to Bangkok?"

"Who go to Bangkok?"

"You, Velveetah and Samantha."

"Why you think we go to Bangkok?" she asks, feigning confusion.

"Because that new dress you are wearing is a United Colors of Benetton dress from Bangkok. Which is lovely on you, by the way."

"Really?" she gushes, stands up, twirls around, then plops back in her chair.

"I wanted to buy that one but they didn't have my size."

"Next time you ask! They have big ladyboy sizes in the back room. We like to use different dressing rooms than you girls. No offense, Susan," she says, patting my knee.

"Did you or did you not go to Bangkok?" I ask, trying to stay on subject.

"My boyfriend bought me this dress."

"I have no doubt about that, Christine. What happened in Bangkok?"

"When?"

She grabs my pack of cigarettes and lights one.

"What happened?" I ask louder.

"Samantha had a job interview with Thai Airways. Did I tell you about that?"

"No, you didn't."

"She had interview to be a stewardess. We went to Bangkok with her for the interview," she explains.

"Really? How did the interview go?"

She shakes her heard and says, "No. Sam didn't get the job. They don't like ladyboys on their airplanes."

"She would be a very good stewardess," I say.

"Vel and I told her not to wear the see-through halter top and denim mini skirt to the interview, but, she didn't listen."

"Yeah. You have to dress proper for those," I agree.

"Maybe next time. She has another interview with Samui Shuttle next month."

"So, that is all you did in Bangkok? Just go with her to the interview?"

Christine hesitates, takes a puff from the cigarette and starts to pet George Bush.

She can't look me in the eyes.

"You know, Susan, you're dumb sometimes, but he's big ass hoe," she says slowly in a low voice.

"I know that, you don't have to remind me," I answer.

"He won't be doing mean things to women anytime soon, I know that much."

"You three beat him up, didn't you. That's why he is in hospital," I say, squinting at the ocean's horizon.

She doesn't answer.

I take a long drink of beer and shake my head. I knew it.

Christine then picks up my lighter and sets the unopened letter on fire. We watch it burn on the beach in front of us. I kick some sand on the ashes, ending a very dark ordeal.

I then tell Christine that Elad went back to Israel early because of the impending war.

"What about Mike?" she asks.

"I have been writing to him but haven't heard anything back. He's probably in the Gulf, too."

"You write again."

"Has Velveetah heard from the Captain?" I ask.

Christine shakes her head no.

"You write to Mike again," she repeats.

"I write to him everyday," I admit.

"Everyday?"

"Yep."

"Susan, you are being a stalker now," she says, and smacks me in the arm.

"I'm not a stalker! I'm just concerned!"

"Write once a week is concerned. Write everyday is stalker!"

She takes another sip of beer and then says, "Let me know when he writes back."

George Bush starts licking her beer bottle.

I take a deep breath and change the subject.

"How did it go in Phuket?"

"My boyfriend went back to Holland," she says.

"Not your boyfriend, the German tourist."

"Where?"

"In Phuket! The German tourist! Fat burrito man with the briefcase! Did you see him there, or around anywhere?"

Christine smiles and says, "I think he gave up."

"Be careful, I'm sure he'll return. Sexpats always return to Thailand. Especially this guy."

"I know," she says leaning back in her chair and looks at the ocean as a content smile crosses her face.

"So?" I ask.

"So what," she answers.

"What are you going to do with it?"

"Do with what?"

"You know," I reply.

"Know what?"

"Stop talking in circles! The money! What the heck are you going to do with all that money?"

"What money?"

"Christine! Stop it! The money from the briefcase!"

"None of your business," she says sweetly.

"Christine! You can tell me! Tell me!" I say excitedly.

She starts to eat and tells me to eat something also. Fine. She doesn't want to talk about it anymore.

Until she does.

"You know what I want to do, Susan?" she says, feeding George Bush a tiny piece of chicken.

"I wish you would retire from your job," I say.

"I am."

"With the money?"

"What money?" she asks.

Argh, she is doing it again, talking in circles. I don't say anything this time. I'm not going to get sucked in again. I grab a stick of chicken and dip it into the spicy peanut sauce.

"I am going to open my own clothing store," she says.

"That's good news, you really should," I answer, smiling.

"I know I really should."

"What would you call it?" I ask.

"Christine's Hot Sex Love Clothing Store."

"You can't call it that," I say.

"Why not?"

"Just don't."

"What should I call it?" she asks.

"Something chic, simple, like Chrissy's."

"Chrissy's?"

"Yeah, just Chrissy's."

She likes that idea.

We then eat and drink a few hours more before she leaves to go visit her mother.

Chapter Thirty-three

I buckle down this final month as I need to wrap up everything at work.

Like the military, joining the Peace Corps involves a lot more than just walking down to the Peace Corps recruitment office and signing up. On average, it takes about a year for the whole application process to go through and being offered placement.

I filled out the initial application, passed a medical exam and background check, and had an interview with the campus recruiter. At the time, four year college degrees were required. If not, a professional trade such as HVAC, plumbing or electrical licenses are valued also. An applicant needed some sort of skill that could be passed on to the people in the host country.

My grades were low average, but my six years in the Army Reserve was considered a great asset. It proved to the Peace Corps I had a desire to serve and the ability to see through the whole commitment, through thick and thin.

When my group of volunteers arrived, we were eager, excited and mostly recent college grads. At least from what I am aware of, no one turned to the opium that comes from the Golden Triangle out of Northern Thailand, Burma and Vietnam. I don't smoke pot, or the infamous Thai stick, but it is available.

However, many, myself included, did increase our alcohol consumption. For the men here, anyway, drinking is part of socializing with other Thai men. For women, some of us drank more because of the stress and lonliness. Many volunteers started smoking cigarettes, almost as a boredom reliever. I started too. There is always gossip that some PC men visit prostitutes, but that is none of my business.

We all became close friends during our initial in-country training. Training to become an effective Peace Corps volunteer before being sent to our sites lasted three arduous months and was the worst part of my service. I hated it. Privacy during training was minimal to none. For weeks at a time the only privacy we had was confined to the gray matter inside our heads.

The majority was language training. The Asian-type juxtaposition of consonants and vowels were strange to my American ears. I still find it amazing that a voice box is capable of making such sounds. I still can't pronounce some words correctly.

The Thai language is tonal, meaning one word, by the five different ways the tones swerve, make it five different words. There are low, mid, high, falling and rising tones.

A misused difference in tone can lead to not understanding at all, or worse, misunderstanding.

For example, Americans often ask a question by making a statement, and raise the tone of the last word to inflect a question.

"You did that." (a straight tone)

"You did that?" (a raising tone)

A popular tongue twister in Thai illustrates the beauty of the tones: "New silk doesn't burn, does it?" In Thai, each word using the five tones, it is "Mai mai mai mai chai mai."

There were several weeks during training when we split up and each moved in with a typical rural Thai families to get a taste of the real life. This was the home-stay portion. We lived with the families at night and during the day had our Thai lessons together.

During training, Henry, the volunteer from Seattle, always asked off topic questions. One time we broke up into small groups to play some Thai language game with our Thai tutor.

"How do you say *poop* in Thai?" Henry asked.

We all giggled like second graders as our Thai tutor taught us how to say it, along with urine, sex and vomit. However, knowing these words turned out to be very valuable.

The volunteer next to me nudged me. Her name was Sandy, and although we didn't know each other in my hometown of Minneapolis, she is from the next suburb over. We often sat in training and whispered about the Vikings, North Stars or Twins. She had a bag made here that reads in Thai, 'Yes, I can eat sticky rice,' which is a question *farangs* are often asked. I thought of getting one that reads, 'No, I can't sing Madonna songs.'

On the other side of me was Jonesy. Whatever crap we sat through, walked through and learned through in PC training, she wore a string of pearls. She's Irish-American, laughs too loud and has big beautiful teeth. JFK-sized big teeth. East coast Ivy League old money big teeth. I absolutely love her because even through the heat, mud and bugs, she wore her pearls with dignity.

"Maybe Henry will ask about squat toilets next," Jonesy whispered, and Sandy and I snickered.

Sure enough, Henry raised his hand.

"How do you use squat toilets?" he asked, even though we had all pretty much figured it out a long time ago by necessity.

The Thai teacher pulled out a thin plastic mat, with the outline of a squat toilet. It was a U.S. Government issued training tool, provided to PCVs in countries where squat toilets are used.

"We are being toilet trained," Sandy said under her breath.

The teacher rolled the mat on the floor.

It's was about three feet by three feet, with a squat toilet in thick, black outline. There were directions on the side of the outline, in equally big lettering.

PLACE FEET HERE
DEPOSIT FECES HERE
USE WATER TO SPLASH AND WIPE

The teacher then stood on the mat and squatted down, as if to demonstrate.

I remember I thunked my head down on my desk and Jonesy and Sandy tried not to laugh. Henry just smiled.

After language training, we split into groups for our technical training phase. I had been assigned to Community Development. So, my group of a weary dozen PCVs headed south to Surat Thani province.

Half of the women slept at a temple and the other half inside a one room shack adjoining a flooded out zoo. The only male in our group stayed with our Thai tutors in a hotel.

I made my nest in the shack by the zoo, along with Beth, who became my best friend, Clare, who quit her job as a New York City prosecutor to join the Peace Corps, Lou Ann, a stubborn older southern woman with a golden heart, and Laura, a hyperactive girl from Maine.

Laura exercised whenever she had one spare minute and could hardly sit still. I don't know if it was nerves or what. When I tried to talk to her, she would squint her eyes and smile, but nothing seemed to register. Perhaps she was too busy calculating calories. Or, maybe she just didn't like me. Probably both.

With no electricity, we all slept under mosquito nets. We bitched and complained to each other and about each other, often all talking at once:

Y'all know there's a bat in here?
It sounds more like a bear eating my sugar crackers.
Where y'all sugar crackers at?
I hung the package outside on a string so the ants don't get it.
I'd rather have ants eat those sugar crackers than a bear.
You guys, there are no bears in Thailand, go to sleep.

Shoot, might not be bears, but there be bats.

And snakes.

Will everyone just shut up?

I'll shut up when that bat gets out of here.

That ain't a bat.

Well, it ain't the bluebird of happiness.

Shut up and go to sleep.

All the men are losing weight here, it's not fair.

Women do something different with rice than men do.

What the heck does that mean?

We metabolize our carbs slower.

I wanna lose twenty-five pounds while I'm here.

I wanna quit smoking.

Let me have some of those sugar crackers.

Does anyone have an extra cigarette?

Thai women eat rice and they aren't fat.

They also don't eat a pack of sugar crackers before bed.

Why don't you share?

You had every opportunity to buy your own.

We finish at five o'clock tomorrow.

I want some cheese.

I want some pizza

I hate learning Thai.

At least Spanish uses the same kinds of letters we do.

Why does Thailand have to use their own set of letters?

It's cool looking though.

It would be cooler if I could read it.

And 'round and 'round it went. Always wondering what the next day had in store. Always trying to figure out Thailand.

Now that we had been in country more than two years, we all could look back at training and laugh. And cringe. We are old timers and gave up trying to figure out Thailand a long time ago.

~~~

On Monday, I walk into my Supervisor's office, take a seat in front of his desk, and tell him that my duck egg project in Ban Tha Kwai failed. I had been reluctant to tell him about this at all. I should have told him a long time ago, he probably could have helped me, but I didn't. I wanted him to think Americans always have things under control.

I tell my Supervisor that the villagers were supposed to raise the ducks for eggs, and sell the eggs for profit.

He sits back and folds his hands across his basketball belly, then asks me, "Why don't they raise the ducks for ducks? Raise ducks and sell the ducks? Not eggs. Duck eggs not that good here, but duck meat good."

"That would be fine too. At this point I don't care, but the problem is, they ate the ducks," I explain.

He sits for a moment, then flicks his head toward the door. That is a sign that he wants me to go. I get up to leave as he grabs his phone and starts dialing.

Within the hour, we are in the back of Boonchu's baby blue truck. My Supervisor is smoking and eating durian in the front cab. Pee Poo, Pee Uaan and I are hanging on for dear life in back.

I realize this is not my duck project, but ours. His. My coworkers. Thailand's. The Peace Corps. Ever lovin' America's. If this duck farm fails, my Supervisor would *lose face* in front of all this. By God or by Buddha, he wasn't going to let that happen.

When we arrive at the village, Pee Poo, Pee Uaan and I are welcomed by the women and led to the open patio in the shade. I see the empty duck pens back in the trees but pretend not to notice. We sit on woven mats, drink hot tea and eat deep fried mung bean cakes and mangosteens together.

Boonchu stays in the truck, drinking Sang Som rum and looking in the rear view mirror at his hair.

My Supervisor is met by the village leader, Pee Nut and the rest of the elders, and disappears into the biggest house.

About two hours later, we all get back in the truck and return to Nakorn. Not much is said, except my Supervisor tells me this, "Susan. Tomorrow go back to the village."

The next day, I don't bother going to Nakorn, but go straight to Ban Tha Kwai.

I walk through the trees and back toward the duck pens. I then about cry in disbelief.

There in the duck pens are not just eighteen ducks like I'd originally given to them, there are at least forty ducks. Thirty ducks and ten drakes. All of them fat, happy ducks!

I am not sure what was said, or how it happened, or who paid who, or who threatened who, or how they got the fucking ducks, but they got them. One duck has already laid an egg that a village woman proudly points out to me.

"Baby ducks! We will sell ducks!" she says with a smile. "We will sell at the market!"

I shake my head. This how it sometimes works in Thailand. Wonderfully.

~~~

On my way back to Sichon, the corroded, orange bus screeches to a halt. A dirt devil whirls inside, powdering the passengers with another layer of red dust. People crawl on, push to get out, dragging cardboard boxes, plastic baskets, durian, chickens, and scrawny kids as they go.

Several lanky boys dangle out the door of the already accelerating bus by fingers and toes. Off we zoom to the next lurching stop.

At the next stop, an ancient, woman with a creased face and baggy body wrapped in a shredded sarong climbs aboard. She squeezes her withered carcass next to me and my big American bones. I'm already sharing a seat with a teenaged school girl, a chicken and three pineapples, but in Thailand, there's always room for one more.

Scratching her weedy hair, she holds her plastic shopping basket defensively on her lap. It's packed with the standard assortment of old Thai women essentials; betel nuts, a betel nut peeler, chewing leaves and a cheap tube of addicting nose inhalant. Some women on the bus don't even bother removing their tubes from their noses, keeping it stuffed in their nostrils for the entire ride.

The sun baked woman pets my hand. From what I understand of her rapid southern dialect, she is telling me I am furry and beautiful. Amazed at the blonde hairs on my forearm, she tries to pull a few out. I stroke her leathery tough skin and reassure her that her arm is beautiful as well.

The old woman silently chuckles through missing teeth and a stream of glinting red betel juice escapes from her stained, crimson lips.

The bus roars under gawky coconut trees and alongside bountiful shrubs loaded with banana bunches. Orderly rows of rubber trees, delicate and pencil sketched, are disturbed by the slightest breeze and shirk at our racket. I stare out the window at the water buffalo in the patchwork of rice paddies, but the old woman's basket recalls my interest.

I realize that there is something stirring underneath the colorful, covered bundle. It's a feebly sort of movement, but definitely an attempt. The woman pats the bag down softly and nods to no one in particular. I return to gazing at the whizzing scenery.

The basket moves again.

This time it's a light pat and several light scratches. The woman puts both hands on top of the basket and slowly crushes down. In return, a muffled pfffft. She looks at me with a slick grin, obviously knowing she has something in the basket that would prefer to be out.

Three deliberate jabs rough up the bag, so the woman bats it down with more force. She then rests her elbow on the irritated lump and it stops moving.

"What is it?" I ask.

The old woman just smiles.

"A lizard?"

She smiles.

"A cat?"

She continues to smile.

"Chicken?"

She shakes her head.

"What is it?"

She wouldn't tell me.

Probably a mammal of some sort. A lizard wouldn't be so active, I think. The bus skids to a stop. Everybody's head ricochets back, forward, then back as we speed off again. Gradually the bag comes to life anew.

The woman winks a black slash of an eye, picks up her steel betel nut peeler and bashes the basket with a vengeance. Thunk! The basket stops moving.

I go back to staring out the window, but glancing at the bundle every minute.

About ten minutes later, the old woman's head falls forward, and she begins snoring. I slowly move my closest hand toward the basket, and gently lift up the rag. A tiny wet nose with about three long whiskers on each side slowly sticks up. I lift the rag a bit more and see two beady round eyes, looking at me like unblinking black marbles.

It's a field rat.

I tuck the rag back in and look out the window. She's going to stir fry that poor thing for supper tonight.

At the next stop, I should just get off the bus and sneak it with me, and let the rat go. Poor little guy. He's going to be thrown in a wok of sizzling oil along with some chilies.

The next stop is coming up, and I'm going to save him. I'm going to rescue him from certain death.

The bus knocks, the gears grind, and pulls to the side of the road. All hands cover their designated noses. The old woman is snoring away.

Then I realize, this rat will be the main course to feed not only her family, her extended family, but probably a few neighbors as well.

Maybe it tastes like chicken.

I go back to staring out the window, defeated. The old woman continues to snore, and the rat settles down, accepting his fate.

~~~

When I get off the bus at the Jet Sipette, the old man walks out from behind the shack. I can't wait for him and Scabby to show me a new trick today.

Except, I don't see the dog.

"Where is Scabby?" I ask, sensing something is off. Real off.

The old man just shakes his head, sits down in his plastic chair, and folds his hands on his lap.

"Where is he?" I ask again.

The old man looks at me with his cataract coated eyes, and I know what happened. His eyes tell me.

"I am sorry. I am so, so sorry," I say softly.

The old man puts his head down.

"Today?" I ask.

He doesn't say anything.

"How?" I ask again.

He doesn't say anything. He doesn't want to talk about it.

"Where is he?"

The old man gets up and leads me around to the back of the shack. Instead of Scabby's hollowed out sleeping hole in the dirt, there is a mound of fresh earth. The old man has lain a small wreath of stringed jasmine flowers on top of it. He then smiles. I can tell by his peacefulness that Scabs died naturally. I exhale.

There is always a moment, one quick second really, a flash, when everything changes. A smoker enjoys the habit for years and years, then one day as he is half way through a lunch break cigarette, one cell in his body defects. The traitor rebels against all the other cells that are trying to keep him alive. It secretly begins to mutate into cancer.

Or, the second when the bullet is one inch from the soldier's helmet. On it's way, suspended in mid air, a second before it rips open his head. Why didn't the soldier just turn to light a cigarette then? Why didn't the soldier bend down to find his lighter?

Then it's over. Just like that. Scabby's time has ended. Everything does eventually.

"He was a good dog," I say quietly.

The old man just stares at the grave.

For what ever past transgressions Scabby's soul committed in his previous Buddhist life, he paid for it in this life. The old man showed him kindness and helped him along the way. Finally, that poor dog is at rest, after being loved as best as the old man could love him.

When I die and go to heaven, I pray Scabby will be sitting by the pearly gates, fully restored to health, and when he gets done smelling his butt, he will escort me in.

I hang my head and continue down the road to the post office. I am not in a good state of mind for the Weasel to mess with me.

Before going in the door, I peer in the window to spy on him.

Weasel is sitting back in a chair, with his feet up on a table, reading a large news magazine. He has an entire stack of them.

Slowly leafing through one, he scans the page up and down, making confused but interested faces.

I put my head closer to the window.

He is holding a City Pages, an alternative weekly news magazine of the Twin Cities. My Twin Cities. Minneapolis St. Paul. The little twerp has again opened my mail. Obviously a friend from home had saved up a bunch and sent them to me.

I barge through the door. I am in no mood to deal with him.

"What are you doing?" I ask with hands on my hips.

Weasel peers over the magazine, and casually shuts it.

"Sawatdee, Susan. You have mail," he says nonchalantly.

"I know I have mail. You are reading my mail!" I answer loudly.

"No, no, not this. This is mine. I will go get yours," he says with a straight face, and goes to the back room to get the rest of my mail.

I crawl under the counter and grab my City Pages, stuffing them in my bag.

When he returns, he knows I had grabbed them, but doesn't say anything.

He hands over a stack of letters, all of them opened and carelessly taped shut. I grab those too.

Reaching in his pocket, he pulls out a tube of cherry chap stick that he must have taken from a different package prior, and puts some on his weasly lips.

For about ten long seconds, I look at this man. Finally, I get it. After two long years, I now understand. I feel a swell of intense compassion sweep over me.

How incredibly frustrating. He sees letters and boxes come in and go out to places he has never been to, and will never see.

My packages are the one thing that connects him to the outside world. To America. To read my personal mail, wear my Minnesota tee shirts, eat my food, use my shampoo, smell my body sprays, that is his connection to America.

He has never taken out the twenty dollar bills that my dear dad sends weekly.

I pull the City Pages back out of my bag, and lay them on the counter.

"When you are done reading them, please give them back to me," I mumble.

"Thank you," he answers, and pulls them toward him.

I make a mental note that when I returned to the States, I would send him packages now and then of cherry chap stick, Big Red gum, and Minnesota tee shirts. I realize I am going to miss him after all.

I spend the next week packing, mailing home souvenirs and shopping for everything I want to bring back to Minnesota. I ship absolutely everything I have ahead of time, as all I want to travel with is my backpack. My threadbare, worn out backpack. My co-workers had wanted to throw a lavish going away party for me, but I emphatically tell them no. It would be too emotionally difficult for me. I just say my goodbyes to them individually instead, and leave the office like it was just a regular day, not the very last one. That is hard enough.

~~~

On the day I leave my serene, little fishing village of Sichon that I called home for two years, Christine comes to pick me up in the afternoon. It is a beautiful February morning. There is a breeze to calm down the one hundred degree heat, the gem blue ocean is lapping in the background, and the birds are calling from all direction.

Every one of my neighbors are outside my door.

Tong gives me a beautiful jasmine stringed wreath to wear around my neck. Pee Poo and two other women give me one also. I want to hug them American style, but it's hard to move. I think I'm in shock.

Tong's five kids rush toward me, and hug my knees and legs. I bend down, hug them all back, and wish I could take them home to America with me. Some of them start crying, step back, and wave their grubby hands goodbye.

Tangmo's mother, father and brother *wai* and give me jasmine garlands along with a huge bag of stir fried rice and fruit to take with me on the train.

Six older Muslim girls from the nearby school are shyly smiling behind their head coverings, and one gives me an envelope, filled with letters, written in English by their class, to me. They *wai* in unison and bow deeply.

I'm about to lose it, and know I have to leave now. My heart is burning and melting at the same time.

I get on the back of the motor scooter with Christine. We head to Nakorn to make the train. She doesn't say much. I can't say anything, otherwise I know I will burst into tears.

Bong is laying in the middle of road, coloring in the book I had given him. He sits up, stares at us, and screams "Get off my cloud!" as we drive by.

"Get off the road, Bong," I yell back, waving.

Passing the post office, the Weasel is sitting outside on the steps smoking. He stands up and waves goodbye also.

We stop at the Jet Sipette. The old man is sitting in his plastic chair, holding something in his lap.

I get off to say goodbye. Then, I see what he is holding. He has a puppy. A fresh, fat puppy, not more than six weeks old.

"Susan! I have new dog!" he says excitedly, and hands him to me to hold.

He is a rolly poly dingo mix of some sort, and smells of that wonderful puppy scent, of innocence, urine and happiness.

"What's his name?"

"Puppy," the old man answers.

"I know it's a puppy, but what's his name?"

"Puppy," he says again.

"How about Pickles?" I suggest.

"What is pickles?"

"Tiny cute cucumbers," I answer.

He nods and says, "Pickles! That's a perfect name!"

I tell him goodbye one last time. He *wai*'s, I *wai*. Christine and I get on the motor scooter and leave. I bury my face in Christine's dark, luscious hair and inhale her Love's Baby Soft perfume all the way to Nakorn.

At the train station, Christine and I eat a bowl of noodles in silence as Boonchu's baby blue truck pulls up to the curb.

Nuang, Pee Poo, Pee Uaan and several other coworkers jump out of the back, and my Supervisor and Boonchu get out of the cab.

I had told them I was leaving next week, because I don't want to go through saying goodbye to them, but word of mouth information gets around quick here in my province, and for once, I am glad it does.

I simply *wai* in front of each of them and say, "Thank you." They all have jasmine garlands for me as well, and place them around my neck.

The train rolls in. Christine walks me on, and I find my seat.

In the aisle, before she leaves, we hug for too short of time. I kiss her on her cheek, and she grabs my hair to sniff deeply one more time.

She waits on the platform as the train pulls away and I wave out the window.

"Be brave, Susan!" she yells.

"I will! You be brave, too!" I yell back.

I wave until I can see her no more.

Chapter Thirty-four

Once in Bangkok at the Viengtai Hotel, Beth's airplane tickets, papers and passport are piled in a small heap in the middle of the bed. She is the first to go. Clare and I are sitting around them like a campfire, just staring.

I don't know what to say. I'm sifting through the extremes of emotions that two years in Thailand has blessed me with.

Just last night, we were all stuffed into a taxi, drinking and laughing. Just this morning, Clare and I were lounging on the hotel's beds, beds with real sheets, and talking about how we soon will be home in our own real beds with real sheets.

Beth is running around the room in a frantic, controlled sort of way, packing a final box of belongings that need to be at the post office before noon. It's now about eleven a.m. She has a million things to do before she leaves this evening.

Clare and I are helping immensely by telling her she should stay a few extra days here with us. In other words, not helping.

She's cramming clothes and souvenirs into the carton at a hectic rate, crushing things to make them fit.

"Can you guys please mail this for me? My final physical was five minutes ago, and I just don't have time!" she pleads.

"Well, how heavy is that thing? Clare asks suspiciously.

Of course we would help, but have to make her properly beg. I push the box with my foot and it doesn't move. I try to lift it up, but can only an inch or so before letting it crash back to the floor.

"Maybe we can get the little bellhop to push it down to the post office on his luggage cart," I suggest.

"That stool under the desk has wheels, we could put it on that I suppose," Clare adds.

"Please you guys, it would really help me out," Beth says again, not really listening to us.

"Clare told me last night never commit to anything that involves responsibility," I say.

Beth is too preoccupied with packing and flailing things about to answer. Grabbing her purse, she heads towards the door.

"Okay, see you guys tonight before I go," she yells back, handing us some money so we can mail it for her.

Before she makes it to the door over the obstacles of backpacks, coke cans, beer bottles and clothes, I call to her, "Where are you mailing this?"

"What?" she answers absentmindedly.

"There is no address here," Clare says.

"Gawd!" she screams, knowing she forgot something, rushing back to scribble down the address before flying out the door.

We don't see her until later in the evening when she comes to get her backpack and luggage.

We all go downstairs and stand together by the hotel door as she hails a taxi. We hug one last time. She gets in, and the taxi disappears into the blue haze toward the airport.

One by one, over the next week, all of us leave to catch our flights back home as the new group of volunteers arrive to begin their training.

And just like that, it's over.

THE END

Epilogue

After I returned home from Thailand, I immediately went traveling and working again overseas, but that's another story. Mike and I simply lost touch. He remains a perfect memory and I wish him the best always.

Elad now plays for the symphony and lives happily in Europe with his gay lover. (Who would have known.) We still exchange Christmas and Hannukka cards yearly.

I don't know what happened to Gaurang, nor do I care.

It was quite a hassle for Captain to marry Velveetah. Her birth certificate had her down as a male, but somehow the Captain greased some palms or pulled strings to change the 'M' to a 'F.'

They returned to the States and adopted a couple of Vietnamese orphan kids from Thailand. I thought I saw her once on the news during an NBA game, holding the arm of a rich, older man.

Samantha was hired by a small Thai shuttle airlines as a flight attendant, flying back and forth from Bangkok to Chiang Mai, Koh Phuket and Koh Samui. For fun, she says, "Coffee, Tea or Me!" to all the horny sexpats. They always choose her.

Christine didn't need me or the United States Peace Corps to save her from anything. She ended up saving herself, and I am sure she looked like a million bucks doing it.

She is no longer an active prostitute. Taking the money from the German's briefcase, Christine moved to Koh Samui and opened up a little clothing boutique. She does, however, like to lecture all the young, drunk, lust-filled *farangs* who shop at her store. With every purchase, she smiles brightly and says to the customer, "Don't be silly! Wrap that willy!"

One of these days I will go see her.

About the Peace Corps

After a day of campaigning for the presidency, Senator John F. Kennedy arrived at the University of Michigan in Ann Arbor on October 14, 1960, at 2:00 a.m., to get some sleep, not to propose the establishment of an international volunteer organization. Members of the press had retired for the night, believing that nothing interesting would happen.

However, 10,000 students at the University were waiting to hear the presidential candidate speak, and it was there on the steps of the Michigan Union that a bold new experiment in public service was launched. The assembled students heard the future president issue a challenge: how many of them, he asked, would be willing to serve their country and the cause of peace by living and working in the developing world?

The reaction was both swift and enthusiastic, and since 1961, 210,000+ Americans have responded to this enduring challenge. Since then, the Peace Corps has demonstrated how the power of an idea can capture the imagination of an entire nation.

The Peace Corps is an independent agency within the executive branch of the United States Government. The President of the United States appoints the Peace Corps director and deputy director, and the appointments must be confirmed by the U.S. Senate.

Established by President Kennedy by Executive Order on March 1, 1961, the Peace Corps was formally authorized by Congress on September 22, 1961, with passage of the Peace Corps Act.

The Peace Corps enjoys bipartisan support in Congress. Senators and representatives from both parties have served as well.

The Corps is a form of foreign aid, but instead of supplying money to developing nations, the Corps supplies the knowledge and expertise of its citizens. The idea stems from the old proverb, "Give a man a fish, feed him for a day; teach a man to fish, feed him for a lifetime."

While building a school or supplying food is crucial for many nations, training teachers or helping them learn advanced agricultural techniques could have a positive affect that lasts decades.

Peace Corps workers are volunteers who not only bring aspects of American culture to places they work, they bring some of that nation's culture back to the United States. There are over 7,000 volunteers serving at any given moment throughout the world.

The Peace Corps' mission has three simple goals:

1. Helping the people of interested countries in meeting their need for trained men and women.

2. Helping promote a better understanding of Americans on the part of the peoples served.

3. Helping promote a better understanding of other peoples on the part of Americans.

Information provided by the U.S. Peace Corps
www.peacecorps.gov

How to help Thailand's prostitutes

Thailand is a source, destination and transit country for sex trafficking according to the recent reports by the U.S. Department of Labor's Bureau of International Labor Affairs. Thousands of uneducated women from impoverished rural villages migrate to Bangkok each year in search of work to support their families. They're at risk of sexual exploitation because they lack the basic job skills and education needed to support themselves.

Fueled by a growing demand, countless women and children from around the world are victimized by gender inequality, poverty and cultural obligations. They are sold or pressured into prostitution and trafficked in and out of Bangkok to sustain an increasingly global network. Estimates are that 80% of Thai men frequent women in bars and 60% of foreign men entering Thailand participate in the sex industry, generating U.S. $1.2 billion annually.

In January 2005, NightLight Thailand was formed to address the lack of opportunity for women trapped in Bangkok's sex trade by providing them with a viable, alternative means for supporting themselves.

NightLight Thailand operates under two branches: NightLight Design Co. LTD, the registered jewelry business offering holistic employment, and the NightLight Foundation, the nonprofit branch focusing on holistic intervention for women in the sex industry. NightLight Design currently employs 80 women in Bangkok.

- Courtesy of Night Light International, Bangkok
For more information, please visit and support
www.facebook.com/NightLightInternational

Acknowledgements

Gratitude and appreciation to SFC Mary Doyle,
You are a true gem and great inspiration.
Anitra Budd, Mike Walton, Sam Aspley and Lissa Marquardt,
Thank you for your professional advice.
Ayden and Ariel,
Be brave and jump into our world with open arms and minds. I'll
make you some warm buttered noodles when you get home.

About the Author

Susanne Aspley served in the Peace Corps, Thailand, 1989-1991 and later worked in Israel and England. She also served in the U.S. Army Reserve as a photojournalist in Kuwait, Bosnia, Panama and Cuba. Retired, she enjoys her kids, rescued American bulldog, surly cat and elderly poodle. She has never learned to eat durian.